I0585268

One Fine Mess

MARK PETERSEN

DUNMORE BOOKS

— 2018 —

Published in the United States of America by Dunmore Books.

First Printing, 2018

ISBN 978-0-692-09760-1

10 9 8 7 6 5 4 3 2 1

PART ONE

I

——

"I finally got Eddie where I want him," Jules Nichols said.

An itty-bitty brunette, she felt the happiness all the way up her throat as she stood at the front door of the ranch house Wesley rented in Burlington. He squinted against the brightness and jerked his head around. He looked as if he expected an entire SWAT team to jump out of one of the sculpted shrubs.

"We screwed up. I know it."

"Oh, come on, we nailed it. Good times ahead."

He gave his shoulders a squirrelly hike. She could hear an edge of anxiety in his voice.

"Aren't you scared at all?"

"Let's go for a spin! Your car."

"I don't know. Jeez, all I see is the blood, all the—"

"I'll drive, for once."

She broke into a sprint. They raced down his flagstone walk and across the lawn. His white classic '69 Mustang was backed into the driveway, the convertible top down. As she plopped into the driver's seat, the big round dashboard gauges reminded her of a cockpit.

When his hand touched hers, offering the keys, she felt a familiar tingle in her chest. She then roared onto the street and knocked off three blocks of well-kept houses and maples in seconds flat. A shapeless man hugging a grocery bag gaped at them from the sidewalk. She noticed Wesley slap his foot down, trying to brake.

Grocery store. Gas station. Whoops tumbled toward them from a basketball court, and she nearly whooped herself. Feeling her own gears rev up, a sense of release rushing through her, she spun the steering wheel. As they squealed around the corner, Wesley clutched the dashboard.

"Slow down," he said. "You really—"

"Oh, sweetie."

Tugging at a strap that had inched out from under her tank top, she let out a laugh. Sometimes it was hard to believe he'd risked his own neck for her. Or that he'd once been such a local hero.

She raced willy-nilly through the traffic on Shelburne Road. The wind playing through her collar-length puff of hair, she cut southeast. A blue pond and sun-bleached barn zipped by. Cornfields. Neat rectangles of plowed Vermont earth. A stretch of woods and a bright ribbon of water.

As they rocketed by a speed-limit sign, he craned his neck toward the speedometer. Just picturing the way *he* drove— shoulders bunched up around his ears, rigidly obeying the speed limit—made her smile. But unlike her own little pickup, wasn't a car like this made to haul ass? His Red Sox T-shirt flapping, he knitted his brow.

"Know we had to do it, I just . . . You don't think they suspect us?"

She waved a hand.

"Relax, for once. Okay? Be optimistic. Remember, we're the good guys."

She slid a little arm out into the wind. This was the beginning of their brand-new life. Even after the big chunk she'd donate to Burlington's Steps to End Domestic Violence program, and paying for rehab for her troubled baby sis, it would be a life with 1 2 5 grand of insurance money. Jules would never have to shake her boobs for sweaty dollars again, or put up with drunks yelling at her to flash some pink. Or tiptoe around at home. After all the black eyes and bruises from her worthless hubby, Eddie, she could finally breathe.

The road dipped and curved. The tires sang.

She saw a flash of movement off to the right. When a squirrel scampered into the road ahead of them, she braked. The chubby critter hesitated, so she swerved to avoid it.

"Go easy, little guy."

A voice from somewhere said, *Be careful.*

Quite what she was afraid of she didn't know. Feeling an uneasiness which surprised her, she checked the mirrors. Maybe Wesley was right? Maybe she should be more cautious? As they hit Keeser Road, she decided to slow down a bit.

She and her sis, Paige, used to sled not far from here. They'd fly down Dyer Hill and then scamper right back up again. They used to ride their dirt bikes all around here too. God. Who could've known then how screwed up things between them would—

Her shoulders tensed as she glanced in the rearview again. Darn.

Near a blocky old brick house, blue lights flashed behind them. The cruiser swelled in the mirror, and Wesley gripped her arm.

"Maybe we can grab his gun, tie him up," he said. "Conk him on the head—pretty hard, but not too—so he forgets everything, and then—"

"Oh, come on, chill out." She checked again. The cruiser was right on their bumper now. Well, great. "I was still speeding. He probably only stopped us for that."

Oh, well.

She had this.

She feathered the brakes and pulled over, gravel rattling the underside of the car. As she switched the engine off, the patrolman strutted over, stone-faced. He was tall and buff, but had oversized ears. His handgun bobbed at his side. When he stopped, he gave Jules the once-over, eyes lingering for an extra beat. He sized up Wesley.

"Your license, registration, ma'am. You aware you were going at least eighty back there?"

Her hand draped on the steering wheel, she studied the nametag on the pocket flap of his khaki uniform, and a nick on his chin from shaving. She shrugged.

"Was I, Officer Gorman?"

"Yes, ma'am."

"Hard to believe."

Trooper Gorman shifted on his feet.

A long moment dragged by.

When Wesley groaned, she turned. He was white as the car's exterior and rubbed his palms along his thighs. He looked about ready to scream, spring outside, and bolt on his spindly legs into the woods. Clumsy as he was, he would probably run straight into a tree. He'd never desert her, though.

Well, all she had to do was play it cool. A part of her brain, though, said something else was off. Humming to herself, she fished her license out of her purse.

"Here you go. Not the best picture. Look at that hair!"

Wesley popped open the glove compartment to grab the registration. She heard him make a sharp intake of breath.

"Oh my—"

When she glanced over, her heart gave a little jump.

She barely believed her own eyes. Between some paperwork inside the glove box gleamed the stainless steel cylinder of her Taurus Judge .45.

Holy shit!

How the hell could the gun be there? Making a panicky little noise, Wesley slapped the lid of the glove box shut.

"Sir," Trooper Gorman said.

Wesley tried speaking—but nothing but a croak came out.

"The registration—"

"Hmm? Oh, yeah!"

Wesley sat still, looking nauseated. He cleared his throat. Twice.

"Um, coming right up. Coming right to you. One . . ."

His hand trembled as he reached toward the glove box again.

She couldn't take her eyes off it. Would he grab the .45 and try something? This could all backfire horribly. After taking a big swallow, Mr. Cool eased the compartment open. Just barely.

She eyed the trooper. She could smell the leather of his belt. Or holster. Had he inched his hand near his gun? He seemed to be studying their hands now as well.

"Sir!"

"Hang on, I think I—"With the glove box still barely open, Wesley rummaged away. His voice was too loud. "Sure is way hot today, huh?"

The trooper said, "You seem a little—"

"Jeez. My head is kind of *spinning* here. Not good, not good."

She feared Wesley was reaching the breaking point as he added, "Um, you see . . . Hot!"

"The registration."

Her sense of alarm grew as Wesley started to pull out what looked like a food wrapper. He made a little sound and shifted uncomfortably in his seat. He then fished around inside the compartment some more. For a second she was tempted to conk *him* on the head. That probably wouldn't look good.

Discreetly, she held out a hand to him, palm down, urging him to calm down. Her own blood felt fuzzy and fast.

While the trooper stared on, a crazy idea floated through her head: snatch the .45 and leave him handcuffed to his car in just his underwear.

She wouldn't hurt the guy. But should she lunge for the glove box?

"Yes, yes," Wesley said shakily. He was a sweat factory now. "Shit. You know, I pay my taxes. For real. Yup, everything by the book. Oh boy, I'll shut up now."

It took another one or two seconds, but he redeemed himself with a quick little grab and whack of the compartment lid. He had done it! God, he had done it. She let out a breath she hadn't been aware she was holding as he continued.

"Here it is. Yup, this car's mine."

Avoiding the trooper's eyes, Wesley handed over the registration and his own license. He drummed his fingers wildly on the armrest. Then he jerked out his phone and gaped at it, as if reading a text.

A second later she saw something flare in his eyes. His mouth hung open so wide she could have stuffed a toaster in it.

What now?

The trooper asked her a couple of questions and apparently hadn't noticed the .45.

"Stay put," he said. "I'll be right back."

She urged Wesley to stay calm. After the trooper swaggered back from his checks, she grabbed her ticket and watched him run a hand along the car.

"Sure is a beauty."

She nodded.

"Thanks."

"Oh," he said. "Had to give you a warning too."

"For what?"

"Why's your rear license plate upside down?"

She didn't flinch. Willed her face to turn to stone. But she didn't understand. *Upside* . . . ? His words didn't click. What did he—?

She bit her lip. They had temporarily taken off the rear plate at the Gorge.

It had been upside down? For three days?

Maybe they should have written WE DID IT in blood across the car's hood.

Well, she needed to answer like five minutes ago. The air had gone dead and heavy. But it was the story of her life. Something good happens. And then trouble.

Nah. Not anymore.

Still, what the hell was she supposed to say? She felt two pairs of eyes on her. The midday heat pressed down. There was the whoosh of a passing car.

Focus.

Answer in your own sweet time.

"So, uh . . . anyhoo," she said. "Kids fooling around?"

She half winced as soon as she said it. Even so, she concentrated on keeping her cool. The trooper stared at her. Was there something combative in his look now? She could feel that her hand holding the steering wheel was damp.

A bird cawed from the evergreens, and Wesley gazed longingly in that direction.

Eddie would have killed *her*, if she ever tried to leave him. He'd said she'd end up in a garbage bag. But would the cops ever believe that? Especially after she'd already fed them a bunch of lies when they questioned her at the New Haven barracks? Maybe she should've opened up to them when she had the chance.

What felt like an hour later, the trooper patted the door.

"Well, fix it. Have a nice day now. Take it easy, okay?"

As soon as he left, she let a "Jesus Christ" hiss out between her lips. She smacked her hand against the dash. She then caught herself. What mattered was that they were in the clear now. Hopefully.

Wesley sat up, letting out a whoosh of air. She restarted the engine, and he eyed her as they roared off.

"Man!" he said. His tongue sounded sticky. "How weird was that?"

"A bit."

For a moment she met his worried green eyes. He wasn't exactly a badass. But from the start, she couldn't resist his goofball charm.

"God," he said. "I think I, uh, just threw up in my mouth a little. I thought you were going to bury that gun."

"That talk about burying it or throwing it in a pond? Ring any bells?"

"Say what, now?"

"You forget about that? You said *you* would."

When she shot him a reproachful look, he lowered his gaze a moment. He thought about it with his mouth knotted.

"Did I?" A realization came into his eyes. "Damn."

"Sweetie," she said, "what were you thinking?" He sat still, not saying anything, so she continued. "Look, we're going to handle this. We will. Just pull yourself together."

He put his hand on her thigh. His grip tightened before he let go.

"My bad."

"It's okay. I'll take care of the gun."

Well, maybe he wasn't the best murder partner. But she really did love the bonehead. He was yummy in bed. And she wanted to have his babies. Still, maybe they really hadn't thought things out so well after all.

"Seeing that pistol right there—shit," he said. "That was . . . My heart was going ninety miles an hour. At least."

As she hurtled by a tractor chugging along on big-ribbed tires, she felt her mind pulling into an ugly place she didn't want to be.

"Poor baby. The truth, though? That rattled me too."

"Yeah, well, you know. Guess I did mess up with that rear plate."

She raised her eyebrows.

"You think? I wonder sometimes, how'd you ever manage? Pushing insurance, I mean. You're such a nut."

They sat quiet a moment. She kept her foot on the gas, and they swung out around a red Ford pickup. Power poles flew by as she tried to ignore her own uneasy feeling. For some reason Wesley had pulled into himself. He looked as if something else was still on his mind. She played a hand through his beautiful chestnut curls.

"Sweetie, don't wig out. For the record? Maybe you were right about not speeding. But nobody knows it was—It's going to be okay."

"Nope," he said.

"We only killed *one* bad guy."

He seemed to mull this over. He then gave a short, shocked laugh.

"Well . . . I'm not even sure about that."

She felt the air go out of her. As she eyed him, he made some kind of desperate sound. There was something he wasn't telling her. She saw it in his face.

"O-kay," she said. "What do you mean?"

Silence.

"Tell me."

His Adam's apple bobbed as he swallowed hard.

She sifted through what'd just happened. Was it something about Gorman? The .45?

She stared at him—waiting.

"That text I got?" he said in a faint voice, as if not wanting to hear himself say it.

"Text?"

The sight of him gave her a slight chill. When she stroked the back of his neck, trying to soothe him, he closed his eyes and shimmied his head.

"I about shit myself," he said. "Heck, maybe I did."

"You didn't really—"
"It was *from* Eddie."

———————

Sipping at a gin cooler on the steps of her cozy farmhouse just outside Monkburg village the next day, Jules drank in the silence and sweeping green landscape, and tried not to worry. Last night she had ditched the .45 into a deserted collection pond. It felt good to wrap her hand around it one last time, then let it fly. As it splashed and sank into the muck, she heaved a sigh of relief. Now, she had her fingers crossed that the cops had no clue.

But obviously, Wesley needed some time to chill as well. A threatening text from a dead man? The stress had to be driving him a little wacky. Wackier. Sometimes there was no telling what went on in that head of his. Although for a sec his claim had stunned her too, he'd produced no proof, saying he'd deleted it. No, he must have been imagining things.

Still, they were in uncharted country now.

Cops aside, Eddie had run with some real baddies. She tugged at the collar of her shirt. She didn't even want to think about any possible trouble from them. At least the rest of her and Wesley's plan had been tight. Despite the scare with Officer Gorman, they were good. Weren't they?

God, she had married young and dumb. That whole union with Eddie had been wrong, wrong, wrong. Why hadn't she listened to her aunt Ina? The first time Eddie had spoken poorly of women, Jules should have known. And stripping? When she'd started, pulling in sweaty cash had seemed the only way to pay the bills and keep her little sis *in* clothes. Should've known better about that too.

Now that she was free, being home felt like living in a palace. Could there be a sweeter place to start her own family?

Her white clapboard home on Plains Road was simple. Inside, faint cracks ran through the walls—along with a fist-sized hole in her bedroom, thanks to Eddie. But the repairs could wait. Set back from the road, the house nestled on a knoll, and she loved the view: broad fields and wooded hills, Black Pond shining beyond her neighbor's dairy barn to the south. It was a little chunk of heaven.

She took a gulp of her cold drink. Screw the past. Screw the faint cracks—of doubt—she felt now herself. Finally, she had room to breathe. And privacy. If things went south, she'd handle them. Hell, she could write her own ticket now. To a new future.

Why dwell on negatives? What was that old saying?

If you call for the devil, he'll come.

2

―――――

She's dressing him up like . . . a *pirate*?

Tucked behind a pine on a rise at woods' edge, Burlington Detective Denzel Burpee gawked through his zoom lens into Jules's bedroom window.

God!

He swallowed.

Wearing stiletto heels, Jules gyrated before her lover, who lay back in bed. A sexy smile lit her face, and she worked her sweet little ass. Slow and sensual, all loosey-goosey. Burpee groaned. It was eighty-nine degrees out. Watching her, it felt a lot warmer.

Clearly, she was not shy. When she'd stripped in Burlington, she used to wear black lipstick and piercings in her nipples.

Now, a red bandanna circled the curls of her slightly built man. But the guy seemed to balk at the black eye patch dangling from her finger. One slow kiss took care of his hesitation, apparently. Whipping on the eye patch, he tossed her down onto the bed.

Well, shiver me timbers.

Burpee had never liked her thuggish husband, Eddie. Eddie had even called him the n-word once, at Eddie's strip bar, the Booby Trap, in Burlington's North End. Burpee had nearly decked him.

It was no secret that Eddie had dealt serious firepower, including assault rifles. Reportedly, some loony named Apache Tait and he had also run a meth lab at a hilltop Lincoln farm. Rumor was that, after a dispute between the two of them, Tait ended up skinned alive. Supposedly Eddie had also smashed in the teeth of one of his drug couriers with an iron bar.

Eddie had been trouble, right down to the cobra tattoo on his fat neck. At one point Jules had taken out a temporary restraining order on him. The prick had apparently bounced his better half off the walls one too many times. Had he given her that slim scar across her right cheekbone?

Still, a murder was a murder. Burpee knew the possibility had to be pursued as he watched her pull a reversal and climb on top of her lover now.

Hmmm.

He drew in a mouthful of piney air. He then turned and gazed off to the south through the branches. A mailbox tilted on a post at the end of the long driveway. A breeze riffled through the young corn across the road. Past a stretch of forest, a white steeple poked at the sky.

Ever since he had heard about Eddie's death, he'd been drawn to the case—partly because not long ago he had been so taken with Jules. Just how naughty had his favorite former stripper been? She'd probably done the world a huge favor by offing her scumbag hubby. But did these two now think their screw-fests were hush-hush?

Still, what was he himself really doing here? Sure, find the bad guys, bring them down—that was his calling. Christ, he'd once even gotten a dimwit perp to fess up by pretending a photocopier could detect the lies in written statements. This case, though? Somehow, he couldn't get it out of his mind.

Eddie's life insurance policy had been fairly big. And there'd been big-ass discord in his and Jules's marriage too.

With some effort through a back-channel source, Burpee had unearthed one interesting tidbit. Days before the murder, Wesley Torrance's credit card had been used at Wal-Mart to buy two pairs of coveralls and a box of 45-caliber bullets.

The Staties had either bungled the initial look into the vic's death, or maybe just didn't give a rat's ass about avenging the death of a shithead like him. Although they'd found faint bloody boot prints at the Huntington Gorge crime scene, they never managed a match. Oddly, the prints were whoppers. Over a foot long—a men's size fifteen. Way bigger than Torrance's would be. That one was a head-scratcher.

Not far from the body, crime scene techs *had* recovered a .45 casing from a gravel patch. Yet without a weapon to try for a match, that didn't amount to jack shit. There were no prints on the casing either, suggesting that the perp had loaded it while wearing gloves. Reportedly the Staties had even lost track of some of the evidence themselves.

The case was still open. Yet Burpee couldn't help but wonder if the Staties were going to just write the crime off as one more dope deal gone bad.

After all, Eddie had been carrying twenty-five hundred bucks. A living-large dope roll.

It also seemed neither Northeastern Mutual's death claim examiner, nor the D.A. here, had much interest in hauling in the hottie widow. Hell, Burpee had no witnesses. No reports of vehicles coming or going in the area. There was also the whole damn jurisdiction issue. Still, fuck it. No matter what, he was going to pursue this one. Whether Jules was clothed or not, in general he sure didn't mind still keeping an eye on her. And he'd never given up on a case before.

Somehow, Jules's pirate lover had won the babe lottery. In high school, the guy had been one heck of a baseball player. He also made headlines a few years ago, when he saved a seven-year-old boy who'd fallen through the ice on Lake Champlain—but then became trapped himself. She was a hero in her own way too. She was a survivor. A scrapper. According to an old co-worker of hers, she'd taken care of a sick aunt for years. And had practically raised her little sis on her own.

Even so, Burpee would love to give her and her man lie-detector tests. He bet the machine would smoke.

He rubbed his beard, listened to the birds. When he looked back toward Jules's bedroom window, framed in his viewfinder she whipped out a gleaming pair of handcuffs. Studying her, he felt himself grin. Before long he lost himself to his own private show.

By the time he sneaked off, nearly half an hour later, he felt flushed and tremulous. He would put aside his copy of *Gunshot Wounds* in bed that night.

Why not romance the wife a little?

But he'd be back.

Who knew what he could uncover inside?

3

In early August a heat wave hit. Day after day the air felt sticky, dense. Wesley gaped out Jules's bedroom window as brilliant lightning, heavy wind, and sheets of rain finally arrived. A lawn chair blew across the yard. The chair rose, then smashed into the ground. The window rattled with two sudden booms.

Earlier, he had already been unnerved. Now, while Jules showered, he dove under her sheets, his chest tightening. Maybe she was right when she insisted he'd imagined the YOU'LL PAY text from Eddie. Maybe not. Either way, this violent weather now was clearly a shitty sign. He was sure he and Jules were in for a load of trouble.

He felt tempted to dial his bookie and start gambling again, just to relieve the damn pressure.

As he waited for her, the rain gusted against the windows. Down came a branch. Her gray cat, Boo, scurried onto the bed.

"Jeez! You scared me, fur-bag."

He petted Boo, until he realized the cat had left and he was stroking the mattress. The faucets in the bathroom squeaked off. The hairdryer hummed. When he peeked out from under the sheets, Jules stood there wrapped in a burgundy towel, skin still pink. Her small, chiseled face squinched up.

"What're you hiding for, good-looking?"

"Not sure, really. Something just . . . All that racket, I—"

"Come on out."

Slowly, she let the towel drop. As her breasts jounced and settled, his heart did a tumble in his chest. He was crazy about her, and he hoped she never killed him.

Looking fresh and young and beautiful, she wet her lips.

"Let's make love. Hard, until it hurts."

He heaved a mock sigh.

"Oh. Gee. Hmm . . ."

Worry-free all at once, he rocketed up, tore off his shorts. In his rush he tangled up in his black T-shirt and banged into her pine bureau.

"Shoot."

A bottle of something clattered to the floor. She let out a bright laugh.

"First one arm, then the other. Don't worry, I'll wait."

A flash of lightning lit the sky as he jerked his shirt off, followed by a thunderclap. She crooked her finger and grinned, revealing the little gap between her two upper front teeth.

"You nut, come here."

He barreled into her arms, making smooching sounds. They kissed long and hard. Everything dimmed around him, and they tumbled into bed.

"God, I love the way you make me feel," she said.

Soon she arched up as he entered her. He watched her perfect face, her bright eyes, and felt her squeeze him. But as he pushed harder, deeper, a crick started up in the small of his back. Then a jolt blasted down his left leg.

"Oh my—Whoa!"

For a second he thought he had been zapped by lightning. He flopped aside, waiting for the blur in front of his eyes to clear.

His agony eased only when he curled up behind her. Clutching her warm teeny waist tight, he didn't dare move.

"Damn," he said, "that—"

"Oh, baby."

Days ago, when they surprised Eddie at the Gorge parking lot and she raised her .45, Wesley had thought he'd die too. All he could hear was the nearby rapids rushing past.

After she fired, he stood there in his coveralls, frozen.

It took the second blast to snap him out of his daze. Once Eddie fell onto his back, she stood over him and kept on firing. The third, fourth, and fifth shots seemed a bit much. Blue smoke clouded the air. Each report echoed off the cliffs edging the rapids.

The amount of blood startled Wesley. It spread across the parking lot at a horrifying rate. His stomach turned. When she reloaded, he knew she *really* meant business.

He kept swallowing.

He looked back from her to Eddie's body. There was so much blood.

"Could be wrong," he finally said, "but I'm pretty sure he's dead."

Apparently she didn't agree. A bunch of additional shots followed.

Now, Jules and he listened to the rain drum on the windowpanes. She turned and ruffled his curls.

"Better now?"

"I don't know. Sure."

"What a storm," she said.

"Yesterday? I started a checklist. A murder cover-up one."

He caught her rolling her eyes.

"O-kay," she said. "You know, you really should get out more."

"I just, well, I just wish we could . . . We can't just sit on our hands. One thing we *didn't* do? Blame someone else."

"Oh, well. Maybe next time."

He lost his train of thought as she laid back and ran a hand across her breasts. She looked and smelled amazing. He craved to touch and taste her. But he still didn't dare move.

"But listen. You said Eddie worked with Kev Bates, right?"

Something flashed across her face.

Fear. That was unusual. She was brave as anyone he knew.

"Yup," she said. "So?"

"That they never really got along?"

She gave a little shrug.

"Eddie fought with everyone. All I know is, they had some falling out over a few workers. That's what Eddie called a kilo of coke."

"Well, anyway, you said Kev was maybe even more vicious than Eddie?"

"What a creep." She made a face. "I'm not shitting you. The worst tats ever. Horns along his bald head. All he lacks is hooves for feet. But what—"

"Couldn't we tip off the cops with a disposable phone? Finger *him* for Eddie's death? Wouldn't that be a badass move?"

She shook her head.

"Nope. Last I knew he was on house arrest, wearing one of those ankle thingies. If he'd left, the cops would've got notice, tracked him. You know, using GPS. There got to be records for those."

Damn.

She took up his hand, kissed it.

"Maybe we're not out of the woods, maybe we could've been more careful. But—"

"We should do *something*, Jules. Before things start to go against us."

She sucked on his finger. Gave him a sexy glance. Feeling her warmth against him, he wanted her worse than ever.

"Chill, sweetie," she said. "Right now I feel so . . ."

"You're distracting—"

"I should hope so. I'm still really . . . Just relax, don't move."

Outside, the wind howled. Holding him with her shining eyes, she caressed a luscious breast and moaned. She flicked at the red, erect nipple. And with her other hand she touched herself below.

Her face was radiant.

"I got an idea too. Why don't you just . . . watch?"

―――――――

Days later in Burlington, Jules tried giving Mr. Crabby a gentle kiss. Putting a bright and hopeful look on her face, she waved a stack of DVDs.

"So! Thought I'd make us a nice healthy lunch. And then maybe we could watch something fun."

She couldn't figure out if his back problem was all due to stress. For someone like him, this killing people thing could get to you. Then again, hearing that her neighbor had noticed something suspicious recently had kind of freaked her out too.

Wesley frowned back at her from his pad on the living-room floor, his lower legs propped up on his hassock. The window blinds slanted shut. Empty pill vials and a heating pad lay on the gold carpet.

"Sorry I've been such a grouch, honey. You're the best—I know that. I just . . ."

When Jules tugged open the center blind, sunlight streamed through the window. Hopefully they could live together soon. Yet that would have to wait.

"I made you a big salad. You got to eat."

Stiffly, he turned away, and gasped. Clamping his eyes shut, he squeezed the edge of his mat.

"Shit. . . . You know, I can't get over a strong feeling I had. That we're super-fucked."

"I'm rooting for you, handsome. You know I'd trade places with you, if I could. What do you say? A movie? You want to watch one?"

She stooped a moment and could sense the turmoil inside him. Stroking his arm, she gave him a sympathetic smile.

Hadn't he already helped rescue her? Shortly after she'd first spilled her guts to him about Eddie, he'd convinced her to try counseling. He'd also helped her come up with the details of their little plan. A remote location. No cell phones, to avoid the towers that could track them. Alibis. He'd even thought up a way to throw off anyone investigating the crime scene.

"You'll be back to normal in a jiffy," she said to him now. "We'll get our momentum back. One other thing, though." She swallowed. Well, here it goes. "My neighbor, Homer? He thinks he saw something the other day. Someone creeping around near my place."

Wesley's eyes saucered.

"You're shitting me."

"Someone who eventually got into what looked like a cop car." She let out a nervous laugh. "That speeding ticket? Maybe I should've paid it."

"Jeez. God. I knew it, I knew it."

"Actually, there could be, uh, all sorts of reasons for them to show up."

She moved toward the window so he wouldn't see her face. Only days ago everything had looked so good. But she had a sense now that the heat was turning up on them. The state police had questioned her, and then left her alone. But were *they* playing her?

Clearing her throat, she turned back to him.

"I bet it's nothing. We're going to have babies, Wesley. We're going to be happy. And I'll go to any length to—"

"Whoever was snooping around, that's another bad sign." With a loony-eyed look, he started counting on his fingers. "There was the trooper who stopped us. The text. There was . . . that crazy-ass storm. Now this. Oh, man. We're up a tree without a paddle. Or something like that."

It probably was time to start taking some action. Dig in more, find out what was going on with the case. Or throw a wrench into the investigation.

Move and exert pressure. Like when she used to show up at the chess club, contest two boards at a time, and win both.

"Sweetie," she said, "where's that checklist you made?"

"Huh?"

"The list. The cover-up-a-murder stuff. Let me take a look."

"I got to explain it then. It's sort of in code."

This whole thing had started with her problem. So in a way, whatever happened to them next was on her.

"For the heck of it, I'm saying."

"It's . . . on my bureau?"

She stared down at him. As he rubbed both hands across his taut face, she tried to put on a little smile.

"We'll do whatever we have to," she said.

He went quiet—digesting her words, she hoped. Maybe he was bucking up?

"Maybe you should just shoot me," he said at last.

She blew out a breath, feeling a strong hint of trouble to come too.

"Let's try a movie first."

4

_____

A day later in the woods behind Jules's farmhouse, Detective Burpee gave in to his impulses and draped the strap of his Nikon digital s l r over a shoulder of his charcoal suit. This case had a strange hold on him and it was time for a little fishing expedition. Even though anything he found would be tainted evidence, he couldn't help himself.

He never gave up on a case. His better half, Flo, always said, if he had to, he'd even turn _her_ in for breaking the law.

He glanced around while pulling on his latex gloves. He then skulked out of the pines in his two-hundred-dollar Bally shoes, using sneak-and-peek movements like a commando and pausing behind a maple tree to double-check Plains Road in the distance. The sun slipped out of the clouds. Her long driveway was empty. All was quiet except for his pounding pulse.

The door to her woodshed was maybe forty feet from the dense trees. There was no cover in between. Only a birdbath.

So close.

Damn.

When a chipmunk scampered by him, he laughed. He flicked his eyes back and forth, and followed. Lickety-split, he sneaked up to the shed attached to her house with a nervous thrill.

Sometimes he felt edgier outside the somewhat diverse hub of Burlington. Traveling through the scratch-ass villages beyond it, making a turn on Main and Cucumber, he often felt that—due to his skin color, and despite his stylish clothes—some of the locals saw him as a shiftless lawbreaker. Still, he couldn't even think about crossing a crime scene tape elsewhere today. A feeling in his gut told him to be right here.

As he moved his eyes toward the road and back, there was still no sign of anyone around. So he pushed against the rough plank woodshed door. It squeaked open and he tiptoed through the entrance. The inside smelled of old timbers. Neat stacks of firewood rose toward the ceiling.

He stepped up to a pair of rubber boots by the inner door leading to the main house. Pressing his ear to the wood, he listened. Nothing. He then slipped inside into the kitchen and froze.

Still quiet. He took a few more steps. The kitchen was painted a warm yellow. Sunlight poured in the big window, potted herbs sprouting along the sill. But he felt himself being drawn by something he couldn't name. He scooted down the hall toward Jules's bedroom.

Her bedroom door sat partially open. He stepped inside, full of an odd sort of certainty. Except for some tiny jeans on the wide-planked floor by the closet, and a hole in one wall, the room looked orderly. Just inside the door, a quilt adorned with hearts covered the bed. Next to it, mostly paperbacks filled a bookcase. There was a wildflowers book. Even a couple of books on chess. Maybe she was sharper than he realized?

He pulled at his beard.

So? What did he have? There had to be evidence. He was sure of it.

On the nightstand sat a framed photo of a man pushing a skinny girl on a tire swing. The colors had faded, but not her smile. He pulled out the drawer below. Only a vial of Valium and a tube of aloe vera lay inside. On a whim, he pulled the drawer completely out and checked the underside. Nothing.

The suspense was making his pulse beat faster. Who really was this woman? He rifled a stack of papers on the bookcase. Rummaged through her drop-leaf desk. Her closet.

Grinning, in her pine bureau he found body gels and handcuffs. Silver booty shorts. Velvet gloves, lacy bras, teeny leopard-print panties.

Digging through the drawers, he hesitated over a sheer pink nightie that cooed *Make love to me*. Drawing his gloved fingers along the nylon, a vague pull came over him—and then a yearning. Though he loved his own wife dearly, he couldn't resist a sniff of Jules's sweet perfume.

His brain swirled with lustful thoughts.

What was he doing? Was he just a perv here? He was supposed to be detecting, and he knew in his gut he was getting closer. Regaining his focus, he riffled through a stack of shirts.

Something stiff stood out when he dug under a lime-green tank top in the back.

Tucked underneath were two snapshots. He raised them. Taking a closer look, he barely believed his eyes.

"Jesus."

Blood rushed to his head.

Bingo!

Jules and her man squatted over Eddie's blimpy body in separate photos. In each one, Jules and Wesley stood with what looked like a .45 in their hands. Worthless gunrunner and drug-slinger Eddie lay on his side, head flopped on an arm.

Jules's canted image maybe was a cell-phone selfie. In it she wore a look that was damn hard to read. Relief from the terror she'd undergone? But why even *take* the photos? To assure herself the sicko was finally history? In Wesley's photo, apparently taken by her, he appeared totally dazed.

Burpee was reduced to dumb shock too.

He heard thumps and realized the sounds were coming from his chest. He shut his eyes. Okay. All right. Well . . .

After putting down the photos, he made his way to the kitchen and grabbed the Dewar's bottle from the corner cupboard. He tossed down a shot. It felt and tasted good going down his throat.

He then scooted back to the bedroom. When he stared at the photos again, his eyeballs pulsed.

Unbelievable. Why didn't they post a video of their crime on YouTube?

Maybe they'd assembled a murder scrapbook too?

Pulling himself together, he photographed the snapshots. He slipped everything back in place, smoothed everything down, shut the drawer.

As he wheeled around, a picture hanging above the bed caught his eye. He looked closer. The picture was heavy with mood and shadow. In it a dark figure raised a scythe up high. Studying the figure, he felt a creep around his heart.

Goosebumps rose on his arms.

Was that the Grim Reaper? Just how many skeletons were in Jules's closet?

Every woman had her bundle of secrets, didn't she? Had Flo ever thought about offing him for a wad of cash during one of their rare bad phases? Shit, he glopped so much ketchup on her dreadful casseroles that she could blend in a whole box of poison and he'd never notice. He loved her too much to complain. Still, he was glad it was his turn to cook tonight. Maybe he'd make a nice stir-fry. Nothing bloody, that's for sure. Thank God for good food. And good women.

The fact remained that Jules had been horribly abused by Eddie. And how many lives had she saved by taking down a shitbag like him? He and his biker buddies sure had been dangerous fucks. Among the items recovered from Eddie's SUV at the crime scene was a pound of c-4 explosive, as well as a deck of smack—100 bags.

When the door creaked open, Burpee stiffened.

What the—?

He whirled around. Totally out of bounds here—no warrant, no backup.

Caught committing a straight-out, illegal B and E.

Body blazing with fear, he yanked out from his holster the .357 that he still carried, thanks to the Chief's okay. He then moved into a combat stance, both hands on his weapon.

"Police! Homicide! Hold it there or you're—"

Meow.

A gray cat brushed against the doorjamb, tilting a notched ear. As it padded up to him, he exhaled loudly, feeling an enormous wave of relief, and uncocked his handgun. Tucked it away. Rubbed behind one of the kitty's ears as it twined around his feet.

Damn.

Well, one more whiskey couldn't hurt.

5

"Forgetting to bury the gun wasn't dumb enough for you?" Jules said.

Wesley watched her wave one of his betting tip sheets next to him on his sofa. She wore a short black top and a highly disappointed look.

Days ago, he had labored his way upright in his striped pajamas, tormented by uncertainty. His back was slowly getting better, but would the freaking pain come back? More important, would he soon be in handcuffs—and not for fun? Snatching up his cell phone, he speed-dialed his old bookie, Cadillac Frank Cannizaro.

Like a dam breaking, it had happened all at once.

"The hell you think you're doing?" Jules said now. "What makes you think you could even win enough to have a stupid golf course?"

"Honey, let me—"

"For fuck's sake, Wesley, you're the one who told me you had a bad gambling problem."

"Right now it's like . . . after your knee lift when you're pitching. I got momentum. I'm serious. Once this all comes together, you'll never have to work again." Although he held his hands out to indicate how obvious this was, he felt himself flushing. Not sure if he was convincing her. "And if we ever need to off anyone else? We can bury them right there."

She stared on.

And on.

Eyeing him as if she figured the crazy bus had come to town. "You're joking, right?"

"Um."

She gave a short incredulous laugh.

"I think you've been taking *way* too many of those pain pills. Really better ease off them." She let that observation soak in for a few seconds. "I need you to focus here. No more goddamn betting, no more harebrained schemes. Don't go looking for more trouble."

He rubbed his palms on his legs.

Hoping to lighten things up, he said, "We're not going to have sex today, are we?"

She didn't smile.

"Good guess. But speaking of evidence stuff? I called the Staties."

He struggled to switch gears. Had she lost *her* mind?

"Don't freak," she said.

"Why would you—"

"To keep up appearances. You know, the innocent wifey checking in on the investigation. Reading your checklist made me think of it. Seems like if I don't call it looks suspicious. Then again, calling too much might . . . Well, I sure didn't demand progress. That would've felt, like, just *too* weird."

Lady Luck would not even flirt with Wesley either. Before long, desperate, wearing his lucky Red Sox hat, he placed a bundle on a powerfully built filly to win. Do It was the eight to five favorite, a sure thing.

"Got it," Cadillac Frank said on the other end of the line. "Keep the damn bets coming. But remember: this ain't no game."

Afterward, Wesley eyed a photo of his brother Drew in Afghanistan. Drew wore khaki camo fatigues and a brave grin. A lump growing in his throat, Wesley gave his bro a thumbs-up. Except baseball before he blew out his arm, he had never been a natural at anything. But now he would prove himself too.

Come race time, as he watched online his blood began to jump in his veins.

"Do it," he said out loud. "Do it!"

Excitement tickled the back of his neck.

Do It threw a fit and bounced around in the starting gate. The gates flew open. Do It then barely broke a goddamn trot—and he threw his own fit.

"Shit! Ah, jeez . . ."

He flopped down on his sofa and squashed his face under a pillow. He then sat up, hurled it across the room.

Later, when he thought about disappointing Jules, he felt a dark dread in his chest. His cell phone was in and out of his hands. He'd end up saying some jackass thing, wouldn't he? Text her? No.

Finally, he dug around for change, in order to mail her an apologetic love note.

By late evening his back was still a little stiff. He felt fatigue weighing in his bones. Longing for the escape of sleep, he eased into bed. He then flipped and flopped around. Killing Eddie, his gambling debts—his mind churned with shitty thoughts. Wasn't it only a matter of time? If he had to, he'd take the rap for Jules.

But *prison*? God! Fear began to prick him like a zillion little knives.

He had about fifty cents left to his name for a good lawyer.

6

———

The following day Jules saw the rifle first.

Her blood jumped.

The man gripping the rifle stood there. Right in the middle of the dirt road. Facing her direction as she slowed her Tacoma pickup. He had orange red hair and looked beefy enough to give a bear a decent fight. The gun was some kind of carbine. He wasn't moving. Maybe he needed help? Directions?

He wasn't smiling, though.

She tasted something unpleasant in the back of her throat. She'd just dropped off some blankets, sheets, and baby supplies at Steps to End Domestic Violence in Burlington. She'd been worrying over why a cop might have been snooping around her place, and then about Wesley losing it lately. Until a second ago, she couldn't get the image out of her mind of him trying to fool her recently that he had everything under control. But now, this dude was creeping her out.

He held up a hand for her to stop. Or was that a kind of wave?

She knew almost everybody in Monkburg. But had never seen this guy's broad face. The jeans and light coat? He didn't look dressed for any kind of hunting.

Not for animals, anyway.

Crap.

If only she had her revolver.

She did have . . . what? That long piece of iron pipe behind the seat. But that was no big help, unless she had to fight the guy off by hand.

She held tight to the shifter. Eased up on the gas.

As she slowed to a near stop, her tires made a crunching sound on the packed dirt.

The rifle wasn't fully aimed at her. Well, it almost was. She was about fifty feet away from the stranger now. The road was surrounded by deep forest.

God, who was the idiot now?

It had to be one of Eddie's drug business buddies. Or one of his gun-running partners. Someone out to avenge him. Someone who'd studied her typical route. But would someone trying to kill her stand in the freaking middle of the road where she could run him over? Maybe if they were crazed on drugs.

She felt things get tight in her chest as the stranger shifted the rifle, then planted its butt against his shoulder.

Clenching the steering wheel, she scrunched down low.

Wesley trudged up to the YMCA's indoor pool and hesitated at the water's edge. He was struck by the sharp chlorine smell, and he heard a rushing noise building inside his head. But he shut it out and set his jaw with resolve.

"Okay," he said out loud.

This water-workout course was going to help his back. That, in turn, would help him get his shit together. Stiffly, he knelt and reached down. The water was warmer than he expected. He rose, drew a breath. The day Jules broke down at his table at the Booby Trap and told him about the beatings, hadn't he sworn to do whatever he had to for her?

Never give up. One thing he'd learned on the psych ward, after his little meltdown when his bro died, was that you had to keep trying. Just like when he used to play ball. He'd never thrown all that hard—but he'd known how to dig his cleat into the dirt, and pitch his way out of trouble.

Jules was freaking pissed now, but she'd be a whole lot happier once he reversed his losses. There'd be money falling out of their pockets.

As he eased into the water, droopy women in loud bathing caps splashed around him. A pop song blared from poolside and echoed across the room.

Right from the start, his wattle-necked instructor, Dora, singled him out.

"Move those bodies, ladies. Come on! You too, Mr. Torrance!"

His cheeks burning, he swished his butt and sloshed his arms about.

"That's better, Mr. Torrance. Relax, though. You look like you're being chased by sharks."

Before long he stopped mid-stroke and lost his breath. The edges of his vision shrank and dimmed.

He couldn't believe it.

He became terribly conscious of his thumping chest.

Floating before him was Eddie's body. Eddie sprawled, facedown. Blood streamed from his chest and swirled about, working its way toward Wesley.

For a moment he was too scared to move. Eddie's blood was coming right at him!

Would Eddie reach for him, grab a leg, and hold him down?

Wesley's mouth hung open. He hacked up water.

He then hauled ass from the pool.

Jules had survived Eddie. Just barely. She wanted babies. A family. But was it all going to end here, behind the steering wheel of her truck? God, she had better get her thumb out of her goddamn butt. Do something, anything!

No one was going to gun her down on a back road.

She had to kill this guy, or die.

Spear the gas pedal?

Maybe she could plow the orange-haired fucker down. Or would he just have a better shot as she raced toward him?

But what if he was an innocent hunter? Christ, he could be. She could never live with—

Reverse?

If she made it around the bend behind her, he'd have no shot. But there might be a damn gunman behind her too. She let out a breath of air she hadn't realized she had been holding.

"Screw it."

If there was another guy behind her around the bend, she would squash him flat.

She stomped the brakes and jerked the shifter, intending to reverse. In her panic, she screwed up and the gears ground.

Goddamn it!

The engine stalled. Fear flooded her body as she imagined a bullet crashing through the windshield. Time. She had no time.

"Come on!"

She nearly twisted the key in half as she turned it. She restarted the engine. Sweat rolled down her back and it took forever until she managed to find reverse.

She raced backwards. Heard a popping noise.

Was that a stone skittering into the truck frame?

Or a shot?

7

———

"Let me in, Wesley—or I'll smash this door down," Jules said outside his house the next day. "I know you're in there."

From inside came a groan.

"Hide on me?" she said. "You're not going to. Hear me? Open the door, or I'll—"

"In a minute."

Yesterday, after hauling ass in reverse, she had raced home. Settling down from the adrenaline dump, she carefully inspected her Tacoma for a bullet hole. She didn't find one. The sound she'd heard? It must have been the pop of a stone flying off one of her tires. She decided she'd worked herself up over nothing. Over a likely squirrel hunter. Or at least she sure hoped so.

Outside Wesley's door now, though, she too was feeling an impulse to kill.

"All right, that's it!" she said. "You're about to have a very bad day."

Him and his dumbass golf course. All he cared about lately were point spreads, exactas, whatever. And he was losing right and left. She'd found his kitchen junk drawer stuffed with overdue bills.

The sick part was, she really did love him. From the very first time she met him at the club, she'd admired his gentleness and how he made her laugh. Even on their first outing together, canoeing on Otter Creek, he had lost his paddle and fallen into the water. And what had she felt when he overturned the canoe as well? Joy. Pure joy.

But fooling herself that she was about to be gunned down yesterday had been the last straw. After getting home then, she'd calmed herself down with some wine therapy. After two glasses, or maybe three, it really hit her that she had to contain things. Then later she could have her babies. And all that good stuff.

To her right, one of the living-room blinds lifted. Two bloodshot eyes peeked out. His voice came from behind the door again, lowered to a near whisper.

"Check behind you."

"What the—What the hell you talking about?" She smacked the door. "What're you doing in there? Talking to your damn Mob bookie?"

"Just check."

She made a small scoffing noise. God, they were *both* getting paranoid.

"There's a hit man with a gun peeping out of the mailbox," she said.

From inside came a loud report.

"What was *that*?" she said.

A sickening rush swept through her gut. Wasn't that a real gunshot?

She clapped a hand over her heart.

"Wesley? Sweetie! Oh my—"

Had he . . . ?

The numbing notion rose in her that it was too late. She should've foreseen this! Lately he'd been hanging on to his sanity by an itty-bitty thread.

She hammered on the door.

"Wesley!"

Or was someone inside after *him*?

She pounded harder.

No. Anything but—

"Hang *on*," he finally said. "Let me put this gun away. Damn."

"What is—"

"Accidentally shot my recliner."

The lock on the door snapped back. When she stormed inside, the dumbass shrugged. His expression was strained. He'd missed shaving for a day or two and was draped in his ratty plaid robe. But he was still the handsomest man she'd ever met. She smelled a trace of gunpowder in the air.

On his TV screen, football players bashed each other. She stabbed it off. Newspaper sports crap covered the coffee table. Stuck next to a crumpled Burger King bag was a yellow Post-it note that said NEVER, EVER BET ON THE KNICKS AGAIN.

Men!

She'd never understood them at all. Not long ago, eyes heavily lined, she'd danced for them, desperate for cash to help her baby sis. Shimmying around and faking willing looks. Yet in the shower one night, she felt unable to get clean, and knew she was doing exactly the wrong thing.

Days later, Eddie—crazed on PCP—had bound and beaten her. Wrapping his belt around his fist, he'd ripped a deep cut across her cheek with the buckle. The next day she had poured gas all over his Escalade and lit a match. No guy would ever mistreat her like that again. No guy would ever degrade her. Or drag her down.

Biting her lower lip now, she glared at Wesley.

"Look at you. You're a mess."

Behind him, the landline phone sat in a bunch of pieces on the end table, and a vent grille was gone from the wall. Like he'd been hunting for listening devices. Besides his debts, the fool had to be still wigging out about the cops.

Apparently unsure what to do, he made a lame attempt to tidy up. He slouched down over the coffee table and neatened a stack of sports sections, and then some scummy-looking plates. Soon, though, he gave his hands a little upward toss. He plopped down on the sofa. One of his feet began to tap nervously.

Standing before him, she shook her head so hard she felt her hoop earrings swing. Most days, all she wanted was to tumble into bed with him and stay there for hours, his hands all over her. But now, what was it going to take to pull him out of this? Since that scare with that orange-haired guy, she was determined not to let their life turn upside down.

She stamped one of her high-top sneakers.

"The cops never figured shit out. No, some days I'm not even sure about . . . But why this gambling shit?"

His tapping foot tapped faster.

"You'd never guess what I saw in the pool—"

"And with a *Mob* bookie."

Spotting the gunshot hole in his recliner, she gave a little groan.

She then stormed across the room. Yanked open the closet. His stupid large trophy for pitching Winooski High's baseball team to a state championship gleamed on the shelf. Below it stood his stupid black-and-gold bag of golf clubs. Exquisitely crafted Callaways, she knew they'd cost him a shitload.

She snatched them up and whirled around toward the center window.

"Whoa, whoa. Jules, don't. I was trying to—"

"What a dick move."

For a moment she felt dark waters rising. The cop snooping around her yard? Maybe Homer had imagined that. At his age, he couldn't have the best eyesight. But right now she and Wesley really didn't need to get tangled up with other, real criminals.

"We got all the crazy we can handle already," she said. "You piss the Mob off, we could *really* be in danger. All I got to say is fuck yourself. And—"

"C'mon, don't throw those!"

With a loud grunt, she heaved the bag through the glass.

8

Each day of the next week, Wesley sent Jules a dozen long-stemmed red roses. He managed another grand of credit, and then kissed it goodbye when Devil Gets His Due came up short in the Santa Anita Breeders' Cup Classic.

It was a teary departure. The loss left him feeling tapped out and sick.

Staring at the replaced window in his living room, he felt like smashing it himself.

When Jules finally answered her phone, Wesley swallowed. As she spoke, her voice sounded tired and hard.

"You got to stop, Wesley. *Now.* If we need to, we'll get you help. But no more gambling." He thought he heard her tear up. "Or that's it for us."

Hanging his head, he stared at the whorls in his carpet and felt a sense of guilt drop over him.

The first time her perfect eyes had met his at the club, something had unclenched in his chest, and he had grinned back. And grinned some more. And then nearly missed his mouth with his Heineken. She was luminous. He knew that for the rest of his life this was the woman he wanted to wake up next to.

"I, I couldn't handle that," he said now. "That's why I left you about eight hundred messages."

A moment of torturous silence went by as he waited for a response.

"You need to chill," she said at last. "We got rid of Eddie, we got the insurance money. Just like my *Murder For Dummies* book said."

"What book?"

"I'm kidding."

"Whatever," he said. "You were the one who told me the cops were snooping around."

"Even if they suspect us, they don't really have anything. God, don't screw things up now."

Another silence gathered on the line. She sniffed into the phone.

"Hear me?"

He froze up a moment, not understanding how it had come to this.

"I do, honey. The gambling and golf course?" He shook his head in disgust with himself. "Not one of my better ideas. You're right, you're right. You're always right. God, I'm a—"

"I warned him, you know."

"Who? Eddie?"

"Told him if he ever even threatened me again, I'd put a hole in him."

The phone trembled at Wesley's cheek. His body ached from restless sleep. Lose her? He couldn't bear that. He felt so full of feeling he could barely speak.

"I made a big, fat mistake," he said. "Sometimes I get excited, and my thoughts run ... crooked. I thought I could be someone."

"You already are. But you're not letting me help you. I need to be able to trust you. God, do something, distract yourself ... before you get any more brilliant ideas. You know we got other things to worry about."

"I'm stopping. Don't know what—No more secrets, I want to make everything right. If I even think about gambling again? May God strike me dead."

Staring out the window past a small red house at the cemetery down the street, he imagined his coffin being lowered into the ground. He felt a chill at the edge of his thoughts and swallowed. He saw no need to mention his bookie had finally cut off his swollen credit line, anyway. He had no way to even keep up the vig, a point a week interest, anymore. He'd even maxed out his goddamn credit cards. He was broke as fuck. And the meter was running.

He shuddered. Maybe it'd be a good thing to *go* to prison.

If anyone was going to strike him dead, it'd be Cadillac Frank Cannizaro.

———

Eager for an escape the following Saturday morning, Wesley figured the opening of deer hunting season was a good excuse to get away and wander the woods—and to carry a gun. Years ago, his happy-go-lucky uncle Max had always taken him and his brother Drew along to deer camp. They had enjoyed the camaraderie of it. Even now, alone, a change of air couldn't hurt. Why not do something smart for a change?

Burlington miles behind him, he cruised southeast on Route 116. Warm air blew from the heater vents. After a bout of heavy rain, the sky was clear and bright. Forests and fields rolled to the horizon, and cruising this scenic stretch usually left him feeling renewed.

But something felt off. From under his blaze-orange hat he darted glances at his rearview mirror. He felt the pace of his breathing increase.

Cutting south, he stabbed the gas pedal. That maroon car had followed him, hadn't it? Appearing like a ghost in his mirror, it had kept its distance. But it had held tight behind him. There had been something sinister about it. Maybe it'd been an undercover cop? For the past few weeks, he had expected the cops to come crashing through his door. He knew better than to think this was over.

Or was Eddie's bloody corpse following him around in a car now? Christ, that was all he needed. His tires squealed as he cornered.

He pulled over to the shoulder and left the motor idling, then flipped up his hat's earflaps. Anybody tailing him would whip right around the corner. Rolling his window down a bit with a shaky hand, he made out the sound of a creek some-where off in the woods. Even louder was the sound of his own heartbeat building inside him.

As he waited, the surrounding forest felt threatening, like it might close in around him. He grabbed his Winchester off the backseat. Slipped three bullets from his pocket into it, laid it across his lap. Drummed his fingers against the steering wheel. Now he was ready for whatever challenge came along. But too bad he didn't have one of Eddie's stolen high-powered weapons, which were still stashed at Jules's place.

Eventually, a tan Dodge pickup rattled by, rifles racked in the rear window. No one else showed around the bend, though. His nerves settling down, he shifted gears and pulled away.

Hell, he was acting nutty.

Once he'd parked in a pull-off and swished through low brush into the woods, his mood brightened. The air smelled fragrant as perfume: pine and moss and bark. The cops, his back, his loony gambling—he had been all worries for too long now. He had been stupid. Somehow he had lost his focus.

Jules deserved better. She was all he wanted, and no one would ever stand in the way of that. Before they met she'd had it so damn rough. Hadn't Eddie once threatened to cut her face off? Once Wesley heard that, he knew he'd do anything to keep her out of harm's way.

He paused on a rutted logging road to re-tie a bootlace. Watching his breath puff out, he was glad for his wool layer. Although he carried his Winchester, he didn't want to kill any animals. Still, the gun did help make him feel secure.

After skirting a swampy area full of deadfall, he gobbled down a turkey sandwich and then moved on and scuffed his boots through the fallen leaves.

Striking white birches had surrounded the family's log camp. Cartons of beer rose up alongside the door. Inside, a cartoon hung from a tack above the table. In the picture a card-playing hunter blasted his rifle into the air to scare off the buck peeking in the cabin window. Captioned "SCRAM!" the cartoon summed up their priorities there.

What he would pay now to be back to those simpler times.

Soon he stepped up to a marsh thick with water lilies, hunkered down by some cattails. Cradling his rifle in his arms, he watched a muskrat waddle through a flattened area. Bathed in sunshine, he inhaled deeply. Filled his lungs with the crisp air and the smell of chilled muck.

When he finally rose, he felt himself smile. His gruff uncles had shared a gift with him and Drew, hadn't they? Life could be pretty damn good, when you thought about it. Or didn't think about it too much, actually.

Time to stop worrying.

Still, was there some way to get the upper hand on Cadillac Frank?

Then again, he had barely handled helping get rid of Eddie. And the cops . . . Well, it didn't pay to think about some things.

It was getting colder, and he looked forward to huddling before his car's heat vents. Unsure of where he was, he clomped south a mile or so.

That creepy feeling he'd had earlier? That was weird, though. Maybe being here wasn't such a great idea.

The dirt path he'd started out on appeared. His Mustang sat only a few hundred feet away then. Gunfire crackled in the far distance as he stopped to blow his nose. The oak trees stood several feet apart, and he leaned his rifle against one.

A moment later the brush rustled.

The back of his neck prickled.

"What the—"

When a huge black pistol muzzle waggled between his eyes, his heart crashed to a stop.

9

———

"I just had this feeling."

Jules stood in her kitchen, phone in hand, picturing her neighbor Emma Mayhew's lined, heart-shaped face. Emma was housebound, and Jules often picked up groceries and ran other errands for her.

"A weird one," Jules continued. "Like something was wrong."

"No, dear, we're fine."

"Well. Okay, good."

"Nice of you to call, though," Emma said on the other end of the line.

"No sweat."

"And you two? How's Wes?"

Jules looked out the window at the rolling hills. In the near distance rolled bales of hay dotted the fields that Emma's husband, Homer, farmed. Despite Emma's reassurance, Jules couldn't shake the funny feeling in the back of her mind.

"I'm home. Wesley's, well, hunting today. Supposedly. Probably napping in the sun, actually."

"I love that young man."

Jules cleared her throat.

"Really?"

"Oh my, yes."

"Hmm."

"So polite. Homer's out . . . puttering, I guess."

"Ain't he always?"

"What'd he tell me? Oh, dear." Emma gave a funny little embarrassed laugh over the line. "Some days my mind . . ."

"That's all right. I—"

"No, no. The pond? Some problem? That's it."

A quick distressful sound came out of Jules's mouth. Something like adrenaline trickled into her bloodstream and she felt herself moving into a colder, more frightened place.

The collection pond?

"*Which* pond? The big one, or little?"

"Oh, let me see. Hmm."

The little collection pond was where Jules had ditched the .45.

"Small," Emma said at last. "Yup, the small—"

"God! What about it?"

There was a pause.

"Tell me, Emma. Quick."

"Well. Too much rain, I guess. It failed last night."

Jules gripped the phone tight.

One glitch that had cropped up at the Gorge was that she'd lost one of the .45 shell casings in a gravel patch. She and Wesley had searched like crazy for the small piece of brass. Crunching around and around. Squatting down. Fruitlessly. If the Staties had found it, and then also got their hands on the .45, couldn't they match the casing's firing-pin marks to it? No matter what, if the murder weapon was found so close to her house, it sure wouldn't look good.

"*All* the water?" she said now.

"The what?"

"All of the pond water? Gone?"

Jules waited and breathed back her own breath.

"Oh," Emma said. "Not sure what he . . ."

"Shit."

"Hmm?"

"Nothing," Jules said.

"Well, dear, come by. When you can."

It was hard enough trying to help save Wesley from himself lately. God, now she had to save them both. Events were spinning out of control.

She had to get that gun.

She let her body slow some, then blurted into the phone, "I'm coming."

"Well, don't—"

"Right now, I mean."

Half an hour later when sunken-cheeked Homer drove off, Jules said another quick goodbye to Emma in person. She then hustled out their kitchen door. The sun beat down on her as she shot past their long red barn. Across the fields. Beyond the giant willow to the clearing.

When she looked, a chill rose inside her.

No.

The collection pond was gone. Or nearly. Only a few inches of water gleamed in its muck-edged bed.

She shook her head.

"Crap!"

She then felt a spark ignite in her bloodstream. Well, she would find the .45. She'd take care of this.

She scurried down the low bank and slogged her way to the pond center, where she thought the .45 had landed after she'd pitched it not long ago. Cursing, she kicked at and dragged her feet through the low water and mud. Soon she was sweating. She could smell herself and all the mucky water around her.

Where was it? Where?

Maybe the water rushing out had moved it? A medium-framed Taurus Judge, the weapon had had a fair heft to it. But who knew how fast the pond water had moved? Her tennis shoes felt like blocks as she trudged closer to the small broken dam.

Where the hell—?

She kept working through the mud.

Nothing.

Maybe it was buried in the mud for good.

Waiting that day at the Gorge, she had pressed the bullets home tight into the .45's chambers. It was the same gun Eddie had pressed to her temple and threatened to rape her with. As she closed her hand around the rubber grip and thumbed back the hammer, the handgun felt rugged. And lethal.

Wesley had insisted on arming himself with a ball-peen hammer. When he had first pulled the hammer out and began gesturing with it, she rolled her eyes. She knew he wanted to help. But knowing him, she was concerned that, if he took a swing, he might smack her by mistake.

Soon he jerked on a black ski mask. First he had it on backwards. When he turned it around, his eyes bugged out of the eyeholes. It had been his inspiration to wear oversized boots to throw off any investigators. But pacing around in size-15 work boots, he looked clownish.

He had puked minutes before on the way there. They had set Eddie up with a phony deal for OxyContin. The wait for him took forever.

When Eddie showed, she felt neither fear nor blind anger. Only an aching determination to save herself.

As she stepped toward him, Eddie's eyes fixed on her with the same mockery she had come to expect.

She leveled the Taurus at his chest. Her finger tightened around the trigger. Did the bastard have a gun on him too?

He didn't move.

Nor did Wesley.

Maybe Eddie wasn't armed? But she could tell he was tensed to try something. Before long a kind of laugh came out of his throat. In the distance water crashed through the Gorge. She expected him to make a stand. To come after her.

For the last time ever.

When he took a step toward her, she thrust the .45 forward.

How long had she waited for this? If he thought he was going to attack her one more time, he was wrong—dead wrong.

"You bitch," he said.

She fired before she knew she was going to. The force rose all the way up her arm and the muzzle flash made her blink.

Wesley, her stone-cold killer accomplice, jumped about three feet. He dropped his hammer. His hands flew up to his ears and—

As she stood ankle-deep in Homer's failed little pond now, a loud rumble startled her. She nervously craned her neck. Scoured the area.

A logging truck rolled by in the distance.

Crap.

Somebody was definitely going to spot her here.

And in these mud-caked tennis shoes, if she had to scoot, she would barely be able to move.

10

Wesley felt his eyebrows shoot up toward his hairline. For a second he ran out of air, his whole world tipping upside down.

Christ, Cadillac Frank Cannizaro! Those dagger-like sideburns, heavy eyelids, fiery eyes! And his goons, Sal and Pino! All three of them loomed huge as the surrounding trees. All three clutched large . . . *Starbucks coffees*?

One also held a big-ass pistol, which was now pointed about four inches from Wesley's right eye. He took that as a very bad sign.

He didn't move. He was too scared to move.

They must have followed him earlier. The maroon car he'd seen. They looked ready to shit on his shoes. Or worse.

Why the hell had he started goddamn gambling again? He'd wanted to prove himself to Jules. Set them up financially for life. But it wasn't supposed to end up involving a freaking gun in his face.

Now he gulped and pictured himself being lashed across a car hood like a dead deer. He gave a frantic little laugh.

"Didn't know you guys h-hunted."

Cadillac Frank twisted up his mouth. He was big as fuck. At least 2 7 o pounds. His face flushed with anger, he stared down at Wesley.

"Got something for you."

The way Cadillac Frank closed and opened his monstrous free hand suggested the gift sure wasn't going to be one of the drinks.

Wesley felt his throat tighten. Despite the gun in his face, his hands came up, fisted.

"No one messes with Wesley Torrance," he said. "You touch me, I'll put you—"

"Funny."

Cadillac Frank shifted his cup to his other hand. He then rammed a fist into Wesley's side.

Wesley doubled over, letting out a whoosh of air. As he clasped his ribs, spots floated before his eyes.

He straightened. Caught his breath. His insides felt aflame.

Out of the corner of his misty eyes he spotted his rifle. Could he turn this around? Or outrun these big bastards? The cold pistol muzzle now pressed against his throat was a big-time obstacle. Could he knock that hand-cannon-of-a-pistol away? Likely, he would wind up just a puddle of teeth and blood. Or facedown with a few bullets in him.

Hulked alongside Cadillac Frank, Sal could hardly stand still. Something about his head looked misshapen. His eyes were lit with a strange excitement.

"Hey, how about the bat?" Sal slurped at his paper cup. "Let's, you know, fuck his shit up."

Wesley took in Sal's comb-over and battered nose and gave out a small cry.

But this was no time to lose his shit. His only hope was to . . . fight. What about his knife? The blade was long enough to do some damage with it. But which freaking pocket was it in? His jacket? No. His pants.

He slid a shaky hand downward.

Lower.

And lower.

Into his pocket.

Okay! There it . . .

He held his breath, waiting for them to notice.

Nope.

He swallowed. But he didn't seem to have any spit left in his mouth. His pocket was tight. Way tight. So now he had to push his hand down hard and—

Cadillac Frank stopped him with a firm grip.

"The hell's the matter with you? Playing with yourself?"

He jerked Wesley's hand back out.

Damn.

"Stab him in the nutsack?" Sal said. "Bitch-slap his sorry—"

"Shut your mouth, Sal, I mean it." Cadillac Frank tugged at a cuff of his teal sweat suit. He shot his goon an irked look. "What I want is . . . you hold his hand."

Sal mouthed the words with a blank look. He blinked.

Cadillac Frank stared at him, lips tight.

"I got to say it again?"

Fidgeting, Sal grabbed Wesley's sweaty palm. Cadillac Frank blew out some air.

"Not like that, moron. Hold it against the damn tree like . . ."

While Cadillac Frank tried to explain, Pino tore off Wesley's orange hat and stuffed it on his own noggin. All furry eyebrows and stone eyes, he jabbed his pistol against Wesley's Adam's apple and stared at him. The muzzle felt hard. And damn cold.

What the hell were they going to do?

Pour an expensive coffee on his hand? Stick a scone in his eye? Then shoot him?

Pino's twisted smile exposed yellowed teeth.

"Like the way that barrel feels? Make you want to pee your panties?"

Sal finally locked his hand around Wesley's shaky wrist—trapping his right palm against the oak. Cadillac Frank then yanked a meat cleaver from some kind of crazy-ass chest holster. Wesley struggled to jerk his hand free, panic flapping through him.

He didn't like the risk class *this* put him in.

"No! Stop. Look, look. Seriously, you don't got to do this."

"You guys hear something?" Cadillac Frank said. "What was that? Some fuck—"

"I swear I'll pay."

Cadillac Frank's dark eyes seemed to swell out from his face.

"You'll pay all right. I want my hundred and fifty thou."

Jeez! Against one, he stood a slight chance. Against three, he'd need a freaking miracle. Still, he had to make a move. His body flexed taut. He felt the anger building in his throat as he lifted his chin.

"Okay," he heard himself say, "you're all—You woke the dragon! It's *on*."

He jerked up his left foot. Tried kicking Cadillac Frank in the shin, hard.

He missed—and his foot smacked into the tree.

"Shit!"

As Sal howled with laughter, Wesley caught the glint of the falling cleaver. With a thwack, the tip of his pinky disappeared.

Blood geysered into the air.

"*Jeez!*"

Snatching up Wesley's coat, Cadillac Frank lurched even closer.

"Not your day, is it? Ten seconds, you shitbag, that's what you got. To gimme a reason not to go on."

Wesley's breath came in little pants as he gaped at what was left of his pinky. Blood! He had to say something—or it might really cost him an arm and a leg.

The cleaver loomed before him.

He floundered for an answer.

He felt his shoulders rise, the blood in his face.

"Screw you, motherfuckers."

"Oh, my."

"I'll have the money! Two weeks? One! All I need is—I'll freaking get it."

For a few seconds there was dead silence.

Cadillac Frank squinted in suspicion.

"All of it?"

"Yes."

His bookie let go of his jacket and nodded. Sal then dropped his blood-streaked wrist. Tears welling in his eyes, he clamped his bandanna around his burning finger. The pain was throbbing and deep. Mentally, he felt as if he was having about ten nervous breakdowns at once.

Cadillac Frank lowered the cleaver. He sipped at his Starbucks.

"Sweating now, ain't you?"

"Damn, my hand . . . *hurts.*"

A bird screeched in the trees as Cadillac Frank snatched up Wesley's Winchester and glared at him.

"You'll pay up, fuckface. Last loser that didn't pay? He got dead."

"Jeez," Wesley said.

Cadillac Frank lowered his voice to a hushed threat.

"Understand what I'm saying? Anything goes wrong, you're Dumpster meat. Ding, ding, bang, bang—we'll be right at your door. We'll hack your damn legs off. Then whack you."

Hack and whack?

"Oh, shit. Not cool."

He felt the sweat of desperation breaking on his neck. He was seeing dead people. The cops had to be after him. Now the freaking Mob was too.

Cadillac Frank glowered on.

"This ain't over . . . Let's go, boys."

Wesley froze, squeezing his throbbing pinky in his bandanna, aware his life was spiraling downward from troubled to worse, while Cadillac Frank, Pino, and Sal lumbered off toward a stand of spruces.

When Pino brushed against a branch, he told it to go fuck itself.

———

Jules grabbed a metal rake from Homer's tool shed. Raced back to his failed collection pond. Double-checked to make sure she was out of line of sight of the house. Began to methodically search the entire pond bed. For a long while she dragged the rake through the muck. Dragged it some more. Dripping with perspiration, feet chilled, she lost track of the passage of time.

Maybe she was too—

Had Homer already found it?

Eventually, the heavy rake caught on something dense. Like metal. She breathed a sigh of relief. Thank God!

She felt a charge of excitement as she pulled at the object. Jerked it up with the rake. Stooped to inspect her find.

It was the rusty end of an old shovel.

Shit.

She had picked the little collection pond because only livestock used it. It was mucky and off-the-beaten path. Basically deserted. Maybe the cows had knocked it around? Trampled it down deep? Used it to rob other cattle? Okay, she was getting punchy.

A little alarm sounded in her brain.

What *did* the cops know? Shortly after the shooting, they had questioned her twice. They hadn't browbeaten her at all. Instead, they seemed more concerned with setting up a time-line of Eddie's activities, and adding to their mile-long list of his enemies. But had she underestimated them? She wiped her forearm across her brow. Apparently even a slug could be matched to a gun. She had to at least get rid of the revolver. In a better hiding place.

She had used it to save herself. She couldn't let it drag her into trouble now.

She kicked her foot into the mud and had a sense she and Wesley were racing down a long, narrowing tunnel. Damn, she could've used his help right now! Why did he have to be out, taking it easy?

When a tan Chevy pickup appeared in the distance, she felt a chill.

Homer?

Already?

How goddamn long had she been out here?

She had to do something. And do it now. So much was at stake. Her and Wesley's plan suddenly seemed so fragile.

Already ankle-deep in muck and water, she squatted lower, hoping Homer might not spot her. She felt like she had jet fuel thrumming through her veins. She and Homer had been pals for years. But who knew what he'd do if he found out about what had happened?

Had Homer already found the .45?

Homer's black Lab, Cody, tore out from behind the nearest barn. He barked. Then veered her way.

Barely a hundred yards away, Homer's truck slowed. She could make out his white mane of hair. Her stomach twisted into a knot as his head turned. Right toward her.

Every muscle in her body was rigid. He had to see her.

Damn.

She squatted there. Braced and tense.

Cody closed in.

Barked again.

"Shush, Cody!" she said. "It's me."

Her calves were already submerged. Was it too late to slip all the way down into the mud?

Busted, she thought.

Apparently Homer didn't make her out. He drove on.

Cody settled down at pond's edge. He let his tongue out, started to pant. A moment later she felt a lifting inside as her eye caught the glint of metal in the shallow water and muck.

The Taurus Judge's stainless steel cylinder.

On Monday, Jules watched Wesley slump back against her floral-print sofa. His pinky was wrapped in a gob of gauze and tape.

"Oh, shit. Shit. What kind of fool am I? A big one." He stared at his bandage, horrified. "Stupid, that's what I am—stupid."

Seated beside him, she nodded in agreement. She kept silent, mouth pursed.

"A first-class bonehead," he said.

After a pause, she said, "You think of that all by yourself? Or did it just come to you? You know, stupid can get you killed."

"Jeez, everything's going . . ." He drew in a deep breath, glanced at her, and then stared into space. "I owe the Mob. I just . . . Hell, maybe I deserve to be punished." He gave a little laugh. "Today's forecast: screwed."

She stood and stared out the window. Minutes ago, she had thrown her hands in the air before him. Despite her best intentions, she was tempted to clobber him. But if she didn't help him keep it together? Things could get really messy. So, what she did was holler, "Enough is enough!" She then nailed him with a now-I-have-to-unfuck-this look.

After a while she rallied to his side, racking her brain for ways to help. He looked so stunned, and she wanted to be encouraging. Given a little time, she knew she'd figure out what to do.

She had decided not to worry him about it, but she hadn't had the best Saturday herself. That close call at Homer's pond had made for an edgy start to her weekend. Besides the big scare then, she could still feel now the ache in her thighs from desperately slogging through all that mud. But standing before Wesley and his bandaged pinky, she wondered if he'd been through enough lately himself.

Perhaps not quite yet. She puffed her cheeks.

"You know I love you, Wesley. You know I'd do anything for you. But maybe you do deserve that. To get punished." Her voice took on some heat. "You are really something."

His face flushed.

"I know, I know." He closed his eyes briefly, as if to let her words sink in more deeply. "I—I must've been nuts."

"Well, duh. You think?"

"Or dreaming. God, they were like monsters. Wham! That shit hurt." He let out a breath with an audible sound. "They even took my hat."

She raised her eyebrows. Messing with the Mob? What had he expected to happen?

"You've said that."

"I liked that hat."

"Enough about the hat!"

"I was going to try some karate shit on them. Give them all a beat-down. Ass was going to be . . . They sucker-punched me, though."

She had warned him about his gambling, but did he listen?

"Right," she said.

"You know? There must be a way to get rid of . . . the whole problem."

"Oh, sure."

"Guess I'll have to go after them."

"Uh-huh."

"Hunt them down myself." He kind of puffed his chest up. He shadowboxed a moment. "I was *so* close to taking care of business."

"Well, while you're at it, make sure to ask for your stupid hat."

She let out a grunt. She'd figure out what to do about the money he owed. If she had to, she would take Cadillac Frank out of the picture for good herself. But, damn! Hopefully the new week was going to be a little calmer. A part of her wished she could take a big eraser and rub it right across the past few days.

She raised a palm.

"Anything else to tell me?"

He looked away nervously.

"Well . . . no. That's pretty much about it."

For a while she just held his bandaged hand. They didn't speak. When at last his gaze dropped toward the braided rug, she sensed he was about to really tune out on her.

She knew him. She knew that the bump on the bridge of his nose had come from a playground tumble. Knew that, as a kid from a poor Winooski family, he had hated being called a "river rat." Knew that, years ago, he had been scarred mentally when he risked his own life saving a drowning boy, Tommy Jenkins. The one time Wesley had mentioned it, she didn't believe him, so she searched the Net. BYSTANDER SAVES

BOY TRAPPED UNDER LAKE ICE, the article headline said. NEARLY DIES HIMSELF.

She knew all his quirks. And a thrill of satisfaction ran through her when she figured out how to play this. She knew just what would take his mind off his troubles now. She would assert control here.

"Anyway, maybe it's time. Time for a little . . . discipline."

Her blood picking up, she began unbuttoning her blouse. She scooted into the bedroom.

When she strutted back in, she wore only a spiked black collar and slinky five-inch heels. She clutched a leather riding crop and a pair of handcuffs. His mouth hung open, and she gave him a good long look.

She could spot that something other than his pinky was apparently throbbing. She narrowed her eyes again.

Thrusting out a calf, she pointed with her crop at her shiny black high heel.

"Now lick my shoe, you little worm. You bad, bad boy!"

13

———

A little later when Jules picked up the kitchen phone, a flash of panic filled her chest.

Investigator Farrs? The state police?

She grabbed onto a ladder-back chair to steady herself. Wesley was snoring away in the bedroom as she scrambled to take stock of the past few weeks. Just what mistakes *had* they made? Was their plan about to lose its wheels?

Wait a minute.

Hadn't she phoned them? Maybe Farrs was only checking things off his own list.

"I'm calling from Trooper HQ, Miss Nichols," said the gruff voice on the other end of the line. "You wanted an update. I know it's been a bit, and, well, I apologize."

When she first met Farrs at the New Haven trooper station, she had been surprised by how dead-serious he seemed. He sounded the same now.

She didn't respond.

"Wanted you to know there's been a development in your husband's case—a big one."

Damn. Scratch this call being a mundane check-in.

As far as she knew, the cops had made little progress. She had kept a cool head that night. And she'd set up a tight alibi. After all, what clues did the cops have? No gun. No finger-prints. They might have found boot prints. But size-15 work boot prints—which Wesley had made an effort to leave behind.

But now she had a sense their present-day life was about to explode.

"Come again?" she said.

"A break."

Everything seemed to slow down.

A torturous stretch of silence passed. A break? The longer she waited to respond, the more ominous Farrs's statement seemed. Her fingers gripping the chair were white. Her legs felt weak. So she sat.

"Well, that's . . ."

Minutes ago, things had seemed to be looking up. She recently had retrieved the .45 and buried it where no one would ever, ever find it. Not even an hour ago, she'd distracted Wesley in bed. After he perked up, buried his head between her thighs, and gave her an orgasm which rocked her whole body, she felt like they'd gotten their second wind. She had been in a stupendous mood, for a short while.

Now, though, she was in a dream.

"God, I don't know what to say."

"Knew you'd be pleased," Investigator Farrs said.

She stared toward the door, seeing nothing.

"Mmmm."

Weeks ago, Farrs had sat her down at a metal table in a gray interview room, and then turned on some kind of recorder. He was forty-something. An intense, husky guy. He looked as if he could use some sleep. When he pulled a chair out from the table to sit, the legs screeched against the floor.

She smelled Pine-Sol. And sweat.

She had agreed quite willingly to go in to talk. Knowing she would be questioned, she and Wesley had even prepped together beforehand. She hated lying to anybody. But she and Wesley had to move forward.

"I just want to help," she kept saying as the interview proceeded.

After signing a consent form, she'd outlined her recent activities. Even faked concern for her own safety. And plowed through a stack of tissues.

"Who might have done this?" Farrs asked.

Eddie had run with a dangerous crowd, she stressed—crazy-ass bikers, other underworld lowlifes, junkies, and so on. To encourage the Staties to cast an even wider net for suspects, she mentioned how Eddie trucked goodies down from Montreal. The falsified freight documents. The hidden compartments under truck floors.

All the while Farrs seemed to be deep in thought, lips pursed.

"Eddie always owed people serious money," she said. "And they always owed him. None of them seemed to think twice about getting violent. Some of them are *out* there, you know? Eddie told me that one crankhead even takes scalps."

When Farrs asked her about guns, she took a long sip of water from a foam cup. Looked hard at the closed metal door. She then fed him info about Eddie's gunrunning, and his last delivery of some kind of foreign rifles. Fully automatic, still in their plastic wrappers. Which he'd apparently sold to some gangbangers.

"Myself?" she'd quickly added. "I'm way afraid of guns."

Farrs had seemed to accept her story. And thankfully the Taurus Judge was taken care of now.

Presently? He must be taping her over the phone line too. And there was something new working in him.

"That night at the Gorge?" he said now on the other end of the line. "It appears we were understaffed. And, well . . . somehow a piece of evidence got put aside. But among the items we collected, there was a leaf."

"A *leaf?*"

"CS-2 9. Well, that's its crime-scene number. Anyway, it was a leaf with a red stain. A leaf with one drop of blood on it, it turns out."

"So . . ."

"For a while there afterward, we had *photos* of the bloody leaf. But not the leaf itself. Stuff happens, you know? The good news, though, is we got it now."

The receiver seemed to go cold in her hand.

"Su-per," she said, maybe a little too slowly.

"And the forensic lab has determined that the blood on it wasn't from the deceased."

"Which means—"

"Now we can search. For a possible match, I mean."

Wesley's new trouble with the Mob was enough to handle. A *leaf?*

One little drop of blood? It wasn't hers. God, maybe Wesley had cut himself that night at the Gorge. She felt a crappy sliding sensation.

The simplest explanation was the most likely:

Wesley.

How?

And who knew if the damn Staties had found the shell casing she and Wesley had lost? After reading Wesley's murder cover-up checklist a while ago, she thought they'd done pretty well.

Apparently not.

What the heck was next? They might have left other evidence behind. Maybe she'd left her library card there too?

"You there?" Farrs said on the other end of the line.

Struggling to pull herself together, she said, "Um."

"Miss Nichols?"

The cops had to know that she and Wesley were together now. If so, now they would want to test his blood. For exclusionary purposes, if ever needed, she had already given a DNA sample. Well, she sure wasn't going to tell him about the damn leaf. That definitely would wig him out.

Was it his blood the troopers had collected at the Gorge? Why couldn't that leaf have stayed lost?

"Wonderful," she finally said.

"Realize this must be hard for you."

"Oh, gosh." Did she really just say that? "You're *so* right." God, Farrs had to sense her lame struggling over the line. She should be acting way more . . . "Well, let me know if I can, um, help in any way."

He made a disgusted sound.

"Granted, Eddie was no angel. No offense intended. Sorry. But it galls me when any killer's still on the loose."

How to react to that?

No problem?

Don't sweat it?

She stayed silent. Farrs cleared his throat before he spoke again.

"The Vermont Forensic Lab?"

"Yeah?"

She glanced toward the window. Maybe they were being watched by the Staties now. The thought of a cop snooping around her yard a while ago wasn't funny anymore. Not one bit. Things were heading downhill faster than she could keep up with.

How was she supposed to take on the state police?

"People lie," Farrs said. "But science? It don't. You know? The lab's top-notch. So when we do start looking for a match . . . Just wanted to give you the good news."

14

"Got a question for you, man," Wesley said into his cell phone a day later.

Make a decision. Act on it. That's what his old shrink, Dr. Chi, had always urged him to do.

He felt charged to be taking this step. Jules's recent dominatrix play had inspired him to get a little rough himself. It was time to make things up to her, and get freaking Cadillac Frank off his ass. He had to take the fight to the enemy.

Did he sound tough enough now, though? Parked in his Mustang at an Otter Creek boat access area, he had been shitting bricks just thinking about making this call.

A raspy voice came over the other end of the line.

"Who the fuck is this? How'd you get my digits, asshole?"

Jeez, what now?

He pictured the horn tats along Kev Bates's bald head that Jules had mentioned before. How she said all he lacked was hooves for feet.

Wesley stared toward the murky creek water. Closed his eyes a moment.

He knew he was sticking his neck out. He had found Bates's phone number on a list that the state cops had recently returned.

Now he could still hang up.

Then again, he needed to get his shit together. Every roll of the dice was a second chance.

"Not important," he said.

"Hell yeah, it is. Nobody got this number."

"A mutual connection?"

"Who the—"

As he cut Bates off, he heard his own voice rise in pitch.

"He's, well, like, not around now?"

"What? Say it, asshole. You mean dead?"

"Yeah."

"Eddie?"

"Something like that."

"So what? We worked together. But I hated that fuck." Bates dredged up some phlegm and apparently spat. "Got some kind of offer?"

Who had *horns* tattooed onto their head? Was that someone Wesley could trust?

He could still end this call.

Horns?

No, that was someone to have on *your* goddamn side. Taking on the Mob wasn't for sissies. Hopefully Bates was off house-arrest by now.

"Easy money," Wesley said. "For one favor."

From the other end of the line came another spitting sound.

"I don't like phones."

Wesley watched the creek water pull at a snagged plastic bag. How to phrase this? Appeal to the guy's animal side?

"It would take some . . . well, firepower?"

"Now we're talking, dude. Got me a SAW. Seven hundred rounds a minute. Same shit the boys in I-raq had."

He nodded, as if Bates could see him.

"That sounds—"

"Slice and dice. More better? The M-40. That's the stealthy shit, my man."

A car thumped along the nearby covered bridge and startled Wesley. He clutched at his chest. A duck or something scurried up the opposite bank of the creek.

"Yeah?" he said.

"Sniper rifle."

"Um. Nice?"

"Say, you like little boys?"

Wesley winced.

Man! Screw this sicko. How was he supposed to answer *that*? Was it a trick question? Was Bates freaking serious?

"Asking you a damn question!" Bates said.

"Uh, no. Not really."

"Don't know what you're missing."

Up until now, Wesley felt he'd done all right. He'd held tough. But now he had nothing.

His Net search had revealed that Bates had been brought to trial on two different murders, but had managed to skate on both. It was believed he'd kept both victims locked in dog crates. Witnesses against him had drowned and died in a car explosion.

Just who was this creep?

Wesley had called the only person he could think of who might be willing to take out Cadillac Frank for a price. Hopefully a price much less than the amount he owed Cadillac Frank. The wheels had been set in motion. But what had he gotten himself into? He felt a surge of fear.

Suspecting he'd just fucked himself good.

There was a long silence.

Then through the receiver came a creepy cackle.

"Maybe, asshole, we can meet."

15

A voice in Wesley's head said, *Go, before it's too late.*

Kev Bates had summoned him to a Denny's restaurant right off the interstate in Winooski. Waiting, pacing the rear parking lot, he couldn't see any traffic. But he heard the distant cars rushing away. Scraggly bushes edged the lot. He smelled car exhaust, and he couldn't shake a sick feeling in his gut.

He braced himself when he heard a motorcycle engine approach. But his unease grew. This was so . . . He halted next to a pale red pickup and eyed his Mustang, which waited near a fly-buzzed Dumpster maybe twenty feet away.

God! What did Jules say sometimes? *If you call for the devil, he'll come.*

Well, he was coming.

Yet he himself couldn't risk Jules staying pissed at him, and maybe dumping his ass.

"Doable," he said out loud.

His body tensed as Bates roared up on a Harley-Davidson to the rear of the broad, nearly empty parking lot. No helmet. Bates's bike was black with leather bags. It had high handle-bars and a little, low seat.

As Bates killed the engine and smacked down the kick-stand, Wesley took in his wide-set, intense eyes. The flat face. Tried not to stare at the dark blue horn tats which ran back from his brow.

The dude was muscled-up.

Wesley couldn't help himself. It was like some invisible force was pulling his eyes. Slowly, he looked down. Beneath the cuffs of Bates's leather pants.

Black motorcycle boots.

No hooves.

When Mr. AntiChrist strutted closer, Wesley extended a trembly hand.

"My man!"

Bates slitted his eyes. They were empty and icy at the same time. Even his body pitched forward at an aggressive slant.

The hairs rose on the back of Wesley's neck.

Aw, shit.

"Okay," he said, "not really a people person?"

Had Bates changed his mind? This was happening too fast. What was the wild-looking dude thinking?

Was Bates going to tear him to bits?

Couldn't they just shoot the shit inside over some coffee and pancakes?

Probably not. The nasty twist to Bates's mouth told Wesley this wasn't going to be good. He felt the sweat soaking through his shirt.

Screw it.

Feeling the high whine of his nerves, he forced himself to stare Bates straight in the eye.

"Hold on," he said. "Dude, back off."

For a few seconds he matched Bates's silence. The sun beat down on them. A plane thundered by overhead.

Bates gave him a quick up and down, stepped forward. Bates then shook his head ever so slightly.

Wesley's anger popped.

"Get the fuck away from me," he said.

"Who you talking to like that?"

Hell.

Okay.

The parking lot was dead quiet. No help there.

Make an all-or-nothing move. He would stab two stiff fingers into Bates's eyes. A hard-core killa for sure. Then—

Somehow Bates slipped in behind him and hooked a powerful arm around his neck.

What the hell! The whole move had been so fast. Was Bates screwing around? Or what?

Wesley had never hired a vicious, bloodthirsty killer before, but this seemed like a really crappy start.

He bucked and furiously tried to pry away Bates's wrist and forearm. Dug his nails into Bates's skin. Bates had him in a brutally tight choke hold, though. Glued to him. His face went hot. As he gasped for breath, he felt what must be a gun tucked into Bates's waistband. Bates reeked of exhaust and oil. Wesley reeled under the weight and smell of him.

Wesley hooked a foot around the bastard's ankle.

But he couldn't budge Bates's leg to jostle him. So he tried banging his head backward, which hurt like hell. Air!

Goddamn it.

He'd been played! Bates was going to snatch the down-payment cash Wesley had scraped up, and then scoot. Or maybe kill Wesley first.

His eyes blurred. He felt Bates's breath on his neck.

He was getting dizzy.

He needed—

Air!

16

—————

Was he really going to die at a Denny's?

This is it, Wesley thought in wonder.

He didn't want to die!

Not now, not like this.

"No fucking around, right?" Bates said. "Easy."

Wesley gasped for air.

No giving in! Growing dizzier, he flailed about. Threw a hand behind him. Where was the bastard's gun?

Was that it?

"Git your goddamn hands off that," Bates said. "Got me?"

"Yeah!"

"Or I'll finish your sorry ass off, right now."

Wesley wondered if he was turning stupider by the minute. *This* guy was his new ally?

"Right."

"Was just screwing with ya."

Once the pressure on his neck eased some, he coughed. Coughed some more. His breathing began to even out.

After he assured Bates he was good for the money, Bates released him.

"So chill, homie," Bates said. "Ain't no need to stress then."

"Let me make something clear. I just want to protect the woman I—"

"Screw that shit. All I need is the cash."

For a down payment on Bates's help, Wesley turned over a banded short stack of cash. Mostly twenties. He had sold his big-ass TV, his graphite golf clubs, anything he could think of, through Craigslist. But he was going to need a lot more.

He rubbed the front of his neck where Bates had squeezed him so hard. Bates glared at him for what felt like an hour.

When Bates thrust a fingertip into his chest, Wesley tried not to stare back at his horns.

"Just don't fuck with *me*," Bates said.

17

———

The following day, Wesley drove down Burlington's Main Street, palms sweaty on the steering wheel. A huge black SUV with a LOVE THE EARTH bumper sticker crept along ahead of him. The downtown skyline loomed closer. It was time to take one more gamble, double down and make a withdrawal from Citizens Bank. With a shotgun.

If Kev Bates took out Cadillac Frank right away for fifty grand, as he'd promised yesterday, it would save Wesley a big chunk of change. Otherwise, if he didn't come up with the $150,000 he owed Cadillac Frank by the Sunday before Thanksgiving, he would be the one getting stuffed.

Previously, he'd thought hard about his next move. Staring at the hacked tendon and bone of his pinky before bandaging it again, he conjured up a solution. It was a weak plan. And he knew it. It might even be a total freaking mistake. He might end up with both wackos coming after him.

But he was shit-out-of luck desperate. And now as he motored into downtown Burlington, despite the sick emptiness in his stomach, he was rolling with the plan. At least he had Cadillac Frank on Bates's most-wanted list now.

Wesley had no kick-ass robbery scheme. He hadn't studied Citizens Bank one minute. But a large red shopping bag waited on the car floor. Stuffed inside were a latex Frankenstein mask and Eddie's sawed-off shotgun. The Browning was loaded with double-aught buck shells.

Two days ago, he had finally told Jules about his vision of Eddie in the YMCA pool. Her eyes went wide with apparent concern.

"He's right behind you!" she soon said.

He panicked and spun around, before he heard her break into laughter. Some things, he decided later, were better kept to oneself. Like this robbery now.

Downtown, off to his left Chittenden County Courthouse rose up, boxy and gray. Its marble pillars ran close together—like giant prison bars. Gaping at them, he swerved into the wrong lane. Then he swerved back.

As he hunted for a parking space, the pressure pinged inside him. He whipped his Mustang around and around City Hall Park. A beat-up Honda finally backed out, and he almost knocked down the parking meter racing in. After he cut the motor, he leaned his brow against the steering wheel. His neck still stiff from yesterday, he lifted his head.

No sweat!

He had already helped murder someone, had half his finger hacked off, and teamed up with a man with horns and the creepiest eyes he'd ever seen. What was the big deal now?

Snatching up his bag, he dragged himself out of the car and then stood before the parking meter. Jeez, how much time did he need for a holdup? Merely thinking about it, he dropped half his coins stuffing the slot.

His eyes jumped about. City Hall Park was quiet for a sunny Wednesday afternoon. A few teens slouched near the fountain. A woman with matted hair shuffled toward a bench. The hotdog vendor on the corner waved away a stray beagle. None of it seemed real. His heart beat too quickly. He knew he had to freaking calm down. So he bought a wiener and a root beer, and then sank onto a bench facing Citizens Bank, and gawked about, and nibbled.

After a while he gaped toward the brownstone bank's doors. An ancient-looking box jutted out to one side. VAULT ALARM, it warned in gold letters.

Quickly he turned away.

Why rush things? He scurried back for another hotdog. His hand shook as he grabbed the squeeze bottle of mustard. When he was done, the pockmarked vendor made a little noise.

"That finger. Want some onions on it too?"

"What're you—"

"Your pinky, dude."

Wesley glanced down. Mustard slopped along his bandage, not his hotdog. His cheeks burned.

"Oh, shit."

"Least you didn't bite it, right?"

With a pained grin, Wesley grabbed some napkins and cleaned up. He then scrambled back to his bench to eat again. Flinging an arm over the bench top afterward, he tried to summon up an air of ease. Nothing weird here, folks!

"Got this," he said out loud.

Somehow things would work out. He had to keep the faith. When the woman with matted hair shuffled up and asked for spare change, he eyed her soiled Batman T-shirt. His heart went out to her, and he thrust a five into her palm. Jerking his head around, he let out a burp. Well, if he didn't do this soon, he'd puke. And be totally broke.

He needed to keep pushing forward.

The run-in with Cadillac Frank in the woods felt seared into his brain. He could still feel the shock deep in his bones. To avoid any more meat cleavers, he had to—

"Mister! Help me find my dog?"

A red-haired, stringbean of a kid stood before him.

"I'm kinda busy," he said.

"Sure don't look it. . . . Hey, there he is! C'mon."

"But—"

"Pig! Here, boy!"

For a minute they chased the kid's beagle dragging its leash around, without capturing it. When Wesley cast a glance toward his bench, he felt the alarm spreading up from his diaphragm.

Christ! His bag!

Where the hell—?

Oh God, the woman in the Batman T-shirt. There she was, shuffling away with it.

"Hey, mister!" the kid said from a distance. "Grab him! Pig's right behind—"

"Hey, lady! *Stop!*"

He had to get his bag and rob the—

"Right there," the kid said.

Wesley stooped and grabbed the pudgy beagle. Pooch in arms, he sprinted to the shuffling woman and then tried to yank his bag away from her.

"That's mine," he said.

The woman held tight. As she kicked at his leg, something warm and wet spread across his waist. His face twisted as a foul smell hit him.

"Oh, shit."

For a second he was tempted to drop the dog.

"Trade you for your shoes?" she said.

"What?"

"For my man."

"You're freaking nuts. Gimme that—"

"Nuh-uh."

He lunged for the bag again. When he pulled, it started to rip.

"*Shit*. Screw it. Take the stupid shoes, then."

He shifted the smelly beagle in his arms and struggled to pull off his Nikes. He pushed them toward her, while barely catching a hold on his bag. He then raced back in his socks to the kid. Handed off the damn dog.

He could do this! Despite the socks, mustard-stained bandage, and pee-sopped shirt, he had to man the fuck up.

He crushed the weakness and the doubt. Everything swam as he took a big swallow and started his movement toward the bank. His head was pounding. In a sec he would jerk on the mask, whip out the sawed-off. But what the hell should he say inside? Sorry, in trouble with the Mob? Need fifty thou to pay off a man with horns?

Nearing the curb, he tripped and lost his balance. He twisted his body as he went down, dropped his bag, and plunged onto the hard street pavement.

The sawed-off spilled out. Diving forward to grab it shot bolts of pain up his hip. The pain was bright and fierce.

"*Damn*."

When a horn blared, he jerked his head toward it and gulped.

18

The next morning, Detective Burpee leaned over his desk, pen in hand, doodling, biting his lower lip. He had finally finagled access to phone records for his lovebird suspects. Not surprisingly, the two of them had been talking up a storm for months. Recently, Mr. Torrance was dialing notoriously ill-dressed Mob bookie Cadillac Frank Cannizaro nearly non-stop too. One particularly busy week there had been 1 3 2 calls to that number.

Street sources said unless Jules's lover wised up, he was about to end up ill-dressed himself—wearing cinder blocks, and with a permanent lake view.

It would be possible to cheat on this one. Burpee could fake evidence, and shop around for witnesses to say most whatever he wanted. The old saying was, a decent detective and prosecutor could put away someone guilty—but it took a great pair to lock up someone innocent. That wasn't his style, though.

Clucking his tongue, he laid down his pen. Oh, well. Even with a slam-dunk case, would he turn Jules and her partner in? Although "hook and book" had been his motto for years, it was clear she had been abused. Horribly abused. Eddie had even put her in the hospital with a concussion once. According to the records, she had facial injuries and whopping bruises on her body. She could barely move one of her legs, and her pee had blood in it.

A dirtbag batterer like him, his death was practically righteous. He'd had it coming.

Who knew what was right on this one? There was just no telling how a battered woman would react. Eddie might have even threatened to off her, if she left him. As things stood, there was almost a kind of rough justice to it all. In his gut he already felt that. Why knock himself out anymore?

Hell, somebody should probably have given her a hubcap-sized medal.

Snooping on her, sneaking into her farmhouse and pawing through her bedroom—maybe he'd gotten too personally involved. He had given the finger to standard protocol. Where was this supposed to end? He was starting to act as unreasonable as his rigid captain, whenever he began digging his heels in on something.

Still, he had to set his uneasy mind at rest. What would keep them from trying to pull something else?

He picked up his pen again, twiddled it. After a while he furrowed his brow.

He then had an idea. He might be dumb-ass wrong, but every instinct told him he was right. Who knew what else they might try? Something dumb as bank robbery? Well, maybe they weren't that stupid. But maybe he could scare them straight.

With a tick of excitement, he phoned Jules.

Wesley hobbled into Jules's kitchen, the ringing phone distracting him from his glass of Jameson's and fantasy of ending it all with the sawed-off. He could feel the tension in his entire body.

What now?

Forget about his debts, hacked pinky, and the botched robbery, his back was trashed.

An eternity after he plunged into the street outside Citizens Bank yesterday, the Saab barreling toward him had swerved away—just missing what was left of his spread fingers. Just missing covering him with tire tracks. Crippled with pain, he finally managed to tuck the shotgun away. And he never even made it inside the goddamn bank.

Now, how the hell was he going to pay Kev Bates, or Cadillac Frank, or whichever crazy dude he was going to owe money to?

Sure, he had the sicko with horns on his team now. But was that even a good thing?

With each step, he grimaced.

"Damn. Ow!"

When he finally reached the stupid phone, he glared at a bluejay raiding the birdhouse outside the window. He snatched up the receiver with a surge of irritation.

"For Christ sakes! What!"

The man's pissed-off tone startled Burpee. A few harsh breaths sounded over the line, like the guy was hyperventilating. Burpee heard something like ice clinking in a glass, then spoke.

"Hello? Listen close."

"Sure! Why the hell not?"

"I got evidence. Incriminating photos of—"

"Bullshit!"

The line was silent a moment as Burpee fumbled for a response.

"Try anything else, and I'll—"

"Oww. God."

The receiver smashed down. Burpee grumbled, harsh echo coursing through his ear.

To clear his head, Burpee sneaked off to a matinee cop flick. He nibbled popcorn and counted seven deaths in the film. Seeing the law depicted in such black-and-white terms cracked him up. When the iron fist of justice came down at the end, and every surviving dirtbag was locked up for good, he chuckled. The Blue Brotherhood had done it again!

Upon return, a stack of messages waited on his desk. He pushed them aside, onto a photo of a folding knife. He knew he should update some reports, but . . . He also needed to yank someone's chain on some way-late lab reports. Screw that too. Instead, he crunched his way through a stack of buttery Ritz crackers.

Well. A good cop never gave up. But now what? He sat there for a moment, rubbing his chin.

What the hell.

Staring at a composite image curling on his corkboard, he again dialed Jules's house—and winced in anticipation. He clenched the receiver six inches away from his ear, half-expecting Satan to answer at this point.

A second later the same voice as before hollered into the line.

"Shoot me! Kill me. Can't take this."

Right away, the receiver smashed down again. A dial tone buzzed.

As he eased down his own phone, someone screamed at the end of the hall, a hysterical gibberish. Wackos! Soon they'd be piling in through the windows.

Full of workaday fatigue, he glanced up at his cheap plastic wall clock. It read only a quarter past three. He pinched the bridge of his nose, and for a split second felt like thumping his head against his desk.

Well, he should return that call from his trooper buddy, Mike Farrs. Respond to Mike's voice mail about something interesting to share.

Who knew what that was all about?

19

Two days later, shortly after Cadillac Frank climbed out of his Caddy, the back of his stomach went cold. Who the fuck was *that*?

In the distance some loony with inked horns on his noggin was coming at him with his piece raised. Using a two-handed grip.

Cadillac Frank's breath came faster.

He whipped out his Glock from his waistband.

He had just parked near the iron gates of Holman Cemetery to pay respects to his old boss, Tony T. The day was overcast, no sun. He could smell the clipped grass beneath his feet. Now, this loony with a piece was a good twenty-five feet away. Horns? What the hell was this world coming to? He looked like the goddamn bogeyman. The bogeyman in biker gear. And as big as if he lived off of steroids.

Where had he even come from?

Cadillac Frank eyed the gates. Should he haul ass inside? Take cover behind a headstone or that granite angel?

No time for—

With a burning knot in his chest, he scooted right. Stopped. Faced the loony. Saw the flash from the fuck's gun. Alongside the iron fence, they fired away. The shots boomed. Why the hell was he firing so fast? God, he was shaking.

His head rang from the noise. Once they'd emptied their pieces, it looked like he'd hit the loony in the arm. The freak's hard, narrow face didn't even change, though. He kept his cool. Like he was ex-military.

Or was plain psycho.

In a ballsy move, the guy charged. He came straight at Cadillac Frank. His tackle felt like being hit by a freight train. They tumbled down, wrestled around on the grass. The fucker was way strong. Cadillac Frank knew he would have to move fast. He walloped the guy with a smashing overhand blow. Then drove his fist into his throat.

"You *shitsack*," Cadillac Frank said.

The blows barely registered. Was the dude amped up on something? Or maybe he *liked* pain.

Was he even stoppable?

Cadillac Frank hammered at the fucker, trying to wear him down. But it was like hitting a concrete wall. And the blows were still coming his own way with a shocking power. When the dude drove a short, vicious fist into his gut, Cadillac Frank gasped for breath. Another blow landed hard on Cadillac Frank's head, coming so damn fast he had no time to react. Then came more close straight shots and things dimmed and cleared up and he shook his buzzing head.

The horned dude's eyes refocused. He pulled himself to his knees, whipped out a combat knife. It had a mile-long blade.

Blood seeped down his injured arm as he smiled coldly at Cadillac Frank.

"Welcome to my motherfucking party," the guy said.

Pitched on his side, stunned, Cadillac Frank felt his stomach turn. He'd had close calls before. But right now . . .

"Fuck you," Cadillac Frank said.

"After? Gonna scalp you. Cut that shit off, inch by inch."

As the demon-looking freak shifted closer, Cadillac Frank desperately clamped his hand onto the guy's wrist. Despite his tight hold, there were less than two feet between him and that monster blade. Maybe he'd had a chance before, but not now. His other arm was pinned beneath him. And the freak was strong as fuck.

Cadillac Frank felt his arm weakening.

It began to shake.

He couldn't hold off that glinting big steel blade much longer.

While he waited for the kill move, he felt the sweat creeping down his brow. Screw this up, and they could bury him next to Tony T.

The freak's eyes had become hard knots focused on him. Staring back, Cadillac Frank felt his fear blowing on through to goddamn rage. Felt himself gain new strength. He gave the dude his *you're screwed* smile.

Okay, asswipe.

Try it.

When the wide blade came down at him, he rolled.

The blade seared into his shoulder. He screamed against the pain.

Gritting his teeth, Cadillac Frank snatched the blade away. His fingers curled around the handle. Hell, this was going to be fun. Screw him and his horns.

He raised the knife above the loser's eye.

"Party's over, fucko."

20

———

Tuesday afternoon, Jules sucked in a calming breath and then dialed her flame-haired ex-stripper buddy, Bree Connelly. If anyone could get Jules some intel, it was Bree.

"What's up, Bree?"

"Well, finally dumped Jeff—my Halloween hook-up. Kicked him to the curb."

"You said he was hot."

"Another man in love with himself! You know? He was more of a sport-fuck, anyway. Should feel lucky you got yourself such a winner."

When Jules peeked around the corner into the living room, she felt a small disturbance. Wesley lay flopped on his back on the rug, feet up on the sofa. He muttered into space, something almost crazy in his look. He claimed he'd been getting strange phone calls lately. She couldn't help but wonder if he'd imagined them—like that text from Eddie from the grave he'd imagined a while ago.

After that troubling call from that Statie detective, she was about half ready to disconnect her own phone. Were they suspects? Didn't the cops usually *not* release evidence details? How the hell was she supposed to strike back on that? For now, though, it was time to deal with Wesley's screw-up with the Mob.

She held her tongue as Bree continued, sounding peppy as ever.

"Imagine counting on a man. To fulfill you, I mean."

"Uh-uh. Nope. Really can't."

"Not much else going on."

"God," Jules said. "Wish I could say that here."

"Just did my *Buns of Steel* workout. About to have me a line or two."

"You slutty cokehead."

As Wesley groaned in the living room, Jules rolled her eyes. She thought about the bloody leaf again. She really didn't want to think about that. She heard Bree chuckle into the receiver.

"Me? Well, gee, thanks. Say, think I'd look good with shorter hair?"

"You'd look good in anything."

"Not too," Bree said, "but, you know."

"Listen, got a favor to ask. A big fat one."

"You've always done things for me."

"Remember that huge sleazeball Cadillac Frank? Came into the club a couple times in such tacky outfits? I wonder if you could get me some info from him."

———————

That evening, Cadillac Frank hunched over a bar stool at his favorite Burlington nightspot, the ABC Lounge. When some dumb fuck bumped into him, he tensed. Was he going to have to kick some ass again?

Was it some loser sniffing at a goddamn craft beer? This might be—

As he turned, his breath caught. It was a red-headed cutie, swelling out of a sheer leopard-print blouse.

"Oh!" she said. "Sorry. I'm such a . . ."

She dropped a hand to the bar. He noticed his oversized salmon pink shirt didn't quite cover his gut, and he sucked it in.

"Looking great, baby! I'm Frankie. How you doing?"

With a wide grin, he begged her to join him at one of the booths, and led her off with a rolling strut. Christ! What good luck he was having tonight. He had hooked her in with his goodfella style.

Seated toward the back, she chattered away to him—about sports, working out, all sorts of crap. As she puckered her glossy lips and leaned into him, he tried acting all decent and shit as he wondered what her bush looked like.

After their second shots of Jose Cuervo, she winked.

"I'm starting to feel good," she said. "And a little bad, if you know what I mean."

Her hand settled on his inner leg. When she gave it a squeeze, the lime wedge he was playing with shot into the air.

"Hell, yeah."

"One more! Let's go for the buzz!"

He laughed, thrilled.

"You bet!"

He waved wildly for the waitress.

Flopping an arm over the back of the booth despite his sore bandaged shoulder, he bragged about access to a truckload of Tommy Hilfiger jeans.

"Maybe you could use a few pair?" He touched his gut where that horned fuck had driven a fist into him. The booze helped some, but it still hurt too. "Hell, maybe I can help you try 'em on. Or take 'em off?"

The fucking cutie chuckled. So he boasted some more.

Scooting closer, she wriggled her eyebrows suggestively. She then eyed the bruise on his face and whispered into his ear that she'd always had a thing for tough guys, and that she was feeling hot all over.

Minutes later, as she danced around, he sprawled across his bed, still wearing his clothes along with a loose grin.

"Oh, baby!"

She swayed her way closer. When she eased off her blouse, he gasped. Giving him smoking eye contact, she slowly played her hands down her sweet-ass body. And to her hips.

Hooking her thumbs around the sides of her pink thong, she paused.

"Do it!" he said.

"Just *one* more drink first?"

"I love you!"

_____

When Jules picked up the kitchen phone the next day, the gruff voice of Vermont State Police Investigator Farrs came over the line again.

Her heart sank.

Crap! She definitely should have disconnected the phone.

Just hearing his voice made her blood race. Had his personal radar picked something up during the last call? Had she screwed up? She planted a hand on the counter. Reasons for another call flashed in and out of her mind. They wanted her to return to that little barracks room for a grilling. Some other new evidence had been uncovered.

She and Wesley hadn't left blood behind. Not a speck.

Had they?

"The other day?" Farrs said. "Something I forgot to ask."

A hard lump formed in her throat.

Handling a pissed-off mobster in your life was stressful enough! Who needed more damn homicide questions?

As she cleared her throat, something like congealed grease stank in the sink.

"Shoot." Oops, poor choice of words. She sank into a chair. An image of prison popped into her head, and she shook it off. "Fire away, I mean." Crap. "Well, anyway! Anything I can do to help."

"About your guns?"

She thought she heard something different in his voice. Picturing a look of stern resolve on his face, she felt herself twist in her seat. Did he have some new info from a source? Had someone seen her retrieving the Taurus from Homer's failed pond?

"It's no secret Eddie had his hands on a lot of weapons," Farrs said. "A way lot. His own arsenal."

She began to get a weird feeling. As if she were outside herself, watching herself squeeze the phone.

A niggling question moved through her brain. Was he building toward a "gotcha" moment?

"Hmm," she said.

"Rest assured, the guilty always make mistakes."

As she cringed, she thought she could almost hear him smiling over the phone.

"Oh, yeah?" she said.

"Anyway, the guns?"

She tried to keep her voice level as she answered.

"He did have quite—"

"Ever recall seeing a .45 ?"

For a long moment she went blank. Some ice cubes dropped in the ice-maker, startling her.

She heard him breathing, waiting.

A sense of defeat came over her.

Was she about to jump off a cliff?

Speak up, idiot.

22

————

An eon later, Jules finally unglued herself.

"Nope!" she said into the phone.

"You know," Investigator Farrs said, "when I have to, I can be a real bulldog."

"That's, um, great to hear."

"Anyway, lately we've narrowed things down."

She felt blindsided again. Shook her head. The Staties must have grown more and more suspicious. He was about to pounce.

But wouldn't he want to do that in person?

"I think you can help us here," he said. "How well did you know Eddie's associate, Joseph Plank?"

Him? Why did Farrs want to know that?

"Not really. Jo-Jo is what everyone calls him."

"Well, recently? We've been looking closely at him."

She practically jumped out of her chair. That could be kick-ass news. A game-changer.

Jo-Jo had made the news years ago, when Border Patrol agents busted him in North Troy. Wearing winter white camo clothing, he'd been nailed pulling a sled loaded with a duffel bag full of drugs across the border. Apparently he and his brother Aaron had never been able to stay out of trouble.

Still worried her voice would betray her, she paused before responding.

"You mean for—"

"He'd been back and forth through the Highgate border checkpoint lately. We finally located him."

"Good."

"Or *part* of him, anyway."

Part?

She felt her concentration slip. Gave herself a moment.

"Huh?" she said. "How's that?"

"We found a cardboard box."

"A box?"

"With his head in it."

"Yuck."

"Freshly severed."

Poor Jo-Jo. Eddie had had plenty of fucked up buds and dealing partners, but Jo-Jo was probably the least sucky.

"It's hard to sort out, but we think Eddie's death created a sort of power struggle," Farrs said. "Between local dope slingers."

She felt another flash of excitement. A freshly severed head? Maybe she could use all this. Could Eddie's skeezy background now be an ace up her sleeve? There had to be *some* damn way.

The stakes could not be higher.

One thing she'd learned stripping was that most every guy could be played. But what story would Farrs buy now? To send the Staties on a wild goose chase, she had lied through her ass back during her barracks interview. Now maybe she could push even harder? The head formerly known as Jo-Jo offed Eddie?

Convince them of that, and no one innocent would get hurt. At this point she sure wasn't going to be causing poor Jo-Jo any further harm.

Fingers crossed, maybe she could throw the damn cops off for good.

Blame the dead guy.

But she couldn't lose her own head now.

"Hmm," she finally said into the phone. "Now that I think about it? Maybe Eddie did tell me something about a meltdown between the two of them."

"Concerning—?"

"Let me . . ."

She hesitated, as if the memory had to be pulled from the back of her mind.

She felt her nerves, firing up her body. She'd nearly flubbed things with Farrs before—but this time . . . Well, this whole thing just might get swept under the rug.

Jo-Jo used to drift around the Booby Trap with half-mast heroin eyes. Not long ago, supposedly he'd flopped for a bit in a junkie camp on Burlington's outskirts, then cleaned himself up. Sort of. The last time she'd seen him, his greasy black hair had been pulled into a tight ponytail. He and Eddie had sat down to a crack pipe and a plastic baggie of rock.

The drugs. Yup, she had to use them.

Her heart punched hard in her chest.

"Eddie said . . . Jo-Jo wanted to step up."

"How so?" Farrs said.

"As far as dealing, I guess. Really not sure. I . . . I know Jo-Jo used to cook for Eddie. Meth, I mean. He supposedly also had access to shady prescriptions for getting pills. But Eddie? He always seemed to have Jo-Jo by the short hairs."

"What do you—"

"Jo-Jo tried pulling something, and they had a fight over some stupid drug."

"Hmm."

If nothing else, maybe Eddie's death would forever remain one of those cold cases. One with questions, but no answers.

She faked a heavy sigh.

"Not sure just what Eddie said. I, uh . . . I guess he took Jo-Jo down with a chain. Whipped him. Maybe, maybe that was *too* much for Jo-Jo? God, I made a point of staying away from all that stuff." She made a disgusted hissing sound. "That drug crap scared me."

She exhaled, almost too loudly.

There!

Enough . . . head games.

Maybe the Staties would focus on catching some real baddies in some legit case now?

She hadn't realized it until now, but her whole body was shaking. Still, it felt good to finally be more in control. All that should keep the Staties barking up the wrong tree.

Relief washed over her as she added, "How could I have forgotten all that?"

23

_____

Thursday morning, Wesley bit at his lips, eyes burning from crappy sleep, as Jules flicked off the flame under a pan of bacon. For some reason, she blew out some air and paused before she picked up the phone.

When she whispered to him that it was Bree, he groaned.

The last he knew, he owed Cadillac Frank $150,025—but Cadillac Frank had been kind enough to knock off the odd twenty-five dollars. Wesley was supposed to drop the cash at the upper gondola station on Mount Mansfield at 1:00 on the Sunday before Thanksgiving, or he was screwed.

The other day, contracting Kev Bates had seemed like a solid plan. Now Wesley had his doubts.

With only a few days left before the deadline, he had tried reaching Bates. Repeatedly. A million times. And then some more. He'd made his bargain with the devil. And needed some goddamn action. There was a clock ticking on the hit—but Bates was not answering his cell. Hopefully, the horned crazy fucker was on the move against Cadillac Frank.

Way back, Wesley had been warned by another gambler about Cadillac Frank. The story was that Cadillac Frank had dumped a body that was later found decomposing in Burlington's Centennial Woods. The victim's hands and feet were bound. For not paying off his debt, the guy had been stabbed over fifty times. Along with the stab wounds, the body had rat bites and empty eye sockets.

Thinking about those empty eye sockets now, Wesley began to feel uneasy about his chances.

Trying to stay positive, he pictured Bates roaring by his psychopath bookie's car on his Harley. In Wesley's mind Bates raised a huge pistol . . . and gunned Cadillac Frank down. Or maybe Bates would just slip up behind Cadillac Frank, like he had with Wesley outside Denny's, and then slit his throat.

Rest in peace, you Mob fuck!

He'd get that son of a bitch.

Wesley hadn't shared his secret with Jules about contracting Bates. He hadn't quite trusted the dude. Nor had he even wanted to think about her coming in contact with someone like Bates. But maybe it was finally time to bring it up?

Or wait! Maybe Bree had news now that Cadillac Frank was history. Please, please, please, let that be freaking true.

For a while Jules muttered into the receiver without saying much.

Wesley shuffled back and forth between the kitchen and living room. Jules's cat made a choking sound behind the sofa, and he nearly made a choking sound himself.

Halting in the kitchen, he stared at the half-browned bacon. The strips lay exactly parallel—like graves.

"What?" Jules said to Bree. "Well, he's been gambling like crazy. I don't know, I really don't, I *tried* to save him. Tried to stop him."

She paused, and her body seemed to stiffen. She gave him a look of alarm. She turned her attention back to Bree.

"Oh, that's terrible!"

He clapped a hand on his brow.

"Well, where's his house?" Jules continued. "Just in case, I have to . . . You know, make a visit."

What?

Shit! Apparently Cadillac Frank was still alive. But a visit? Was she nuts?

She finally dropped the receiver into its cradle, tears in her eyes.

"Damn."

"Well?"

Her face tightened.

"Jeez!" he said. "What?"

She sounded frightened as she said, "What a mess this is turning into."

"Jules, tell—"

"Bree says . . . he might whack you, no matter what."

He felt a sinking sensation, and she receded in space.

"Oh, shit."

"And listen to this. We *almost* got lucky. Too, too bad. She said he had a bandage on his shoulder. Guess he got into some kind of shootout."

No.

It couldn't be.

But the more Wesley thought about it, the more certain he was something had gone terribly wrong.

"What?"

"Frank bragged the other dude would never be a threat again."

His vicious, bloodthirsty killer.

Dead.

Bates was dead.

Cold sweat broke from Wesley's pores. He'd been backing the wrong . . . So much for his game plan. Where did that leave him? And what did that say about his own chances?

"Goddamn. Oh, Christ."

"Oh, sweetie. You screwed up. But come here, let me hold you. Just let me hold you tight a minute."

He took in her words, but seemed to be hearing her from afar.

"Don't worry, you knucklehead," she said. "Chill out, don't panic." She squeezed him hard, and let out a little laugh. "Maybe we should take out some life insurance on you, though."

"That's not funny!"

———————

Detective Burpee's cell phone buzzed. When he checked, he saw an incoming text. It was from his former occasional informant, Bree: HI HANDSOME. GOT SOMETHING 4U.

He pictured her pile of red hair. Her big shining eyes.

He smiled and then typed: I WISH.

There was a brief delay.

Then: THIS IS GOOD.

He answered: BET IT IS.

REALLY. GONNA B TROUBLE. MT. MANSFIELD. TOP GONDOLA STATION. I ON SUNDAY.

He scribbled the info down on a legal pad.

Then he wrote: MY DAY OFF?

After another delay, he read: come on. MIGHT EVEN GET TO FIRE UR GUN. COME BY, WILL FILL U IN.

———————

The ringing phone assaulted Cadillac Frank's ears. He blinked one aching eye, then the other. He squinted toward his alarm clock and tried to focus, but gave up.

"Oh, God. What . . ."

The past few days had been full of surprises.

First, there'd been that attack by that loony with inked horns. The one he'd stabbed right in the eye. Even before the dude showed up, Cadillac Frank had been in a mean-as-fuck mood. The brief fight made his day.

And his little adventure last night? His hangover now from that made him feel as if *he'd* been stabbed in the head.

He could barely remember his own name. The goddamn phone rang, and rang, and rang.

He groped for the phone. When he eased it up, a vaguely familiar female voice jabbered into his ear that Wesley Torrance was scared shitless, and was going to be able to pay off his debt. He'd do whatever he had to.

The voice cut right into Cadillac Frank's head.

". . . no need for guns. Nobody got to get hurt, do they?"

He staggered to his feet as the voice screeched on. When he flicked on the switch in the bathroom, the light drilled into his eyes. He winced. Grabbed a sink edge.

When he squinted into the mirror, his face was gray. How many damn drinks had he had last night? What had he done with that hottie? Somehow there was a big hole in his memory. He half-pictured her foxy face. And her feeding him a lot of booze.

Somewhere in there, she had asked him a lot of damn questions. Was this her?

"Hold on a—Who'd you say this was?"

When the woman on the other end of the line hung up without answering, he ripped open the medicine chest. Vials rolled into the sink. He blinked down at them.

"Oh . . . forget it."

24

———

Early that afternoon, Jules slid behind the steering wheel of her burgundy Tacoma pickup, mouth lipsticked and eyes lined. She felt sharp and determined. As she zoomed out of town, fog was rolling across the hills. Wild turkeys pecked their way through the stubble of a cornfield.

She had lots to do today.

She had shot Eddie full of holes to free herself. And the cops seemed to have bought her story. And she was not going to be denied now.

Well, there was that leaf. The single drop of blood. God, she hoped that wasn't ... Could the Staties also test that blood against a sample from Jo-Jo Plank's head?

What else had she missed recently? She was only about a mile from Swamp Road, where the stranger with the rifle had appeared. Had that orange-haired guy actually been after her? Eddie had had such shady connections. Maybe someone from that circle really was pissed.

Had she and Wesley teed off whoever had offed Jo-Jo Plank?

Outside, the sun was bright through the leafy treetops. Yet she felt something heavy building inside her chest. Ahead, she spotted a deer moving through a clearing in the trees. At least *it* had survived hunting season without incident. Thanks to Wesley's stupid gambling, the stakes for them had been upped even further. They were supposed to be free now. Now, not only might they be charged with murder, they could also end up dead themselves.

A little buzz of adrenaline began to tick in her blood. Well, she was not afraid of Cadillac Frank one bit. She would help Wesley pay him off. Or get rid of the bastard altogether. If she had to, she would track him down and put a bullet in his skull.

Anyone else? She would handle them too.

"Screw 'em."

Minutes later she strode inside Green Mountain Bank. Her heels resounded across the tiles, and her big black purse swung at her side.

Well, this was it.

The easiest way out.

She surged up to the teller counter. Paused. Gathered herself.

She had a plan. Help Wesley. However she could.

As far as she knew, the Mob probably didn't coddle people who didn't pay off their debts. Hadn't Wesley already risked a long, long prison sentence for her?

What else was she supposed to do to raise cash? Cook up some meth, like goddamn Eddie would have? Deal some of the fentanyl-laced smack he called "Crusty"? She half-wished she still had the large freezer bag of coke she'd found after offing Eddie. She'd dumped it, though, refusing to get involved with that shit anymore.

Time was running out.

She stared at the teller. Exhaled. Then filled out the government form for a large withdrawal and cleaned out her whopping savings account. She loaded her purse with stacks and stacks of cash.

"There!" she said to herself. "That's a start."

Feeling masterful, take-charge, she paused in the lobby. Collected herself. She then strode into the loan office. The loan officer wore black-framed glasses that sat slightly askew. His hair was cut short as a bristle brush.

After planting her ass into a chair across from him, she also finagled an immediate emergency loan, secured by her home. She was only getting started.

A little later Jules parked her Tacoma near the PLEASANT ACRES sign. Climbing out into Homer's barnyard, she breathed in the richness of the soil. As a little girl she had learned to raise calves and drive an old Ferguson tractor, and visiting here always brought that back. Barn swallows slid by as she called out.

"Homer?"

She strode into his red gambrel-roof barn, hay rustling beneath her feet. The sweet, sour smell of manure rose from the gutter. A few stalls down, Homer stooped forward, speaking to one of his Holsteins in a soothing tone. She greeted him, and his knees cracked as he gripped a pipe stanchion with one of his work-beaten hands and stood.

"Jesus, ain't you a sight for sore eyes today." A smile lit his lined face. "Pretty as a picture."

The cow swished its tail and mooed. It dropped its head to the feeding trough, quietly working its jaw. She scratched behind its ear, facing Homer.

"That's sweet. Thanks."

"These critters sure keep me busy. Ain't got time in the day." Pulling a handkerchief from the front pocket of his overalls, he honked his nose. "Anyhow, how're you?" His face screwed up and he let out a chuckle. "If you ain't here to run off with me, what about some coffee?"

She gave out a groan of frustration.

"Need some money. Wesley's in a heck of a bind."

His brows knitted in concern.

"Well, sorry to hear. He's gotta be better than that Eddie. What an a-hole. Come along, then."

His ATV sat next to the post fence by the machine shed. He hesitated before straddling it, as if he ached. When she plopped down behind him and clasped his sides, she smelled his pipe tobacco on his shirt. A breeze rippling through the surrounding fields, they puttered up to his rambling house. After he paused to brush off some bits of hay and scuffed his gumboots on the doormat, they stepped inside to silence.

"The old bird must be asleep." He grinned. "Lord, she's cranky as ever lately."

Jules gave a short laugh and felt a rush of affection for him.

"Nag, nag," he said.

They squeaked down the cellar stairs. The air was musty and cool. Grabbing a canister off his workbench, he pulled out a fat roll of bills.

"Here."

No questions asked, he lent her nine grand.

Another neighbor, an old schoolmate, Ray Turcotte, was ready to kick in $3,000. A lean musician with a scraggly beard, he loved his weed.

Pushing his long, straight brown hair behind his ears, he had to think for a minute to figure out where the money was, though. Jules glanced around his pine-paneled, cluttered living room. She shrugged.

Unwilling to slow her undeniable momentum, she thought she'd have to call her baby sis in San Diego, and she winced inwardly. A while ago Paige had dropped out of the Navy, and had apparently blown through most of her savings on meth. At one point she'd been caught with a bunch of boxes which held the fixings for a portable meth lab. In place of 200 days in jail, she'd gone to rehab, which hadn't done squat.

Since then, Jules had sent her ten grand to help pay for a longer rehab. Maybe Paige had turned things around and could pay Jules back?

Right.

Not likely.

Jules still felt safest when they were a few thousand miles apart.

Worst-case scenario, maybe she could slip into the club-house of Eddie's old biker buds, the Pagans. That would be way dangerous. But there had to be a stash of cash in there.

After a few more bar chords and puffs of sweet herb, though, Ray pointed toward the coffee table.

"Dude! Those songbooks? Try under there."

Jules raced home. She slipped into the house and sneaked up to Wesley in the kitchen, electric with success.

"Ta-da! Ka-ching! I did it."

She made a little hop in the air. She then waved stacks of cash in his stressed face. As she plopped the money down next to the sugar jar on the counter, he clutched at his chest.

"Jeez! Oh, God."

She gave him a thumbs-up.

"Got it! I got it."

He made a little noise.

"Not cool. You scared the *hell* out of me."

Feeling a stab of sympathy, she skidded a hand along his curls, looked into his eyes, and studied his mouth. He wore a blue denim shirt and jeans. Although he looked tense as a caged cougar, she wondered if he knew how handsome he really was. Probably not.

"You are kind of . . . pale."

He nodded his head in a kind of weighted way.

"You know, right now I'm worried about me, yes—but way more concerned about you. Maybe you should skip going. To Stowe, I mean."

"Well, I feel great."

"At least you came through." He managed a smile, for the first time in a long time. "Honey, you rock."

She stared into his emerald eyes. His hands, even the way he stammered sometimes—she loved him. He didn't seem to know it, but he was a good man. Flawed, but good.

"Well, maybe I can shoot *them*," he said.

"Anything you say."

"Fire off a few quick—"

"Oh, sure. Shoot 'em just like you did your recliner? You know, we should celebrate. Let's go out, if you can manage. Or straight to bed. Let's get a little weird and wild, have some fun."

But first, maybe it was time to ask. Get the big question she had out of the way. She had spared him from freaking out further by not telling him about Investigator Farrs's phone calls—but she had to at least find this out.

"One thing," she said. "Did you cut yourself?"

"What?"

"You know."

"I don't—"

"At the Gorge."

His eyebrows went up.

"Then?" He thought a moment. "I—I don't know."

A small chill ran down the length of her spine.

Christ. Did he fall and scrape his hand? Or what?

How could he *not* know?

A bang made them both jump and she realized she had slapped her palm down on the stove.

"Jeez," he said.

"Oops. . . . *Think*, sweetie."

Worry had washed over his face again. He thought for so long, she finally waved a hand in front of his face.

"Hello? Wesley?"

He needed to shave. He rubbed his stubble for a few seconds more before replying.

"No. Uh, I guess not."

She eyed him with disbelief.

"Come on."

His lips parted, as if he was about to say something. Then they closed. She heard the wind outside.

"Well?" she said.

"Really not sure." He gulped. "Why?"

He looked like he was telling the truth. What could she say? Could the cops be messing with her? Were they lying?

"Just . . . Never mind." That wasn't going to do it. "Actually? Just making sure nothing went wrong."

Oh, well. Hell, maybe it was better not to know.

"In a way," she said, "we're still on thin ice here."

He was quiet for a long moment. He had a distant look in his eyes.

"You know, I really don't like that saying."

After a couple of days of rest, Wesley's back was settling down. All they had to do now was avoid getting zotzed on Mt. Mansfield, and drop the money. And hope that that they had gotten away with murder.

25

———

Time to strike back.

Wesley lowered his binoculars the following afternoon. When he swallowed, he could taste his fear and excitement. He had scoped out the tan split-level house for any sign of activity. There had been zilch. A dog barked in a nearby yard, but no one came outside. He wiped his face.

He moved out.

As he headed toward the house, his sneakers squished from wading through the small creek that ran behind the property. He vaulted a post fence. He could do this thing. He could not afford to be standing still. Sure, Jules had raised the cash they needed. But his plan now? It was even better.

Scratch the drive to Stowe! Scratch the money drop! This was pure genius.

Scoring 23 bags of heroin in Burlington's Old North End had been a breeze. For twenty bucks, the third person he whispered to knew exactly where to go: a dude who lived on a beaten-up stretch of Elmwood Avenue.

Now, wearing dark sunglasses and a black baseball hat for a disguise, Wesley bolted to Cadillac Frank's double garage. He pressed his back to the wall outside the side door. Took a deep, shaky breath. The air was still and quiet as he eased open the door to the dank-smelling garage.

When he peeked inside, Cadillac Frank's Caddy was gone. In the adjoining space, a blue car cover shielded another vehicle.

After pulling himself together, Wesley had thought further about Jules's idea of paying a visit here. With Bates dead, he would have to take care of his psycho bookie himself. Now he was jacked to take care of business. He could still get the upper hand.

With fumbling excitement he dashed into the garage, and knocked over a goddamn empty black plastic trash can and then banged into an aluminum ladder.

He nearly peed himself in fright.

Before he could even look around further, a car honked outside. He whipped his head toward the sound. What the—?

Should he bolt?

But he had to plant the freaking heroin. He was going to make all this go away. Send Cadillac Frank's ass to prison. Save himself right now. He had one shot at this and he had to do it right.

But was that motor idling? Or had it stopped? He held his breath as he waited for some kind of sign. He strained to pick up sounds.

When he heard footsteps, his sense of danger tripled. Christ! Had someone seen him? Had they honked now to scare him off? Maybe he *should* bolt. He glanced desperately around the garage. Or could he fit in one of those trash cans? What was he supposed to do if he got caught with 2 3 bags of smack? Or was someone only picking up one of the neighbors?

His heart running like a small animal, he snatched a pipe wrench off the plywood work bench. Heaved himself into a garbage can. Tried to scrunch down. The inside of the can stank. And he didn't quite fit.

He couldn't quite get out either.

He clapped a hand over his nose and mouth to keep the stench away. This had to be his all-time shittiest idea! Stuck in a goddamn trash can in a killer's garage. What could he do now if someone came in? Hurl the pipe wrench? Tip the can over and roll them down? Then try to strangle them with the strap of his binoculars?

Well, he would fight.

Or roll, anyway.

He would stop at nothing to see this mission through. As he held the pipe wrench ready, his blood ticked.

"I *will* be okay," he whispered to himself.

The longest ten seconds in history passed.

A car door thumped closed. The sound of a car engine faded. Apparently someone had been getting picked up.

Jeez.

He managed to jerk himself out of the can. He threw himself back to the work bench. He ditched the pipe wrench and stuffed the dope behind a jar of screws and can of paint at the rear. He blew out a breath, a great weight lifting off his shoulders. Mission accomplished. The tables were turned now.

"It's *over*," he said out loud.

Well, screw Cadillac Frank. Might as well have a little fun.

He grabbed an awl. After bending down by the covered vehicle's front, he raised the awl.

"Take this," he said.

He plunged it into the tire's sidewall. He then lifted the car cover.

"And *this*."

He raked the tool tip across the doors.

Yeah, bitch!

He was only getting started. Grinning from ear to ear, he returned with the pipe wrench, and swung it hard into the covered windshield. The heavy tool sank in deep. He spit on the concrete floor. Did a little fuck-you-Frank dance.

"Wesley! In the house!" He raised a fist in triumph. "Whoo!"

Score one for the good guys.

He whirled and threw a karate kick at a door.

"Ow! Shit."

A second later he was hobbling toward the wooded line by the creek.

As he phoned the cops, he could barely believe how slick his plan had gone. He'd done it! He felt the tension that had gripped him for so long start to ease. Who needed Kev Bates? Soon Cadillac Frank was going to be stuck in jail. Jules would be so proud of her crafty man.

He brushed his hands.

He was a hero, plain as day.

———

A little later, Wesley told Jules in a voice tight with excitement how he'd sneaked up to ninety-one Crestview Lane and set up Cadillac Frank by planting heroin, and then grinned.

"After?" he said. "I felt just like when I used to strike out a final batter. Kick-ass. Nothing better."

Her eyes flashed. She made a face.

She didn't say anything.

He stared at her for a good five seconds. What was wrong with her? Why wasn't she jumping up and down with joy?

Was she actually jealous of his plan? She should be even more thrilled than she was yesterday.

"What?" he said at last.

She shook her head.

"Well, good try. I guess."

"Huh?"

"Did I say Crestview Lane, sweetie?"

"Yup, you sure—"

"Well, actually?" she said. "I meant *Viewcrest*. Guess I said Crestview because that's where my uncle Jesse used to live."

"*Damn*."

An embarrassed smile flickered at the edges of her mouth.

"Oops. That's on me. Maybe all this stuff is getting to me too."

26

Early Saturday evening, Jules and Wesley gathered up tooth-brushes, a change of clothes, handcuffs, a Colt .45 handgun, the grenade launcher from Eddie's cache, and a tiny battered pink suitcase stuffed with $150,000. She watered the plants, poured out extra Cat Chow, and kissed her cat Boo on the head. They then loaded everything into the Mustang to drive to Stowe.

When they were finally ready, she held out her palm for the car keys.

"You don't look . . . I better drive."

They climbed in. She adjusted the rearview mirror and seat, raised her eyebrows.

Chewing at her lip, she went over everything in her mind again. First, deal with Cadillac Frank. Hurt him, if she had to. Hit him first. Second, deal with the cops. Throw them even more false leads, or whatever. Eddie's buddies? She'd handle them too, if she had to. She had to keep up.

And keep Wesley from flipping out.

At least he had tried taking action yesterday. She still felt embarrassed about that one.

"So. All set?"

He gazed at her as if he hadn't understood a word she'd said.

"Oh, God," he said.

"I'll take that as a yes."

———————

Wesley started chain-smoking right away. Yesterday he had been so sure his troubles were over. Now he tried to steel himself.

Before long the ashtray overflowed with stubbed-out Marlboros. The air reeked with an acrid tang.

Jules turned her head his way.

"Can't believe you're smoking again."

Off to his right a farmhouse sagged beneath the gray sky. Barren apple trees covered the hillside. Everything looked shut down. Bleak. As he stared at the dark peaks in the distance, his stomach churned. Wind whistled shrilly at the top of his window.

"What? Maybe I'm a little bit nervous."

"Where's that water bottle?"

"I say we turn our asses around, head somewhere else. Like Mexico. That way we stay alive, and out of prison."

When he groaned out loud, she rolled her window down even further to let more smoke out.

"I love it here. We're *not* leaving. Ever. Try and relax."

"Or Vegas. Well, maybe not—"

"Wesley."

"What?"

"Calm down, listen to me. You're going to have a stroke before we even get there. Look at me. Take some slow breaths, think about something peaceful."

Last night Eddie had stolen into Wesley's sleep. Eddie laid there at the Gorge, moaning. Bleeding everywhere. But then he popped back up.

His head swung toward Wesley. Eddie was trying to say something. His pale lips were moving. But Wesley couldn't make out the words.

Raising an arm, Eddie pointed at Wesley in condemnation.

The dream had scared the freaking crap out of him. Afterward he had flown out of bed and into the shower, obsessively scrubbing his body with soap. Bouncing his leg up and down now, he wondered if the dream had been a sign.

"Relax? How do I do that? I'm dead. Pushing up daisies, dead as a—"

"Didn't you get the memo about growing a pair?"

"Memo?"

"You'll drive yourself crazy thinking like that." Stroking his arm, she gave him a hopeful smile. She looked confident. "Maybe you're stronger than you think."

"Nah, probably not."

"We'll be all right."

"You hear a buzzing sound? What is—"

"Think of this as a . . . mini-vacation."

"I'll be okay, once we're there."

It looked like she was holding in a laugh.

"Sure you will . . . . You know, you've already proved yourself a hero, is the way I see it. I love you. Hear me?"

He nodded, without answering. The flame on his lighter quivering, he lit a Marlboro. Then he realized he already had another one going next to it.

He dragged deeply on both of them, the mountains looming larger, and larger.

At last he said, "Do I look like I'm afraid of a fight?"

"Well. Actually—"

"We got a lot of guns. Let's show these fucks how we roll. It's *on*."

27

"That sorry sack of shit," Cadillac Frank said to himself.

Thinking about Weaseldick as he thinly sliced two garlic cloves, it was damn clear to him. He had a plan. When Sunday came, he wanted a nice early lunch and a couple of espressos, then he wanted his 150 grand from the fucker for a late dessert. With football season kicking in, he was making kick-ass vigorish. Still, every once in a while you had to set an example for the bettors. Whatever he did to Weaseldick, he didn't want any of his clients thinking gambling was just a game. Screw that shit.

He'd granted the dipshit a high line of credit after being assured that a big insurance settlement was on the way. But apparently Weaseldick had exaggerated his share of the settlement. Still, he'd get his own cash soon. He could almost smell it as he chopped an onion in half.

Easy money.

One-fifty large.

He loved to watch his clients squirm in striking settings. And Vermont was full of scenic backdrops for threatening and killing. Covered bridges. Sweeping big-ass orchards. Fucking lakes, and whatever.

So, who knew? He had never shot anybody on a mountain-top. That might be kind of cool.

He'd noticed online that Stowe was going to be extra busy on Sunday. The First Annual Numbnuts Mountain Bike Race up the toll road on Mt. Mansfield was expected to draw hordes of new dumbass tourists into Stowe. Since women planned to race too, feminists had reportedly protested use of the term "Numbnuts" in the race name. God, it was kind of scary. Women were rising up everywhere these days.

The one article photo showed them picketing with NO BALLS! signs. What a crazy-ass state this was.

Screw the expected crowds. Maybe he and the crew could even stick up some of those dumbasses.

He felt kind of like a stud since his hook-up with the hottie from the ABC Lounge. He gave a sigh of satisfaction now, sure he'd shown her a glorious time between the sheets. He was a goddamn stud. Wiseguy killer by day, dream lover by night.

About the only thing bothering him lately was being stuck with a neon-pink Focus rental car while his Caddy was in the shop. Hell, he might even whack Sal if he called him "Focus Frank" again.

———

Jules thought up all sorts of plans. Blast Cadillac Frank and his thugs' gondola with the grenade launcher. Arm herself like crazy and give them the fight of their lives. Go in hot and hard. And so on.

She was tough, a Vermonter. No bad guy was going to screw her over.

Shortly after eleven a.m. on Sunday at Stowe-Away Cabins, she was about to tug on her jeans. Despite everything, she felt hopeful.

She and Wesley would get through this, and then start the family she had always yearned for. Hopefully without killing *too* many people.

She would end this thing. Right now she wasn't going to worry over any crime-scene blood. But if she had to, she was going to draw some blood. She would nail Cadillac Frank.

She was coming for him.

"Almost ready, tiger?" she said to Wesley. "Let's do this. Let's rock this bad boy."

She didn't plan on him handcuffing her to the gleaming brass bed frame. A feeling of delight came over her. The blood pulsed in her head.

A pressure-relieving quickie would be a treat.

"Oh, baby."

But when she took a look at him, the pieces fell together in her mind. The nut planned to head up the mountain alone! She felt her face harden. Striding toward the door, he looked half crazy. But there was also a focused intensity along with it. And why was he wearing a wig? And a dress under that sweater? She stared on in disbelief.

"Wait a minute. Where you think you're going?"

He winked at her, as if this was all nothing.

"I'm off."

"Off?"

"I *got* this. No biggie."

"Come back here." Flopped on her back, she screamed, to no avail. "Stupid shithead!"

"Let me do what needs to be—"

"I'm supposed to be saving *you.*"

So that's why he'd spent the last half hour strutting around like John Wayne! She bit her lower lip. Her throat tightened and she began to fume.

"At least come give me a damn kiss . . . . Oh, you ass."

He was going to get himself killed up there.

"Watch yourself!" she said. "Try not to screw this one up."

———

Wesley had a plan. Though the mere thought pitched him into a cold sweat, he'd head up the mountain, try to make the drop, and hope everything worked out, going in and getting out as quick as freaking possible. But he'd also be prepared to bolt in case things looked fishy when he showed up. Without Jules.

He would do this alone if it killed him.

She'd probably kill him afterward, if he survived. Still, he didn't want her around if Cadillac Frank decided to create trouble.

It took a huge effort, but by the time he had handcuffed Jules in their cabin and spun around, he felt super-charged. At last, he would prove himself.

The Valium, slug of Jameson's, and stainless steel Colt .45 strapped over a Kevlar vest and under his disguise were helpful. On the other hand, her screams weren't. Nodding to her, he strutted out of the swear-filled room, and then yanked the door shut behind him.

Man, she could yell.

He felt like a real man—except for the puffy blond wig, lipstick, and flowery dress beneath his rag wool sweater. Cadillac Frank had insisted on Wesley delivering the cash in person. But if things looked iffy when Wesley showed, being in disguise couldn't hurt. You could never be too careful. He slipped on his wraparound sunglasses.

Whoa. What was that?

A discarded NO BALLS! placard tilted in the lawn. For a moment he thought he was cracking up from the stress. Whatever! He wasn't going to make any mistakes this time.

Hadn't he vowed he was going to be someone who counted, someone strong?

"I'm on this," he muttered.

He pivoted with a flourish. Watch out, crazy motherfucker coming through! He tugged his dress into line, jumped into his car.

Downshifting, he headed up Mountain Road. With a quick glance into the rearview mirror, he watched the cabin disappear. SLOWER VEHICLES USE RIGHT LANE a sign soon said, and a boxy truck revved up before him. A few hundred feet further, the remains of a skunk smeared across his lane. It was a mess of hide and gristle. Meat and blood.

How destroyed the poor thing was. Gone forever, whacked by a car. Whacked? He felt a tremor in his resolve.

Hell, this could go wrong twenty different ways. What if they really were planning to zotz him?

Mount Mansfield's dark expanse soon loomed up to the northwest. He knew the Abenakis believed the peak had taken on its upturned-face profile after a crippled brave dragged himself up it to prove himself, and then died there. He appreciated the story—but didn't like the ending one bit.

Buildings gave way to evergreen trees. The road climbed steeply. Wind buffeted the car. His pulse whooshed in his ears.

Thirty feet before the turn for the gondola station, he downshifted and screeched to the side of the road. The car slid to a halt in the gravel. Hunching forward, he thumped his hand on the steering wheel. Despite the web of ski trails and a few antennas, the mountain shot up with a stark power. Dusted with snow, it towered. A massive rise of trees and rock.

It dared him to approach.

The fear that had been with him for days rose up in his throat.

The wind had whipped hard that wintry day he had dropped into Lake Champlain too. Ever since then he'd felt like the whole world was a sheet of ice that could give way at any second. Shatter into a million pieces. Now, how the hell was he supposed to survive?

Kev Bates hadn't even bested Cadillac Frank.

———————

Minutes later, Wesley paused before the ticket window of the gondola station. The whip-thin ticket vendor eyed him closely and grabbed his shaking twenty-dollar bill.

"Round trip?"

Wesley's voice came out tight.

"Round, um, trip?" For a second he lost himself to the deep thrum of nearby machinery. "Hell yeah! God, I'm not really *trained* for this. But of course I'm—"

"O-kay."

His Mustang was hidden behind a storage shed. And he carried a couple of survival essentials. In the suitcase in his maimed hand he lugged $150,000—bundles of mostly one-hundred-dollar bills. Holstered under his sweater was his Colt .45. But he also had a shitty feeling he'd forgotten something. His head buzzed, though, driving him to distraction.

Something wasn't right. But what? He couldn't put a finger on it.

Screw it.

He had to get these thugs off his back. Get the job done.

His lips moved in a low whisper.

"Never give up."

Once trapped inside the otherwise empty gondola, he thumped his pink suitcase down and pressed his brow to the plexiglass. Forest and rolling hills closed in all around. On the trails, fake snow churned out here and there. The gondola lurched with the wind. Yet it kept hurtling upward.

Not an hour ago, he'd imagined looking Cadillac Frank straight in his cold dark eyes, suitcase in hand. With a tough stare, he would pay up, then call it a day. But as the gondola whizzed into the upper station now, his nerves seemed to eat up the air.

In his mind he heard the ice creaking. He tried to ignore it and think about what was ahead.

Even Detective Burpee had a plan. Screw department regulations. Screw having some backup. He had his own backup with him—his two buddies, Smith and Wesson. Who had time for fighting crime with all these regs and details? That morning he had cooked Flo a nice big breakfast. Afterward, he'd loaded his handgun's swing-out cylinder with equal care.

As he exited the interstate now, his blue Ford Crown Victoria bucked. It seemed like it wanted to lose power. But then it surged on.

He pictured himself waiting in hiding, finger by his .357's trigger as he savored the mountain air. Surprise was one thing he had in his favor. But if he had to, he would smoke Cadillac Frank and his thugs' asses. Hell, he hadn't shot anyone in years. Like a true badass, he figured he could handle them alone.

A while later reality sank in, when he took a scenic detour and his Crown Vic crapped out on a remote Stowe back road. God, it was probably the damn alternator. He whipped out his cell phone. No reception. He slumped in his seat, glanced around. Broken glass glittered along the road shoulder. Trees rose all around, and a railed bridge crossed a river in the distance. Cursing, he climbed out.

For twenty minutes the road was empty and quiet. The air barely moved.

When finally a Mercedes Benz sedan swerved around the bend, he waved his badge wildly.

"Stop! Police emergency!"

His brow broke out with sweat. Time was running out. He kept waving his badge around in the center of the road, yelling.

He waved and waved.

"I said stop! *Stop!*"

As the car closed in, the blue-haired woman in the passenger seat threw him a look of contempt. The codger beside her spun the steering wheel.

Burpee scrambled toward the ditch at road's edge, tempted to fire off a round at the old farts to try to save himself.

28

Wesley stepped out of the upper gondola station, thirty-three minutes early. He then spent what might be his last moments alive furiously pacing against the bracing wind outside Cliff House. Boulders piled up beyond him, and the blue sky boomed above. His dress billowed. Panicky thoughts whirled inside his head.

Last loser that didn't pay? Cadillac Frank had said in the woods not so long ago. *He got dead.*

Wesley scuttled back and forth, back and forth.

The clock was ticking.

What was a sensible gal to do?

―――――

Cadillac Frank parked his Focus rental car in the lot below. He could still taste the garlic from his lunch as he waited for Sal and Pino to lumber out of their old chocolate-brown Chevy van and join him.

He noticed Sal was empty-handed.

"Hey, dumbass."

Sal blinked toward him.

"Huh?"

"Forgetting something?"

"Uh-uh, I don't—"

"The sugar cookies!"

"Oh, Jesus. Sorry, boss."

Cadillac Frank wore a brand-new sweat suit—lilac and turquoise stripes. As they boarded the gondola right on schedule, he thought maybe he would grow a sexy mustache. Go cooze hound, all the way.

As for Weaseldick? Fuck him.

He was going down.

The gondola whizzed up the mountain.

Right now things couldn't be better. Fresh air. And violence. What more could a guy want? God bless fucking America.

———

Higher up the mountain, Wesley dashed behind a huge boulder off Cliff House's north end, face strained. He clenched his suitcase's handle with his maimed hand. The Kevlar vest shielded his chest and back—but what about the rest of what was left of him?

There was no sound, except the whistling wind.

He waited, waited, waited.

Finally, he gaped at the watch on his shaking wrist—12:59.

This was freaking it. Point of no return.

Soon, he heard Cadillac Frank, grumbling about not enough marsala in his zabaglione. Behind the boulder, Wesley tensed.

He told himself he had to stay alert. He had to . . . Oh, man. As he edged closer, neck stretched taut, the rock felt deathly cold against his hands. He could feel his thumping heart beating against it.

He was getting an increasingly bad feeling about this. There was a tightness in his chest and throat as someone burped. Cadillac Frank then spoke again.

"Remember, the brain. Always put one right there."

Wesley almost fell over.

They were going to whack him!

He tensed his muscles, poised for action. Should he jump out and start blasting away?

Twenty feet away, Cadillac Frank watched Pino screw a silencer onto his piece. Pino flicked his cold eyes toward him while racking a round.

"You know, boss, hate to say it. You're wrong—"

"Whoa, whoa, whoa."

"Way I see it, was just the right touch of marsala in the zabaglione."

"Get the fuck out. I tell you, I didn't like it."

"That veal? Dry as a damn bone, though."

Cadillac Frank rubbed at his mouth. He turned. What was that tall blonde over there up to? Why was she shaking her way toward the building's corner like that? Tiny suitcase in hand, she kept trying to avoid his eyes—coughing to one side one sec, and flopping a hand over her brow as if it hurt the next.

Christ, she looked white as chalk.

Hmmm.

That jumpy-looking face seemed familiar. She was a looker, in a way. Even the narrow sunglasses were kind of hot. Where had he goddamn seen her before?

That half-crazy scared look? That stubby little finger? Finger?

That blonde hair was fugazy, fake!

"Son of a bitch, it's him! There he is, guys. Dressed like a chick!"

Before Cadillac Frank could even point, Wesley gave a sudden cry. Legs exploding beneath him, he burst up the slope to the west.

"Ah, shit!"

A jerky panic ran through him. And he zoomed along. His cross-trainer shoes slapped against the snow-dusted rock. Pouring it on, his muscles and lungs searing with the effort, he weaved through clumps of hikers and up and over boulders and through a set of switchbacks, suitcase swinging in his hand.

"Excuse me. Sorry! *Move!*"

The trail forked. Zipping left into a stretch of stunted evergreens, he seemed to levitate. His breaths grew ragged. He kept waiting to fall. But it was like the mountain told him where to go: *Stick one foot here, the other there—keep moving.*

He did.

Beyond a patch of loose gravel, the trail narrowed. Then it climbed. Up, up, and up. He strained, judging his footing in sweat-blurred flashes. By the time he puffed his way up close to the open ridgeline, he felt half dead from exhaustion.

He faltered and weaved.

Legs wobbling, he fell over the last of the stunted brush. Sinking to his knees, he gasped for air.

A stiff wind swept past. But he was so pumped up he barely felt the cold. The summit towered above him.

"Always put one . . . in the brain?" he muttered.

Wasn't there any way he could just pay them off? Christ, no, the crazy fucks would zotz him anyway.

Once he caught his wind, he jumped up.

Screaming wildly, he scrambled up onto the stark gray ridge.

———————

Amid the spindly, low evergreens below, Cadillac Frank and his crew flopped down on the cool bedrock near a cliff edge. All three of them were panting.

"Say, Sal, how about one of them cookies?" Pino finally said.

The chill in each gust of wind sent tiny frigging icicles into Cadillac Frank's lungs. His sweaty clothes felt clammy. For a moment as he stared down into the valley, the rolling landscape seemed to hold an answer to something he wanted. He was struck by the silence. The few cars moving around looked like goddamn toys, and he doubted a bullet would even reach them.

Mountain after mountain rose in the far distance. It was a hell of a thing, seeing all this. After he torched up a Camel, he turned his head.

"Quite the view, eh, guys?"

A few feet away Pino coughed lightly.

"No shit."

"Trees up the wazoo."

"Nippy . . . but nice. That's, like, you know, fucking nature out there."

Cadillac Frank rubbed at his ears then drew in a drag of his smoke. Exhaling, he wiped at a spot on one of his shiny black loafers.

"Probably should get our asses in gear. Kill that sucker. But, hell, gimme one of them treats too."

Sal handed over another cookie with a pout. He pointed forward.

"Hey, what's that mountain over there? You know, the tall damn one."

"Hell if I know."

Sal laughed.

"Dumbass mountain."

They smoked in silence, and then flicked their butts down. When Pino spoke again, his voice was touched by wonder.

"You know, Sal? I'd bet my left nut that ain't even Vermont anymore."

―――――

Up above on the ridge, Wesley stopped too. He gasped, drenched with sweat on the Lower Lip of the mountain's face-like profile.

Snow-dusted rock around him, a sea of trees below, he had to choose a route. Pick the Nose? A cut to the Chin?

Damn, what should he do!

Should he sprint down? Bushwhack and dive on a chairlift?

Where were they?

They would find him. Kill him.

It was hard to think over the terror. Clamping his eyes shut, he thought of Jules—her brilliant eyes, her perfect lips—and felt a rush of concern. Jules. She seemed a long, long way off. He had to get back to her. Make sure she was okay.

He opened his misted eyes. Took another look north.

What the—?

A hundred feet north along a sag in the ridge huddled a group of women. Some of them were so brawny they looked like men who had cross-dressed, as he had. Who the hell were they? Something told him to hide. So he gaped around, searching for a spot.

Gray rock.

Crevices.

More damn rock.

A few feet away the lichen-daubed bedrock jutted out. He inched down near the overhang, wedging a foot in a crack at the top of a steep rock wall. And then almost slipped to certain death.

Jeez.

Scratch that freaking idea. Once he clambered back up with his suitcase, a strong gust of wind knifed along the ridge. The cold bit at his cheeks. Gulping, he shaded his eyes and then gaped around again.

Soon, his stomach went cold.

Oh, shit.

Right there.

Cadillac Frank and his goons! With squinty glares and pursed mouths, they searched through the group of women.

Cadillac Frank turned his head. He pointed, eyes hooded with rage.

"Over there, Pino!"

Whirling around, Wesley bolted to his right along a narrow point of rock. A moment later he regretted it.

The lake valley glinted in the sun to the west. But he wobbled at a cliff edge—a sheer million-mile plunge.

"Oh, man," he said.

When he looked down, the entire valley seemed to rush up at him and recede again. He felt a tingling at the base of his spine.

He wheeled back around.

Trapped.

Not under the ice of Lake Champlain this time. But once again, with nowhere to go.

29

***

While Sal held his ground in the distance, Cadillac Frank and Pino hulked closer. Wesley dropped his suitcase. With a woozy feeling, from his shoulder holster he jerked out his Colt.

He bobbled it a bit.

Cocked it.

The .45 shook in his hand—so hard he was afraid he might accidentally shoot himself in the foot. The barrel was pointing all over the place.

Get your shit together, the ghost of his brother said in his head.

Okay, okay. Hell, he was a bad dude with a gun. Should he attack them? Try and . . .

Probably not a good idea.

In a flash he realized with terrifying clarity he couldn't shoot anything. Finally he remembered what he'd forgotten.

Bullets!

He almost pitched the gun away.

The wind moaned. Less than fifty feet away, closing in damn quick for such a big goon, Pino raised a black pistol with a long barrel. His eyes were large and bright from the hunt.

"You piece a shit! You die!"

Wesley's stomach slid around. He was only realizing now how outmatched he was. They were gaining on him. How could they be so fast?

They almost had him.

Damn! This was his payback for helping get rid of Eddie. What to—?

How the hell was he going to get out of this? He didn't have a prayer.

He looked down at his .45. Clamping it in both hands, arms waggling, he slipped his finger on the trigger.

"I'll shoot!"

A shot rang out and skittered off the rock beside him.

Someone screamed.

Well, bluffing sure wasn't going to work. Since he had no bullets himself, he tucked his .45 away. This was no time to be a candy-ass. He had survived before and he would survive now. He would have to make a stand right here. Could he charge them, fists flying?

Or maybe . . .

There was only one thing to do.

He picked up a fist-sized rock. Before he messed up his rotator cuff, he used to have a hell of an arm. He hadn't even tried to throw a ball in years. But what freaking choice was there now? He'd been bold yesterday. He could do it again today.

Hadn't he somehow pitched the Winooski High Spartans to a state championship? He had been hot shit then. A phenom. He'd never forget all the hooting and high-fiving and foot stomping in the stands.

Now, he waited.

A chilly blast of wind roared in. The bottom of his dress ballooned.

Cadillac Frank and Pino closed in.

Another shot cracked along the ridge. Wesley swallowed hard. Man!

Pino squinted, like he was sighting for the kill.

Wesley half-expected to melt into a pile of quivering jelly. But instead he felt steely resolve. It was now or never. Picturing himself in his dark blue Spartans baseball jersey, a white 17 on the back, he stood up straight. He then leaned into his windup. The glory of those days came rushing back.

You can do this.

Back then he couldn't hit or steal a base to save his life. But he could throw. He could nibble at the plate. Could drop curveballs.

Now, the rock felt cold in his hand as he aimed right between Pino's bushy eyebrows.

"Fuck you," he said.

With all his might, he hurled the rock.

His old split-finger fastball.

Strike!

The stone hit Pino directly in the forehead. He wavered and lost his balance and Cadillac Frank lumbered into him. Both of them swayed with their arms flailing. They then keeled over like bowling pins.

Sal raced toward Wesley.

Wesley felt a bullet crease the air. In response he hunched forward against the wind, grabbed his suitcase, and sprinted away.

Yeah, bitch!

Gunshots popped behind him. He heard cursing. The wind shoved at him. It roared. At first he felt like he was pushing against a heavy door. He then had the sickening sense that he was about to blow away. But he tucked his chin into his chest and fought his way through it.

A minute later a stocky male Green Mountain Club caretaker clomped after him.

"Hey, careful of the plants! They're endangered!"

"So am I!"

———————

Wesley stumbled down the slope. Falling over rocks. Gasping for air.

He dropped onto a side trail. Maybe he had escaped? He stopped to listen. At first all he heard was his own labored breathing. An airplane rumbled high above.

Then came distant voices.

His heart clenched.

The thought of one more bullet whizzing by him seemed to give him wings.

As he scrambled through a cluster of boulders, he spotted a bike racer on foot, and halted. Apparently the race up the toll road had ended. The narrow-faced racer's nose was red with the cold. But it was his yellow bodysuit and helmet that caught Wesley's attention.

The racer turned as Wesley stumbled forward. After sweating so much, his skin was steaming. He had to force the words out past his ragged breaths.

"Take off . . . your clothes!"

He popped open his suitcase. With a desperate smile, he waggled a packet of bills.

The racer inched away.

"Beat it! I'm straight."

The man backed up against a boulder and cursed as Wesley groped inside his own sweater. Hell, it was just a matter of time before . . .

"Hey, look, I'm desperate," Wesley said.

"Get any closer, I'll—"

Wesley jerked out his gun.

"Strip! Now."

The racer gasped, and gaped back in horror. He stripped naked. The wind swished along the slope, and he covered his eyes with a hand, shaking.

"Well, go ahead . . . ."

"This dress. Might want to put it on."

"Oh, God."

"Then again, that could get you killed—"

"Jesus, no."

"—by Mob hit men."

The biker gave him an utterly panicked look.

"*Hit men!*"

"So maybe just head off like that."

"Yes! Thank you."

———————

Wesley stuffed himself into his new bodysuit, jammed the bike helmet over his wig. He whipped the cash out of his suitcase and crammed it into the biker's daypack, stressing its seams.

"C'mon, c'mon," he said to himself out loud.

Five minutes later he was wheezing for breath again. Stuffed into a gondola car, he felt so winded he could barely hold himself up.

Next to him, a tubby boy in a bright orange scarf fidgeted.

"There were guns everywhere. There were!"

A barge-like woman twisted her neck in response.

"Calm down, I said."

"Hey, look it that. Down there, Mom. There! A guy riding down the road, nothing on!"

Wesley slumped against a window. Shaking hard, he drew stares as they descended. No bullets, he thought. What an idiot! Thought that was *it*.

His legs felt full of lead.

As the gondola whizzed into the station below and the other passengers began to stir, he spun his woozy head. DANGER—MACHINERY IN MOTION said a large sign outside. He clasped his hand to his wig, bit at his lip.

Staring at the sign, he scrambled to jog his brain.

Those crazy bastards had to be right on his freaking ass.

30

All of a sudden Wesley felt a flash of hope. He wobbled out of the gondola.

"Hey, hey, you!" He jerked at the apple-cheeked attendant's sleeve. "Up for an easy grand?"

He tugged off the daypack, dug his hand into it. Pulling the teen aside, he stuffed $1,000 into his hand.

"Keep the lift stalled ten minutes, and that's—"

"You tripping? No way! My boss will—How about five minutes?"

"Just do it."

"Deal, dude!" They bumped knuckles. "I mean, ma'am? I mean—whatever."

Wesley zoomed back to the cabin, hands white on the steering wheel. He demolished the NO BALLS! placard outside, screeching to a halt on the lawn. He was hyperventilating and tried to calm himself by drawing in a couple of deep pulls of air. His mind raced too.

A part of him felt giddy. He was alive! A survivor! But now he had to face Jules. He flung his car door open—and almost fell out. She must be nuts with worry. She was going to have a fit.

He was glad he was wearing the helmet and Kevlar vest.

Feeling ragged and weary, he eased open the door.

"It's me, honey! Now, don't—"

She lay shackled to the bed's brass frame, stretched out and serene. Her light snores filled the cabin with a stirring grace. He felt like hugging her shamelessly and weeping with relief.

He plunged closer. Grabbing her tiny shoulder, he shook it wildly.

"Jules, Jules, wake up. Wakey-wakey. C'mon, let's go!"

Stirring, she opened her eyes. Her hair stood up and her face was creased with sleep. She blinked.

"Huh?"

"Nothing worked! I waited, and then, bam, ran my ass off. I was very sweaty. It was—nuts." He gave out a few *whews*. "I just about crapped my pants. Now they're God-knows-where."

"You're okay?"

"Where the hell's that key?"

"What—"

"Shit. Goddamn it. Oh, there it is."

As he unlocked the handcuffs, all at once his throat felt cracked and dry. Flinging off his helmet and wig in the kitchenette, he slurped down a stream of water straight from the faucet. It was cool, and pure heaven. He had never tasted anything so delicious. He splashed some on his face. When he finally sloshed back toward her, she made a spinning motion with her finger.

"C'mon, let's roll!"

They bolted outside, dove into the car. They jerked their doors shut. Slamming the car into reverse, he backed around and glanced left on Mountain Road. She shook her head.

"That way? Uh-uh, I bet they come that—"

"Stowe will be packed."

She twisted toward him and made a noise with her mouth, as if she disagreed.

"Trust me," he said.

Giving her his best decisive look, he stabbed the gas pedal and the engine roared and the car leaped forward. They raced north, away from Stowe, Mount Mansfield rearing into the sky before them.

————————

As the Focus and old Chevy van streaked down Mountain Road, Cadillac Frank spotted the white Mustang hauling ass the other way.

He and Sal punched their brake pedals, and their brakes screeched and their tires squealed hideously as they made sharp U-turns.

Cadillac Frank pushed his Focus. He kept accelerating. He redlined the motherfucker.

A minute later they caught up to the Mustang.

"You're screwed now," Cadillac Frank said.

He pulled out his Glock. He lowered his window and tried firing outside of it with his left hand. The muzzle flashes exploded into the air.

The cars ahead dodged to the shoulders.

As they carved through a set of curves, the Mustang kept pushing on. Who the hell was driving it? Weaseldick? He wasn't bad behind the wheel. The only way Cadillac Frank was going to catch a muscle car like that was to really push things crazy-fast.

Despite a near crash with a little black car pulling onto the road, he pressed harder on the gas. The engine screamed. And he closed in.

"Got you this time," he said.

But the Mustang's driver braked hard.

The fucker!

To avoid a crash, Cadillac Frank stabbed his own brakes again. His car lurched toward the road shoulder. Bounced along it. Screeched to a hard stop. Behind him, he heard the van scrape against something metal like a guard rail, and then a high-pitched keening sound as if a chunk of the vehicle's body had ripped right off.

A split second later the van crunched into the rear of his car and halted behind it. His car's air bags failed to blow.

"Jesus. Jesus."

As he gathered himself, he felt no pain. Thank fucking God, he seemed to be all in one piece. He unlocked his seat belt. Pulled himself out of the goddamn car. Clenched his hand into a fist as he stared at the car's crumpled back end. What a pain-in-the-ass day this was turning out to be.

He lumbered up to a stunned-looking Sal, still in the van's driver's seat.

"What the hell, Sal?"

"Oops. Sorry, boss."

"You dumb shit!"

Cadillac Frank leaned into the front of the van.

"You okay, Pino?"

Pino pulled out a Camel.

"What're you gonna do, huh?"

———————

Wesley exchanged a panicked look with Jules and pinned the gas. The car surged like a rocket. His palms felt slick with sweat.

"Shit, that was close."

"See? See?" She threw a hand up. Her face was pink and annoyed. "I told you. Way to go. Really should've—"

"I told you."

"Don't be an ass. Christ, this is one fine mess you got us into."

He swerved around a silver Explorer and they flew over a bump. The car jumped off the pavement, came down, bounced. He swung his head around.

"Have I ever let you down? Have I?"

She gave him a look. Her lips drew into a bud.

"What're you trying to do, punish me?" he added. "You really don't have to." His eyes darted to the rearview mirror. "Oh, forget it."

They fell silent. As the climb steepened, stone outcrops crowded the road shoulder. Snow frosted the trees. Near the windy crest, the Mustang swaying, they hit a patch of black ice. Feeling only pure surprise for a fraction of a second, then panic, he pumped the brakes.

The car fishtailed.

They skidded sideways to the road edge. A blue-gray rock face looming before them, he jerked crazily at the steering wheel, a roaring in his head.

A gust of wind rushed against the car's side.

The moment stretched out endlessly and then stopped. At last the tires grabbed the pavement—and they missed smashing into the rock by inches.

Still, they kept their mouths shut.

Once the Mustang crested the hill, Jules locked her arms together. Another gust of wind rocked the car, and she glared at Wesley for a minute, face set tight. She saw his pulse beating in his temples. He smelled of stale sweat. His arms shook.

The dumbass had bungled it all. Apparently he had bled all over Eddie's crime scene, and now goddamn this.

Trees and fields rushed by outside. Finally, she couldn't stand it anymore. She gave him her best disgusted face.

"This all started with your idiotic betting, this is on you."

"God, my feet hurt."

"I warned you," she said. "I give up even trying to help you."

"This has been one of the worst—"

"You screwed up the one chance we had."

"Up there? Thought I'd had it."

"You know, that was some outfit you had on when you headed up. Gender fluid is cool, but what's next? You going to start wearing high heels too?"

"I was freaked the hell out. At one point, though, it was pretty sweet." He held his head up. "I held them off with just a rock."

"Right."

"No, really."

They zoomed by a shiny diner and cluster of clapboard houses in Jeffersonville. Then came a small shopping center. Near an old stone house, she watched him shoot another glance at the rearview mirror. His face was tense, scared. She wanted to clobber him. And she wanted to comfort him and kiss him.

All of a sudden he hollered.

"Pink! Ain't that car pink?"

She felt a chill. The Mustang swerved over the yellow lines. She thought she heard a shot whang off the pavement.

"Damn," he said. "It's them."

She snatched up the Colt from the floor.

"Step on it!"

"They're demons! They can't be stopped."

Eyes wild, he stabbed the gas pedal.

The valley widened out. Just beyond a corrugated metal building, they hit open roadway. Farmland spreading out alongside them, they rocketed by one car after another—a flat-out, sound-barrier-busting burn.

She braced herself as they shot between a rattletrap pickup and Volvo sedan down the middle.

A horn blared.

They were going about a million miles an hour now. The engine whined in high rpm. If she and Wesley had to run for now, so be it. But screw those bastards. She was going to take them down.

She waved the Colt in the air.

"Punch it. Go! Go! Go!"

"Jeez, careful with that thing. Shit. . . . No, never mind—the bullets are in the trunk."

3 1

At noon the next day, Cadillac Frank turned his slightly crumpled pink Focus onto Jules's raised long driveway in Monkburg. A short distance ahead of him, the front bumper of the van clanked up and down. A rabbit scampered for cover.

Cadillac Frank saw Sal point toward the bunny from the van. God, sometimes the guy acted like he was three-quarters retard.

Pino turned around in the van's passenger seat, cradling the Kalashnikov. Checking for the sign from Cadillac Frank. Pino was smiling that weird little smile of his as he pulled back the gun's cocking lever. There was still a red mark on his brow from the rock that Weaseldick had pelted him with.

Cadillac Frank gave him a thumbs-up. Yesterday had been a goddamn embarrassment. Today would be different.

Today Weaseldick would die.

Dressed in a gray sweater and Levi's that hung low on her hips, Jules peeked out the back door.

"Here they come!"

She and Wesley were expecting company. But they didn't plan to clap them on the back in welcome, or to serve them coffee. All too often her life had seemed like one long battle: endless skirmishes with a groping uncle, abusive lovers, and her own flaring moods. Now it was psycho wiseguys. But no Mob bastard was going to defeat her.

She felt a heat rise up inside her, flushing her neck. It was time to kick some serious ass. This was her show.

She had the dummies on her home turf now.

With a high fervor, she grabbed her double-barrel Remington shotgun. Etched along the stock were pheasants in flight. She crowed as she bolted out of the kitchen.

"Come and get it!"

———————

Wesley jerked open a living-room window. He felt ragged from stress and lack of sleep as he leaned forward.

Outside, gravel crunched under the oncoming vehicles' tires.

All morning he'd been trying to bury his fear. Hour after hour he and Jules had waited, weapons nearby. He had checked and rechecked his Colt .45. In a daze, he turned the cylinder and listened to the small clicks it made. Jules, meanwhile, had looked composed and unflinching.

Now, the waiting over, his eyes felt huge. His oily-smelling handgun waggled in his hand.

"Oh, boy."

This time he had ammo. A box of bullets sat beside him. If he could have, he would've crawled right into it.

But he had to be tough.

Closer and closer the car and van pressed in.

Forty feet.

Thirty feet.

Jules raced by down the hallway.

"Don't get shot, sweetie!"

"Oh my God."

"Let's do it. Be strong. Time to kill some more baddies."

Then he was alone. His breathing grew harder and shorter, and he gave a low moan.

32

___

Not far away outside, Detective Burpee braced himself against a stone wall. Thanks to a last-minute tip from a street source, he knew Cadillac Frank was still on the warpath. The ruthless scumbag had also supposedly boasted about planning to pull off a home invasion today. Given Wesley Torrance's reported huge debt to the mobster, Burpee was willing to gamble himself that this was right where Frank intended to strike.

Only a short while ago Burpee had met with Jules and her man. As he had approached the door, he took a deep breath.

Just how far was he supposed to go to help keep these two *out* of trouble?

After ogling Jules from a distance and digging deep into her life, it seemed odd to finally meet her. It was exciting. But also somehow embarrassing.

Stammering out his own name, he felt strangely torn. He was supposed to assign guilt. Was he freaking nuts for overlooking her and her man's actions? Had he betrayed his badge?

As he shook her tiny hand, though, he thought of all the horrible abuse she'd endured, and of Eddie's umpteen other crimes. She did not belong behind bars. He could never know what it was like to be a battered woman. Hell, it was surprising that women didn't shoot most of the men around.

Burpee felt an immediate intimate bond with her. Still, he hesitated before he spoke again.

"I know. . . . About Eddie, I mean."

She paled, held her tongue.

"You know," she said at last, "he deserved it."

"I believe you."

"He was a bad, bad—He swore he was going to kill *me*."

"Well."

Her statement made sense. It was what he suspected all along. And Eddie had been a piece-of-shit trafficker. In her own way, hadn't she balanced the books? She had guts. Sadly, though, the Staties had a piece of evidence with blood on it from the crime scene. He probably couldn't help her there. Who knew what would come of that?

He was reluctant to let go of her small, warm hand.

After a while she said, "You can let go now."

"God! Sorry."

Despite the urgency of the moment, they both laughed. They then hatched an on-the-fly defense.

Waiting now behind Jules's stone wall for the attack, Burpee could just make out her seamed-faced neighbor Homer at the corner of her house. Draped in the bulletproof vest provided by Burpee, Homer jerked up Eddie's stolen grenade launcher to his shoulder. For what seemed like forever, he squinted toward the sight.

Homer had only one load, so it had to count.

The old-timer set his tongue between his teeth. He then fired toward the approaching car and van. With a crackling whoosh, the projectile flashed across the yard.

As the rocket shot by, the pink Focus screeched to a halt. The rocket also missed the van. But the van veered right, and it hurtled off the driveway embankment and crunched into a huge field boulder and pitched on its side.

Flames shot up from a tractor down the road. Black smoke billowed into the sky.

When the bulky van driver squeezed out of his window and dropped to the ground, Burpee popped up from behind the wall. With both hands, he steadied his .357 Magnum.

This was his time to shine: The Ultimate Police Machine. He had just called for backup, and state troopers from the New Haven barracks were on their way. The forces of justice were closing in!

"Halt! Police! Drop that—Ah, screw it."

He squeezed off two quick shots, smoke curling up from the muzzle.

Apparently dazed, the van's driver scrambled around. When a shot hit near his foot, he dashed to his left, head down. Another bullet kicked up the dirt before him. He then ran in a crouch to his right.

Each round that snapped by the guy sent him scuttling in a new direction. Soon, he thunked right into the Focus's front passenger side. He scurried over to join his *goombah* at the car's dented rear.

Burpee hollered again.

"Throw down your weapons! This is—"
Return pops reminded him to hurl himself down.
"Hey, hey!"
He pressed low behind the stone wall, a bullet skimming off it inches above his head.

33

———

Jules thumped upstairs in her turquoise slippers, flooding with a dark anger and clenching her shotgun. It was time to lay down some hellfire.

"Somebody's going to get killed," she said. "Somebody's going to get *hurt*."

This was supposed to be a safe place. The place she would raise her kids.

With a hoot and string of curses, she popped in and out of the two dormer windows in the spare bedroom. *Kaploom*! *Kaploom*!

Faint doughnuts of smoke spread out from the shotgun's muzzle.

The room flashed.

The ceiling angled down sharply above her, so she had to duck her head as she scooted back and forth past the old dresser between the windows. But she could see down on everything—the overturned brown van, the two attackers huddled behind the car in her driveway. From behind the stone wall, that Burlington cop began laying down crossfire.

She pushed round after round into the Remington's chambers. Buckshot roared down on the car below.

"Eat that, fuckers."

The gun butt kicked her shoulder. But she took her time to make each blast count.

Hollering with a crazy glee, she fired.

———————

Downstairs, Wesley waggled his .45 from side to side, thumbing back the hammer and clamping down on the trigger. He pulled away—the muzzle flashing, the shots jolting his hands, the stink of gunpowder in the air.

"Take that!"

His shots pinged into the distant mailbox.

"There's more where that came from."

He seemed to be seeing himself from a distance as he wiped the sweat off his palm, jerked open another box of ammo. Bullets flew everywhere.

"Damn."

He plucked up what he could see, and kept shooting his Colt dry.

———————

Cadillac Frank crouched low behind the battered Focus. The firing had picked up even more, coming in from everywhere. He knew he and Sal were pinned down, and he felt overwhelmed.

They swore in unison.

"Jesus fucking Christ!"

Bullets tore into the ground. They whizzed overhead. They thwacked into the rental car and flattened its tires.

He and Sal could barely get a shot off. Cadillac Frank yanked out another clip from the pocket of his crimson sweat suit. He smacked it into his Glock 19.

Sal scrunched lower. Turning to Cadillac Frank with a panicked look, he shouted against the racket.

"I'm scared! Really—"

"Shut up and fire, you moron."

"Pino's dead. When the van flipped, he—"

"You should've grabbed the AK."

Sal gaped as a divot popped from the ground only a foot away. Rounds streamed from behind the wall to their left, ripping into the car's side.

"We gotta get out of here. They're every—"

"You whack job, for now keep shooting. Then you're gonna get me that AK."

Cadillac Frank braced himself against the cool metal of the car and fired at the house, scowling. A shotgun roared back.

Buckshot blasted out the car's windshield.

Squinting, he inched his head up. Smoke hung in the air. Weren't those Weaseldick's curls at the bottom of that window lined with flowers?

That asswipe!

He squeezed off another shot.

Wesley held his .45 high and his head low. Everything was *way* too loud.

After he ran out of ammo, he dropped a hand on the windowsill and peeked out toward the driveway. Then he ducked his head.

Crash!

A window shattered to his right. Shards of glass skittered across the floor.

From upstairs came the heavy slam of Jules's shotgun.

Outside, Bree's friend, the Burlington cop who'd showed up, hollered to Cadillac Frank to give up. When Wesley stole another glimpse outdoors, someone hurled Jules's cat. Boo hurtled through the air, yowling. Springing to his paws, the cat dashed away.

A round whizzed by Wesley's ear. It smacked into the wall behind him.

"Holy shit."

He ducked—and couldn't help thinking of torn flesh, shattered bones. After another deadly round drilled into the fireplace mantel, he was about ready to haul ass and hunker down in the closet.

But he couldn't fall apart now.

He was strong. He said it to himself: *I will be strong.* Feeling a measure of control come back to him, he clenched a fist then hollered wildly out the window.

"I'll burn your houses down!"

34

Jules thumped down the stairs by threes with the shotgun. What now? As in chess, superior position would be the best way to kick ass. How could she get that? She froze a moment and then raced into the woodshed. Fighting off a pulse of fatigue, she told herself to relax. Let the air in. Let it out, let it in.

Slow down.

She steadied herself and her body settled. She had been too far away to take them out. It was time to get closer, get this over with.

She had to attack.

When she poked open the woodshed door, Boo scampered inside. The good guys were going to win this.

She had some killing to do.

As the gunfire spluttered to a stop, Cadillac Frank glanced around. He felt super-fucking-alert, aware of everything, the clouds drifting across the sky, the smell of sweat and something coppery.

"No sweat, right, Sal? . . . Sal? Sal?"

When he looked down, his spirits sank. Beside him lay Sal's bloodied body. His still eyes seemed to search the sky. His comb-over flopped back into the dirt, and Cadillac Frank patted it back into place.

"Oh, Sal," he whispered. "Rest in peace, you moron."

As he stared dumbly at the ground, he felt short of breath. Pino down. Sal down. Now he really was in deep, dark shit.

There were more pops of gunfire.

Time to get the hell out of here. But no way could he survive trying to jump into his car. Or bolting for the AK 47 in the van. He shot a glance toward the tree line. He'd never goddamn make that either.

Okay, this shit wasn't over yet. This was no last stand.

Good thing he still had a hand grenade.

———————

Detective Burpee crept closer to the house behind the wall, clenching his Smith and Wesson.

He lifted his head quickly.

Ducked it.

When a bullet cracked against the rocks, he froze. A surge of adrenaline zinged through him.

He took a moment to try to listen for a siren. Where was the damn backup he had called for? Moments ago he had dropped one of Cadillac Frank's *goombahs*. Now he would have to take out Cadillac Frank too. The main thing was to close in. So he eased another few feet nearer. Stopping, he dropped to one knee. Paused. Stealing another peek over the wall's top, he raised his piece.

He had a clean head shot at Frank.

"Come out! Or I'll drop you."

With his hulking target at the rear of the car in clear view, Burpee swallowed.

Pow! In his mind he could already see the spray.

He squeezed the trigger—but heard a flinty click. Out of bullets himself, he stared at his revolver.

Turning his ringing head, he cheered, though. A horde of grizzled farmers in John Deere and Caterpillar caps marched up the field to the south. They wore looks of quiet determination and clutched carbines. A pack of mutts yapped at their heels. Sighting on the Focus in the driveway, they opened up with a rapid fire.

The noise was immense.

Bullet holes blossomed in the car's body.

———————

Jules crept out of her woodshed with the Remington up and ready. She stopped behind her surplus wood stack. Leaning forward, she braced herself and then cocked the hammer.

Bullets snapped through the air. Mutts howled. A sweat-suited mobster swore his head off only a few yards away and scrambled for better cover behind his car. Despite the ruckus, she felt fully at the center of things, and in control.

This would work. This had to work.

"Say your prayers, wiseguy."

As she shifted her weight, a corner of the woodpile slipped. Pieces of ash clattered to the ground. But it didn't rattle her.

Aunt Ina used to say that Jules was probably the best shot in Addison County. Not that it mattered, this close. The barrels of her Remington were poised straight ahead of her. Her little hands steady, she aimed at the big mobster. As far as she could tell, he was the last bad guy standing.

The bastard had attacked her home. Had tried to kill her and her man. Her anger welled up.

She would end this, now.

Her breath tightened as she laid her finger in the curve of the trigger.

Got you.

Screw with me, I'll screw you right back.

Men swarmed toward Cadillac Frank, rifles raised. The metal *thunked* nearby him. Bullets pounded into the dirt. They had outflanked him. His options were narrowing with each passing sec. What the fuck was coming at him next? Goddamn fighter jets? From close behind him came an odd clatter.

Hand grenade in hand, he spun. His hair dripped sweat.

Oh, Christ.

Against the sweep of forest and low sky, two narrowed eyes stared back at him above two gun barrels.

Well, this was it.

He grabbed hold of the grenade's pin.

She had no clue. She was already dead.

All he had to do was—

But the bitch fired.

Kaploom!

The blast blew him right out of his white Italian loafers. Steel shot ripped into his butt. Keeling over, he let out a high, fierce howl.

35

Jules dropped her shotgun. Racing past two armed neighbors to the side door, she flung it open, scrambled for the living room.

"Wesley? You okay? You all right?"

Bullet holes pocked the walls. Plants spilled across the floor, and blue smoke hung in the air. Glass shards crunched under her feet. Otherwise, there was a strange silence. Why was it so quiet?

Something was not . . . She felt scared in a way she had never felt before.

A strange tingling went through her.

"Sweetie?"

Something horrible had—

When she jerked her head to the left, her heart heaved.

The air retreated around her. The room pitched and surged.

"Oh, no! No. No."

He sat slumped over next to the pine stand, spent .45 casings all around him. A broken fern frond hung in his pale face. His lips were parted, his eyes closed. Blood stained his left arm and the side of his chest.

"Wesley!"

She flew across the room. Bursting into tears, she flung herself to the floor. She hugged his limp body tight.

"Oh God, oh God." She convulsed with loud sobs. "Stay with me! *Don't* leave. Don't let go."

She pressed her knuckles against her mouth then gave out a little wail. Collecting herself, she steadied his head with her hands. He was warm to her touch.

She could save him!

Was he even breathing? He had to be. She had no idea how to do CPR. Would a quick thump on his chest work? A hard smack?

"Open your eyes, sweetie, look at me! Someone call 911! Help!"

Wiping away her tears, she wasn't sure what to do. So she slapped him in the face. She then searched for his wound.

Wesley finally came to, eyes fluttering. What had happened? What was . . . ? Jules kneeled at his side, her face red and puffy, as if from crying. He couldn't move. His body was hardly there. His bandanna-wrapped arm throbbed. The smell of burned gunpowder seared his nostrils.

God, he'd been shot. When he spoke, his ears rang so hard, he could barely hear his own voice.

"Really bad, no? Sure it is, can tell."

He glanced toward the sopped bandanna and winced. Staring into Jules's glistening blue eyes, he felt a rush of tenderness. He squeezed her warm little hand.

"Before I kick, there're some things I gotta say, honey."

"Wesley—"

"I love you. So much."

Everything around him seemed askew and fuzzy as her slippers.

"Wesley! For Christ sake—"

"Did I get them all?"

"—listen to me."

Feeling woozier, he held up a hand. How many seconds did he have left?

"Let me talk, I'm the one dying here."

"Actually—"

"Sharing life with you, it's been . . ."

Tears filled his eyes. He was losing blood. Weak. Running down.

He could sense his end coming, rising and swelling like a wave.

"Oh, God."

She let out a laugh. Hugged him hard.

"You lost some blood, but dying? You're not. There's a gash, but it—"

"What?"

"You're all right."

He felt a lifting inside. From outdoors came the bloop of a siren as she caressed his cheek.

"We're going to be okay, you idiot. It's all over."

He straightened up.

"Then we nailed that shootout, didn't we?"

36

As Jules sipped at her morning coffee in her overstuffed living-room chair the next day, she smiled and felt a surge of triumph. Earlier, she and Wesley had swept up all the debris into the snow shovel, and had taped cardboard over the shattered windowpanes. There were still other unmistakable signs of gunfire. And the house continued to feel a bit different. Still, their efforts had helped.

For a while there yesterday the yard had been choked with state patrol cars, ambulances, and news vans. It had been a downright spectacle. Easing back now, she pored over the article splashed across the front page of *The Burlington Free Press* again.

Headlined ATTACK IN MONKBURG KILLS TWO, not much of the article was true—including the mention of Cadillac Frank Cannizaro's attempt to extort insurance money from her. It carried a couple of complementary quotes from Detective Burpee, though. As she reached the second quote again, she felt her little face flush with pleasure.

She's a brave woman, Detective Burpee had said. *They shot up her home, but she wouldn't give an inch.*

"Damn right."

When a Burlington cop had showed up at the house yesterday, her breath snagged. Did the guy know something about Eddie's death? Had someone figured out her lie about Jo-Jo Plank? She vaguely remembered Burpee's face from her days at the Booby Trap. Bree, she gathered, thought well of him. But just what kind of cop was he? An honest one? Or not? Could he be trusted?

Or were she and Wesley screwed?

After all they had been through, was it over now?

But it was soon clear he was on her side. And he helped save them in the end. What a good man he turned out to be. She would never forget the favor he'd done her.

Scanning the Town News section now, she chuckled: a separate blurb related the mysterious explosion of a tractor down the road. Throwing the paper aside with a sense of renewal, she stretched, arching her back.

Well, enough of that.

Still smiling away, she started fixing some pancakes and bacon. As she poured discs of batter into the skillet, Wesley stood behind her and kissed her on the neck. A large square bandage covered his bicep.

"Baby?" she said.

"Hey, what?"

"When I saw you yesterday, slumped there like that . . ." That moment had almost broken her. She shook her head. "I'm just—I'm so glad."

"Mmm."

"Your arm okay?"

Barely skimmed by the bullet in the shootout, his bicep had suffered only slight soft-tissue damage. The ER staff had only had to treat the wound for infection and put him on an IV sedative for shock.

Now he brought his hand up and rubbed his thumb along the back of her neck.

"A little tender. The doctor said—"

"How about grabbing some plates?"

He set the table, and put out some of Homer's best maple syrup. Not one bullet whizzing through the air, they ate in contented silence and at a leisurely pace. She relished his every gesture, and finally she blew him a little kiss. Thank God, he'd survived.

Finished eating, he set down his fork and patted his belly.

"Going to explode. Wow. That was perfect."

"Good."

She smiled to herself when he started clearing the table. Maybe they weren't out of the woods yet. Maybe they were even headed deeper into the woods. She was still hoping that their troubles would all go away. At least, though, they had survived the crazy gunfight.

"Thanks, honey," he said. "Think he's pretty pissed?"

"Who?"

"*Him.*"

"Oh," she said. "Cadillac Frank? It's probably a great thing he's headed for jail."

"Couldn't he, like, get out somehow?"

37

———

Days later, Jules's cell phone trilled as she was grocery shopping at Shaws. When she saw who was calling, she felt her pulse bump up.

Oh, God.

She gripped the handle of her shopping cart. She debated not answering. That would be the smart thing to do. She felt her recent sense of triumph threatening to deflate. This was just going to be aggravating.

Not today.

Why should she . . . ?

Well, it had been nice to feel content for a little while.

"What do you want now?" she said into the phone at last. "I asked you *nicely* not to call anymore."

"Did you?" Paige said. "That any way to treat your sweet baby sis?"

Jules's wingnut sister, lately based in San Diego, was a heavy druggie. A loose cannon. Whenever the local Vermont cops used to pick her up, Paige would call Jules and claim she was merely holding something for a friend.

Jules had tried to help her baby sis before. How many other times had Jules answered her phone only to hear Paige's complaints? One complaint after another. Someone had taken her car keys and was chasing her. Or she was spitting up blood. She'd split from rehab, but met a nice guy. That guy that had seemed so nice? Well, he'd hit her with a tire iron in a little dispute.

Jules had tried to pick Paige up every time the world knocked her flat on her ass. But Paige would do anything to run from withdrawal. "The sick," she called it. For a while apparently, she was into back-to-backs—shooting smack, then smoking crack for a chaser. Otherwise, she was all about meth.

Jules thought about the choices people made in their lives. She could tell now from Paige's irritated tone that she had not cleaned herself up. Who knew where the money Jules had wired her for rehab had really gone?

At times, Paige creeped Jules out even more than Eddie's old partner, Kev Bates, had. Paige didn't have horn tats. But Jules had no problem picturing her unleashing the gates of hell.

"You know," Jules said now, "right now I'm shopping. I—"

"Yeah! Well, fuck you, Jules."

Something else in Paige's voice sent a chill rattling down Jules's spine.

She and Wesley were in enough trouble as it was. Now, though, she had a sense of fault lines about to fracture out of control.

"I bet you're so sorry to have Eddie gone," Paige continued. "That one sure seems damn fishy."

Jules felt her heart stop in mid-beat.

The bitch!

Always trying to stir up trouble. Paige had never seemed to get over the loss of their parents to a car accident on Route 7; Jules wasn't sure she had herself either. Still, Paige *thrived* on turmoil. And hitting the pipe had unhinged her further.

But this? Had a crazy tweaker like her put two and two together about Eddie?

Jules stared at a frosty cooler door, trying to tamp down the little voice in her head that said that this call was the start of something really bad.

"I gotta go," she said. "Got things to do."

No way would she ever let her wacked-out sister get in the way of her own dreams. Hell, what was she even doing talking to someone who'd been so heartless as to steal meds from their dying aunt? Paige snorted on the other end of the line.

"Right!"

"Paige, I've tried to help you."

"Something's fishy, fishy, fishy."

Something deeper *was* at play here. Oh, she could wring Paige's neck.

"Many, many times I've tried to help," Jules said. "Sent you cash. Gave you my time and all sorts of goddamn good advice."

"Sure there's nothing you're—"

"But if you ever show up in Vermont again," Jules said, "I'll scratch your freaking eyes out."

She stabbed off her phone.

Who needed that shit?

Christ. Wesley had forgotten that one on his murder cover-up checklist: Make sure your nutjob sibling doesn't suspect you.

That evening, Jules tossed and turned in bed. All that murder stuff was finally behind her and Wesley now, wasn't it? No, things were shaky—she felt it. Yesterday, Burpee had shared some surprising secrets with her. But Paige and the Vermont State Police were another matter. The Staties still had the leaf with the blood on it from the Gorge.

That ridiculous damn leaf.

3 8

The same day Detective Burpee earned a promotion for nailing him, Cadillac Frank came to with a ragged butt wound in Burlington's Fletcher Porter Hospital.

Post-surgery, all he seemed to do was down pills to fight the pain and infection, and pills to fight the side effects of the other damn pills. Once his skin grafts began to heal, he could finally lie on his back. But he shrank from the walleyed nurse who came to change his bandages. Every time she drew near, he jerked the sheet up over his face.

"Go away! Go away!"

According to his doc, forty-seven pellets of steel shot had ripped into his ass. The way he saw it, he was goddamn maimed. And the guards! They watched him eat, watched him snooze, watched him take a crap.

One day as the sun began to set outside his window, a pair of FBI dweebs showed up. They told him they had the goods on him. They wanted to offer him a shot at the Witness Protection Program. He knew his old life was over if he flipped. He'd be the feds' bitch from then on.

But he could have kissed them.

Staring at the green cubes on his dinner tray, he made a face. He folded in seconds flat.

"One last thing, though. Before I talk, I gotta have a prosciutto sandwich. A nice fat one. And some espresso and cannolis for dessert."

He couldn't believe his good fortune. No jail. And some day, some fucking way, revenge against Weaseldick.

Cadillac Frank went undercover, and the feds got tapes. Lots of tapes. And they got busy digging for bodies with backhoes.

Afterward, he sweated it out as a snitch in U. S. District Court, squealing on his former *goombata* in back-to-back trials. The entire process was hell on him too. Everyone and their brother wanted to bust his damn chops.

Dubbed "Half-Assed Frank" by a wag reporter due to his injury, the name stuck.

By his last grueling day on the witness stand, he veered close to a total nervous breakdown. His spooked eyes darted around the mahogany-paneled courtroom. He'd been hammered with questions now for what seemed like years. He was being treated like a goddamn criminal.

"So maybe I chased a few jerk-offs with a bat." Dressed in a loud checked suit, he shrugged. "That was . . . business."

Bags beneath his eyes, his face clenched, he knew he looked worse than Leo Marino, the defendant. A wall of agents had swept him into the building earlier, but who knew what else had been slipped in?

Jesus, wasn't that Nicky the Mole Testa in back there, shaking his head? Nicky looked hot as a pistol, and mouthed the word *motherfucker* at him.

Hurriedly he turned away. He gulped down some water, hand trembling.

Marino's silver-haired prick lawyer, his black-framed glasses halfway down his nose, flipped a page on his pad.

"Business? I see . . . . But would you answer the question?"

Half-Assed Frank jerked forward, close to the rail, face twitching. He felt like a damn moron.

"What question? You trying to break my—"

"Yes or no?"

"Yeah! But that—that don't make me no bad witness . . . ."

As his voice faltered, the room seemed to tighten. Nicky Testa's eyes burned into him. He tugged at his collar, desperate for some breathing room, trapped in the witness box.

Testa jumped up.

"You rat! Your time's up, Frankie."

It seemed there was no air at all in the courtroom.

Judge Horvath shot out a spindly arm and banged his gavel, hard. When Half-Assed Frank lunged to the floor, the room erupted in laughter.

Fifteen days later, the goddamn hoopla and trauma of testifying behind him at last, Half-Assed Frank swallowed, cinched his black Adidas baseball cap a little lower, and limped down an Alaska Airways ramp. The sky was overcast and close.

Nome, Alaska! A marked man! He scanned the tarmac with narrowed eyes. How the hell did he get into this?

He felt as if he had a huge bull's-eye target on his back.

Quickly, an icy wind cut right through him. Cold sleet came lashing down, and the wind shuddered his yellow sweat suit.

Shivering, hunching deeper into it, he yearned to whip right around and shoot Weaseldick dead.

PART TWO

39

Forcing herself out of the house, Jules pushed Junior in his stroller to Maine and back, it seemed. Her cheeks puffed in and out with the effort. She loved these strolls. And she was determined to stay strong. And to be a Supermom. Dewy mornings, sunny afternoons—she kept at it, ever alert for errant cars and lunatic would-be abductors.

On Lancaster Road, she paused to let Junior take in a herd of cows lazing in a field of brilliant grass. New blossoms scented the air. The sky was a perfect robin's-egg blue.

"Moo," she said. "Moo!"

Junior cooed from his stroller. His eyes shone.

Despite some initial doubts, she had quickly adjusted to being a mother. And with every glimpse of her little one's wide blue eyes and chestnut curls, she floated off to Mommyland. She vowed that no one would ever hurt Junior. Ever.

It had been over a year since the shootout at her home. But she couldn't help but worry Half-Assed Frank would show up again. She knew the thought was barely rational—he was in the Witness Protection Program, and reportedly lived far, far away. Still, the sense of a danger approaching from afar nagged at her.

As she rolled Junior past the long red barns at Maple Meadow Farm now, the fear hit her so hard, she crouched down and clamped her hands on her knees, suddenly faint.

She waited, gathered herself. She then grabbed the stroller handle and rose. When she smiled at her little angel, his body jerked slightly as he hiccupped.

"It's okay, Junior. Mommy's okay. Maybe that was too much exercise."

God.

Was she was turning into a scaredy-cat like Wesley?

She figured her hormones were out of whack.

———

"Go outside," Jules said soon afterward.

She threw Wesley one of her hard-pressed looks. For hours he had been slouched in his black T-shirt and cargo shorts in the rocking chair, gazing across the living room into space.

Half off his rocker.

Lately he had been acting like he had a question mark stuck in his head. He gave her a confused look as she shooed him toward the door.

"What?"

"Get off your butt, get some fresh air."

He raised his eyebrows.

"Fresh what?"

"Air! That stuff you breathe."

"Oh."

A minute later she peeked out the kitchen window.

"Oh, Wesley."

He was sinking—dropping lower and lower as his aluminum chair's green plastic webbing gave way—and didn't even seem to notice. What was up with him? Were his feelings of guilt about Eddie back? She was seized by a dark thought. Did he sense something? Maybe her hormones weren't out of whack. Maybe something bad *was* headed their way?

Rushing outside, she brought him a different chair.

"Here. God, you look . . ." She leaned down and kissed the top of his head. "What is it?"

"Nothing."

She laid a hand on his shoulder, squeezed. Gave him a supportive smile.

How was she supposed to help him now? Was he going to go totally bonkers and spill his guts to the cops? Thankfully, she hadn't heard from them in a while. Not even anything else about what Investigator Farrs had called CS-2 9—that leaf with blood. And that was plenty fine with her.

Way troubling, though, in his last update Farrs had said that they had ruled out Jo-Jo Plank as a suspect, as well as his brother, Aaron, by determining they were in Springfield at the time of Eddie's death. And when Farrs added that the reward might help, it startled her. Reward? He explained that a while ago Eddie's family had posted a reward for info leading to his killer's arrest. It was only for five grand. But, still. She wilted when she heard that.

Probably Eddie's brother, Travis, had raised the cash for that. The day Eddie was buried, Travis had stood apart on the grassy hillside in Holman Cemetery. Scowling. That had creeped her out. Who knew what he suspected? Maybe he'd been forming a grudge right then, even before they shoveled the dirt onto his brother's coffin.

Eddie had come from a rough family. Even his mother had been what Eddie called a "batcher," and had blown up her own house once while making something named "Nazi cold meth."

Nor did his family look down on violence.

"Fingers crossed, right?" Farrs finally said on the other end of the line. "We've hit some brick walls in the case. But even that reward? It could lead to a break."

Here in the backyard with Wesley, it struck Jules again that more serious trouble was headed their way. A sparrow landed on a post at the corner of the garden. She watched it, worked her hand over the back of her neck, and turned back. What else didn't she know?

"So, is your brain coming loose again?" she said to him. "Or what? Tell me."

"I just . . . fuck. I'm not sure."

She steeled herself.

"Take your time."

Was he about to drop a bombshell?

"It's like, I don't know. Postpartum stuff?"

She tried not to roll her eyes.

Some bombshell.

"Mm-hmm."

He sighed, a small sound.

"I'm serious."

She planted a kiss on his cheek.

"I got you. Whatever's bugging you, it'll be okay." She tried to think of something to say, something to lighten his mood. "Just tell me if *your* nipples start getting sore."

He half smiled.

Okay, so that wasn't the horrible bombshell she'd expected. But why did she still feel like one was on its way?

40

Limping down Nome's Front Street for the first time, Half-Assed Frank raised his eyes at the junk-strewn yards and drunks staggering out of the bars. The losers here scraped by on the edge of Norton Sound—only 200 miles east of Siberia, and even closer to the damn Arctic Circle.

Despite the "There's No Place Like Nome" slogan to attract tourists, the town was no fucking Paris, France.

"Alaska, my balls!" Half-Assed Frank had told the feds when they informed him he was being relocated there. "You kidding me? I ain't gonna live in no damn igloo."

They told him to dress warm.

"Might as well call it East Bumfuck," he muttered now to his rangy marshal escort.

"Yeah, well," Jeff Ainsworth said. "It is a *bit* rough, I guess."

Half-Assed Frank's breath blew out in clouds. A tired-looking man in overalls hollered from a doorway.

"Git out, you two! If you're gonna fight, take it to the street."

The wind knifed into Half-Assed Frank, and his teeth chattered. There wasn't a single goddamn tree or bush in sight. He and Jeff stopped by an A-frame roofed with rotting tar paper.

"Supposedly?" Jeff said. "Reindeer herding pays fairly well."

Half-Assed Frank clapped his big palm to his brow.

After shaking Jeff's hand goodbye, he lumbered back to his dingy room, churning with frustration. Of all the places to send him, why this dump? He hurled his parka to the floor. He then flopped onto his squeaky bed, afraid he'd flip out. In the tiny bathroom a few feet away, the sink's tap dripped. Dripped. Dripped. The wind roared outside as he torched up a Camel.

"Stay here," he muttered to himself, "and I'll turn into a headcase. Start banging musk ox or something."

Sucking hard on his cigarette, he couldn't help fantasizing about revenge.

———————

At first Half-Assed Frank felt exposed as the wind-lashed town of Nome itself. He imagined hit men in nearly every face he saw. Who was this guy? Who the hell was that guy? Christ, that old broad looked sort of like Bobby the Beak!

He dug his nails into his blue-black stubble and whirled his head repeatedly. Would it be today? Tomorrow?

You never goddamn knew. Like when they popped his Pop.

He steeled himself, though—keeping Frank Senior's end in mind. Hell, what better place to stay under the Family radar?

"I'll give it a shot," he soon told Marshal Ainsworth.

The fed marshal, who had helped set up Half-Assed Frank in town, was a definite stiff—right down to his cheap-ass windbreaker and wingtip shoes. But Half-Assed Frank did admire his nine-millimeter piece as they shared a drink.

Jeff grinned from his bar stool.

"Lie low, Frank. Keep your mouth shut, and you've got a free pass."

"At least I ain't living in no igloo."

"That's the spirit. Seriously, though? An igloo? We did give it some thought."

Half-Assed Frank vowed to get cruel payback. He felt as if he had a ticking clock inside him.

———————

For now, with some help from the feds, Half-Assed Frank started up a restaurant close to City Hall. Just getting ready was a challenge. But mentally rolling up his sleeves, he ripped the crappy paneling from the leased building's walls. He painted and cleaned until the stainless-steel kitchen gleamed. He sank extra nails into the wind-scoured clapboards outside.

Desperate to keep busy, he hired contractors and staff. Nearly ready, he named the place "Mama's," in honor of his late mother.

His true miracle was the menu. He slaved over it. One of his initial pork dishes tasted like particle board. But he kept cooking. Soon the jumbo shrimp Fra Diavolo tasted delicious, and just spicy enough. The veal scaloppine, perfect. He remembered his Mama bustling from one shop to another to prepare for dinner, and he sweated on, the air fragrant with garlic, tomato, fresh basil, baking bread.

Yet, right from the start, it seemed the asswipe locals didn't want to try something new. His place was a graveyard. The fancy-ass glassware sat untouched. Even the idiot tourists were more interested in panning for gold than in eating Italian.

Plopping his hands on his hips, he swore out the door as one body after another scooted by.

"Get in here, you stupid fucks!"

When U. S. Marshal Ainsworth phoned, Half-Assed Frank couldn't help griping.

"I miss Vermont. Miss my crew."

"Yeah, well."

"Even though, sometimes, I was tempted to bang their heads together like goddamn cymbals."

The next day, he thought he'd freeze his nuts off just limping his way to work. The wind screamed by, whipping his clothes and hair. His feet crunched through the snow crust. He slitted his eyes against a sudden stab of ice crystals. He gave a start when he crashed into a frozen animal pelt—a damn wolf?—hanging from a jutting beam.

Stumbling inside MAMA's front door, he yanked off his mittens and rubbed his big frozen hands together, trying to get the blood back. He unwound the scarf pulled over his stuffed-up nose.

"Shit," he said to a passing round-faced waitress, Cora. "What a raw day!"

"Enjoy it now," she said.

"What the hell you talking about?"

Cora touched a hand to her helmety hairdo.

"Tomorrow's supposed to be a real doozy."

Half-Assed Frank's feet were like ice. He jerked his bulky parka's zipper down. Wind that bends signs? Blows roofs away?

This was bullshit.

He glanced out the window.

"What the—?"

A huge, scary-looking polar bear lumbered by down the street.

"Jesus!"

He couldn't believe it.

That night, he dreamed he was stranded on a tiny iceberg. The blue-white ice was rough. It creaked, and cracked.

All about him swelled a gray sea, floe crashing into goddamn fucking floe.

41

"Get out!" Jules said.

She watched as Wesley shook his stupid head. He stared toward the red-brick fireplace and then turned back.

"Honey, you need to—"

"Now."

He slammed the front door, and then thumped back and forth across the porch. At this point, she wasn't even sure anymore just what they were fighting over. His so-called baby blues had lasted a week. Apparently he'd suffered a special variation, one which included lounging on the sofa and eating lots of potato chips.

The cops, taking care of Junior—she had enough on her plate lately. She needed a partner—not another baby. Sometimes Wesley was about as stable as her loony baby sis. So, before Jules let Mr. Gloomy Puss back inside, with satisfying fanfare she slapped a hand-made sign outside the bedroom. DON'T EVEN THINK ABOUT IT.

She figured he was lucky she didn't smack him with the ball-peen hammer he had carried—and dropped—at the Gorge.

The next time she passed by him, she could tell he was bursting to talk. When he tried blocking her in the living room, she knocked his hand away.

"No."

He made kissy sounds at her.

"Come on! Say, somebody who said she was your sister called. Never told me you had a—"

"I really could slug you."

He raised his hands in surrender and turned away.

"Okay, uh . . . good chat."

How many times had he given her little hopes, and then wrecked them? And what about the *really* screwy stuff? Mobsters attacking her house? That was a bit messed up. Would his kooky behavior drag the whole family into trouble some day?

She felt an unexpected weight of emotion. God, he sure didn't always make it easy for her to want to help him. For all she cared, he could take a flying leap. And so could her damn troublemaker sister.

For a brief spell, nothing seemed to make sense to Jules. The next day as she stepped up to her mailbox, she had an unpleasant premonition.

Crap.

She clutched a donation check she wanted to mail off to Steps to End Domestic Violence. The money would help add kiddie play grounds, with ladders, slides, and swings, to one of their Burlington shelters. Yet she considered turning right around and scooting back to the house.

Nah. Hell, she was the one acting kooky now.

She brushed her tiny rush of fear aside. Tugged open the mailbox.

Inside the box sat a single white regular postcard. It was postmarked Nome, Alaska.

There was no return address.

When she flipped it over, she went rigid. She felt adrenaline coursing through her.

The message was short.

Four words.

In big block black letters, it said I WILL NOT FORGET.

Five lines were slashed under the NOT.

42

Jules finally locked eyes with Wesley in the kitchen. She watched his throat work. When he lowered his glass of water toward the counter, he nearly missed the edge.

"You're not planning to shoot me, bury me in the yard, are you?" he said.

She stared at him for a long moment.

"Hmm."

His eyebrows soared.

"Oh, Jesus."

"Not a bad—"

"I'm sorry, honey. So, so . . . You're a better woman than me." He gave a weak laugh. "Person, I mean. You're—You're all I've wanted since the moment I met you."

Out of reflex, she shot him a stony look. Or was it time for them to hash things out? In twenty minutes she had to leave to give Homer's typically housebound wife, Emma, a ride to see her doctor.

Jules had stonewalled Wesley for three days. And she'd decided to ignore the postcard for right now. She would not forget, either—but Alaska was a long ways away. Screw him too. If he wanted a fight, she would give it to him. Personally. Her last phone call from Investigator Farrs still resonated in her mind as well. But for a while, just a day or two, she needed to not think about all that stuff. She had to pull back from the threats and danger.

Last evening, she had headed barefoot out the side door. As she ambled into the soft grass, moonlight silvered Junior's sandbox and the thirty-three birdhouses on poles that Wesley had built during a nervous spell a while ago. For the first time in days, she had a springy, hopeful feeling.

Now in the sun-washed kitchen, she unraveled her balled fists and wondered if any discussion with Wesley was even necessary.

Right here in the kitchen, Eddie used to cut up his coke with other powders. A scale and baggies nearby. And his .45. Every so often FedEx used to deliver an appliance to the door. Hidden inside would be black tar heroin. Living with a dealer? That had sucked. Hadn't Wesley helped her escape all that?

She thought about him being trapped under ice. How nearly turning into a Popsicle could freak out a person. How he had sacrificed himself for a kid. Not long ago, she had vowed to save *him*. She had to keep remembering that.

She drew closer.

Thought about first meeting him. How she knew she had finally found the thing that was missing in her life. Well, besides a big pile of cash.

Her pulse picking up, she stepped so close she smelled the soap on his skin.

"Hush."

"I swear, I'll—"

She held a finger to her lips. He seemed to have learned a lesson. Wouldn't it be nice to just make love now? Forget everything else?

She eyed the clock. She had to leave. Soon. And she could hear Junior fussing in his crib. On her way to Emma's house, she probably also should check the mailbox again for any more notes from loony mobsters.

Was there even time for a quickie?

Maybe first, though, she should at least tell Wesley about the note? Nope. Some intense sex would be more fun.

And if anyone really threatened her little family, she would kick major butt.

"Sure is something." Standing alongside Jules by the rocker the next day, Wesley smiled into Junior's crib. For a moment he felt lucky. Blessed. "Look at him."

Junior kicked off a dinosaur slipper, his tiny tongue sticking out. Jules touched Wesley's shoulder. She gave the mobile of pink and blue fish above Junior a spin. She then spoke up in a sweet tone.

"He's sure going to favor you."

Her eyes changed. She seemed to go inward.

"I worry sometimes," she said. "You'll always be there for him? Never let anyone hurt him?"

He looked around.

"Me?"

"Don't joke. Yes, you."

He had resolved he could handle this parent thing. Could he do any worse than most people? Now, standing by Junior's crib, he made a little sound in his throat.

"Of course."

"Right. And I'm the Easter Bunny. . . . You know, we might've really gotten in trouble if they'd ever found the .45."

He froze for a second.

"Where'd that thought come from? You did bury the gun, didn't you?"

"Sweetie, I thought *you* were going to."

"Oh my God."

"Gotcha!" she said. "Wow, you're gullible."

Wesley watched Junior gape at the fish circling above him. When Junior hiccupped, Jules rubbed his tummy. But from out of nowhere Wesley heard the gunshots all over again. Not long ago, he had dreamed that the Gorge flowed with blood.

"You know, I still feel sort of bad for him. Eddie, I mean."

"Hell." She put her hand to her cheek, feeling the scar there. "I wouldn't mind driving to the son of a bitch's grave right now and shooting him again. But what you said before? About always being there for Junior?"

"Uh-huh."

Her mouth twisted into a shape he couldn't read. She shook her head.

"I'd like to believe that. But really don't. Lie, lie, lie."

43

———

Shit!

Later that week, Jules nearly sideswiped an oncoming tiny blue car with her Tacoma.

"Paige?" she said into her cell phone.

"Hello, Jules."

Her drug-fried baby sis? This couldn't be good. Was she still on the pipe? Jules was tempted to hurl her phone out the window. She punched her truck's brakes, jerked at the wheel, and pulled over to the roadside. The truck skidded on gravel as it came to a stop.

She imagined Paige, all skin and bones and matted ginger hair, lurking in the nearby stand of trees.

"Still in San Diego?" Jules said.

"You don't need to know that."

"I just—"

"Like you really freaking care."

Jules wished she could slap her through the phone.

Despite her own troubles, Jules had at least done *some* good in the world. Helped the aunt who raised them. Helped her neighbors and friends. Donated to local women's shelters. What had Paige ever frigging done, besides hurt people? Over and over again.

"Let's not get into—" Jules said. "Let's not argue again."

On the other end of the line Paige snorted.

"Ha!"

Jules stared at a crow picking at something in the road. The two of them had never managed to get along. And never would. Even if they both ever made it to being white-haired old-timers with walkers, they would still be scrapping. And ever since Paige had dropped out of the Navy, her life had been one long ugly downward spiral. At one point Jules had found her sis squatting in an abandoned house in Burlington. The place was filthy—even for a shooting gallery, or whatever. Paige had torn up the smelly carpet for a blanket.

"What is it this time?" Jules said. "Money? You need—"

"Little Miss Perfect."

"I won't keep supporting your, well, stupid habit."

"Little Miss Perfect . . . *Murderer.*"

44

Jules gazed out the windshield, without seeing anything. Did her tweaker sis know what she was saying? Wesley had freaked out that morning when Jules told him she was knocked up again. He practically bolted out the door. That really pissed her off.

Now this. Everything was tilting sideways. But she was not going to let Paige intimidate her.

"What?" she said to Paige. "What're you—"

"I tried telling you before. Way back. I know what you goddamn did. I mean, to Eddie."

"You trying to . . . *frame* me?"

"Can't frame the guilty."

Jules felt her muscles tense.

Her breathing had revved up. She wanted to yell.

"You don't know what the hell you're talking about. It's all those drugs. You're—"

"Right. Sure. How many times did you tell me you'd like to kill that son of a bitch?"

Why had she ever shared that with Paige, of all people?

"That don't mean shit. You know that."

"You're so dumb, Jules."

Jules grumbled.

Lately she had hoped, she had prayed, that Eddie's case had come to a screeching halt. Too much time had passed. And apparently the reward hadn't done squat. But if Paige struck her goddamn tweaker nose into the case . . .

Or found out about the reward . . .

One thing Jules knew about her sis was that she was capable of awful things. Paige would trade away everything that mattered for one more high.

Jules had a *new* family now. Who needed this crap?

"Man!" she snapped into the phone. "You're not even making sense. I'm going to hang up."

"Oh, yeah? You don't think I know what went down?"

"You *don't* know what happened."

The line was silent a moment. Then Paige snorted again.

"Evidence? I'll testify that, that . . . you admitted the whole thing to me."

"Like they'll believe *you*."

"They might. No, they will. I can be a pretty good liar."

Goddamn. Paige was right about that.

God help her and Wesley if Paige went to the police. If the cops ever hauled Wesley in for questioning, how long would it take for him to crack? Ten seconds?

Five?

No way in hell was she ever going to let the state swoop in and take away her children. She held her tongue.

"Come to think of it," Paige said, "you did confess to me. Wow, you know, it's all coming back."

Jules smacked the steering wheel. A huge truck thundered past, rattling her pickup.

"Why now?"

"I might even have a friend who was there too. Eddie's biker buds? One of them might just be happy to help out."

Jules struggled to clear her mind. She heard the sound of her breath going in and out of her lungs. What the hell should she say? Her and Wesley's freedom was . . .

If they threw her in the slammer, she'd never be able to raise her own family.

The meth head must need cash.

"What do you want?" Jules said.

"What? You're so—You called me!"

God. Paige's brain was really scrambled.

"Paige, just tell me what the hell you—"

"You always treated me like crap. Always thought you were better. *You.* A fucking stripper, a fucking killer."

Anger made Jules's hand shake. But she felt something else too: strong fear.

The last real fight they'd had, Paige had bit Jules in the head. No doubt, in the future their relationship would be marked by more blood.

Or worse.

"Paige—"

"Big Sis don't always have the answers, does she? *Suffer,* bitch."

45

Squeezed into lime green pants and a plum shirt one evening, Half-Assed Frank frowned toward his restaurant's near-empty tables. Lately he had been clamping his achy eyes shut, willing customers to appear. He had thrown himself into his business, heart and soul. But he'd never realized how goddamn tedious honest work could be.

He knew he couldn't last here much longer. The clock inside him sounded away. Tick. Tick. Tick.

Briefly, he considered bombing the bustling Polar Club Cafe just down the street. He then grunted.

"What do I do, Mama?" he asked her spirit. "What do I . . . This ain't no damn fun."

What did they want him to serve? Spaghetti and moose balls? Blubber parmesan?

No way.

The next day, Half-Assed Frank ran a hand over the top of his head as he gaped through the small window in the kitchen OUT door.

Is it?

He hulked forward, dishes clattering behind him. The dining room lights were dim. Wasn't that Big Lou DiBono by the wall, digging into a salad?

That beard and hat, they had to be a disguise.

Should he call the Marshal Service? There was no goddamn time for that! What kind of pansy was he turning into?

He snatched up a nine-inch knife.

He raced out.

As he closed in, he bumped against a table. Catching his balance, he jerked the monster blade up high, ready to lunge.

The bearded man blanched pale as the linen tablecloth.

"No! Don't! *Don't!*"

Half-Assed Frank couldn't place the voice.

"What the hell?"

He leaned closer.

Squinting for a better look, he saw it wasn't Big Lou.

Barreling back into the kitchen, he halted under a row of hanging copper pans. He barked at his startled flat-faced busboy.

"The hell you looking at?"

"Nothing! I swear."

Half-Assed Frank waggled the huge knife.

"Pull your thumb out of your ass. Do I not have enough on my mind?"

Something smelled like it was burning. One of the sauces again? His head whipped to the right. Steam rose from the big pots on the range.

"Angelo, what the hell?"

"What?"

"That gravy! It—It smells smoky."

"Shit."

Did any of his dipshit staff have even half a brain? Surging with irritation, he waved the knife toward the busboy again.

"Weaseldick? Man, he's gonna suffer."

"Hah? Who?"

"And when I'm done, he'll have flies walking across his eyeballs."

"I don't—"

"Get your lazy ass back to work. *Move*, asswipe."

———

Not long after Half-Assed Frank thought he spotted Big Lou, his head chef called in sick. Minutes later Peggy Ivu, his best waitress, did too. Scowling as he tried to fill in, he slapped down menus before his customers at table seven.

"How you doing. Here's your damn menus."

The smiles dropped from the faces of the gangly young couple holding hands. They wore matching puffy vests, and matching startled looks. Half-Assed Frank loomed there in his polyester shirt and glared.

What the hell had happened to his life?

Had someone given him the evil eye and cursed him? He was stuck in the ass crack of Alaska.

"Be back in a minute to take your damn orders."

"Say, what about the specials?" the woman said.

"Screw the specials."

Minutes later he barged out of the kitchen, reeking of garlic, his hair crimped under a net. The one night he gets a decent-sized crowd, he's short-staffed! As he limped up to table twelve, a gigantic tension rose in his chest. Staring down a burly dude with a buzz cut, he bellowed.

"Got a problem, shithead?"

The talking and tink of silverware around them stopped. The man pointed at his salmon appetizer.

"As a matter of fact—"

"Got some kind of bug up your ass? Do you?"

"The manager? Get me the—"

"I own this place. Complain again, asswipe, I'll strangle you. I'll pistol-whip your corpse—then shove dynamite up your ass!"

He could barely hold onto himself. Back in the kitchen, the phone rang, and rang.

Another waitress, Tina, began yammering about her calamari. Where the heck was her calamari? And she *hated* table nine. He felt like strangling her too. Behind him, the kitchen staff squabbled away.

"I'm trying, I'm trying!"

"You got it? Do you?"

He grabbed a pile of plates. Smashed them. Then he dragged a hand down over his tight-feeling face. The dishwasher chugged and clanked as he muttered.

"What a damn . . ."

He couldn't bear much more of this bullshit. Time was running out.

When the lights flickered, then the power failed, he felt like whacking somebody.

Maybe it was time to launch his little surprise in Vermont?

46

"Things aren't so bad, are they, Junior?"

Wesley shot Junior down a short section of the slide in the park next to Town Hall. Lately, to help out he had been lugging the little guy here—to play, to let him gawk at other babies. The fresh air did Wesley a world of good. Often he just chilled at one of the picnic tables by the small bandstand and let Junior roam in the grass.

Junior grinned at the base of the slide.

"Ba, ba."

Wesley inhaled the sweet scent of the greenery.

"Daddy's pulled himself together."

Heck, he could handle the new pregnancy. He had kind of wigged out the other day, when Jules told him about it. Well, actually he had groaned out loud as if she'd kicked him in the nuggets. But what was one more kid? She had always wanted a bunch of them. How could he even think of letting her down again?

He could survive anything but losing her.

For the past couple days, they had barely touched each other in bed. But without her holding a gun to his head, he'd washed her pickup, mowed the lawn, tackled the leaky bathroom faucet.

After returning with Junior from the park now, Wesley also cooked Jules her favorite dinner, his killer Chicken Boursin. As they sat down to it, apparently she was pleased. When he reached over to stroke the back of her warm hand, she did not draw it away. She did seem a little preoccupied. Lately she had been a little on edge, overall. But she appeared stunning as ever. God, he was so, so lucky to have her.

As they finished up the meal, he caught her eye.

"You know, I'm really, really sorry I hurt you. I want to, um, just start over."

She stared back at him, a surprised look on her face. What he saw in her eyes was something he had never seen before.

She seemed to be very carefully weighing what info to share with him.

Finally, she said, "Well, I've made some mistakes too. There are things you don't know."

He studied her tight expression. All of a sudden she looked way serious. Between them the candle flickered. As she stared down into her empty plate, he felt something gripping his insides. He held his breath, waiting for her to go on.

It was still hard to believe she had a sister he'd never known about. What was up with that? He had only talked to her sis on the phone a sec, and he pictured her now as a milder version of Jules. Maybe a mellow school teacher. Or a librarian. Someone who clipped coupons and always obeyed the speed limit.

But who knew what else Jules was holding back about?

What mistakes did she mean?

The silence stretched on and on.

"Jules, what—"

She jumped up from the table.

"Great job on the chicken. Delish."

———————

In mid-June, Wesley started golfing again at Patten Brook Golf Club. On his second outing, he helped make up a foursome.

"Be the ball," he soon said—and he ended up in the rough.

Jowly Hal gloated around his unlit cigar.

"That a boy, Wes! Pay up, fellas."

Wesley hunkered down with a crazy focus. But with one thwack after another, he drove into the trees, ponds, bunkers. Hacking away at a little white ball took his mind off things, though. Thankfully, he hadn't seen any dead Eddies in a while. But occasionally he still had a sickly, guilty feeling about all that. Didn't everyone have to pay for the things they did?

Each time he flubbed up, his golf partners whooped and hollered. They cackled.

On the back nine now, he shrieked and kicked his ball out of a sand trap with his foot.

"Damn. Tits. Fuck!"

Reese grinned wide, making a screwy gesture with a finger.

"Really got a hold of that one. Smooth!"

Wesley stared back. Hands on his hips, he tried to summon up a badass glare. The midday sun beat down on his face.

At last, he smiled.

"Aw, who gives a shit?"

Their heads flew back. They all laughed so hard their eyes flooded with tears.

Reese said, "You really murdered that one!"

———————

"A present for *me*?" Wesley said that evening.

Jules nodded and held out a closed fist.

Uh-oh.

An uneasy feeling rose in his chest.

He braced himself.

No.

Phew. She wore a grin.

"Now, don't freak out," she said. "It's only a little ... gag gift. A joke."

He'd lost heavily on the golf course earlier. All during dinner, he'd been keyed up about that. Now, he sipped at his Heineken as she extended her closed hand.

Slowly, she eased it open. Revealed her palm.

Sitting there was a miniature police cruiser.

He spat out his swig of beer.

47

Well, this was going to be interesting.

The day after giving Wesley his little car, Jules had tracked him down in the kitchen. She took in a breath, handed him a shovel.

"Here. Take this."

His mouth opened in a look of puzzlement.

"Um. Thanks? *Another* gift?"

After receiving the mysterious postcard, she knew Half-Assed Frank was out there—waiting for revenge. She hadn't told Wesley about it, though. She hadn't wanted to worry him. But how could she play this new situation without freaking him out?

As if it had a will of its own, the damn .45 was in danger of being exposed. Again.

No way could she chance that. There were three threats to deal with now—the gun, Half-Assed Frank, and her damn sister. It was bad enough that Eddie's family had posted that $5,000 reward.

"I don't really want to talk," she said now to Wesley. "I'm still mad at you for the way you ran out the door when I told you I was pregnant again."

"Well, I did—"

"And for other stuff too. But soon as it gets a little darker, we're going out. For a change, you're going to help *me*."

Leaning the shovel against the counter, he pushed out his lips.

"O-kay."

"Junior's with Emma."

Emma's heart-shaped face had lit up when she and Junior stopped by. Despite Jules's worries, for a few minutes she had dropped into a wicker chair on Emma's porch, and then cooed and murmured over Junior with Emma, while making fun of their men.

"You and I are going to do some digging," Jules said now.

"Some digging?"

"Moving some—"

"Dirt?"

"Right," she said.

"For—?"

"You don't need to know."

Shoot. Awkward! She should've thought this out better. Hell, she probably should've thought the whole gun disposal thing out better.

Wesley took a moment to think, apparently. She sensed he wanted to help—or at least knew he'd better help. But obviously he was puzzled. He made a humph sound.

"I don't need to know?"

"Right."

She hadn't even told him about the first problem with the hidden .45 either. Nor had she told him about Paige's recent phone threat. Did a guy have to know all of a woman's secrets? But now she could barely look him in the eye. She didn't feel so smart herself as he spoke again.

"Digging for something, but you can't . . . Course I got to know." He raised a hand in plea. The smile on his face was getting strained. "Anything for you, honey, but you know I don't like the dark. And I kind of wanted to catch the Sox-Yankees game."

She made a disappointed noise with her lips. Threw him a straight hard look.

"I imagine they let you watch all the sports you want in jail."

He gave a small yelp of surprise.

"What?"

"Well." She cleared her throat. "Maybe I do need to—"

"*Jail?*"

"Crap. I was going to tell you when we got there, so you wouldn't wig out right away."

He winced.

"That doesn't sound—"

"The .45. We got to keep someone from finding it."

He stared at her with his mouth open.

"What?" Giving a little groan, he shifted backward and brushed against the leaning shovel. It clanged to the floor. "You—You shitting me?"

"Nope."

"This isn't another joke? Like the cop car? Actually, not long ago, you did—"

"Nope. Not teasing this time."

"*That* .45?"

"That darn thing won't stay hidden."

As Wesley clutched at his chest, she explained how an hour ago she had driven by the house of her old science teacher, Mr. Modele.

"So?" Wesley said.

Her heart revved at the memory.

"When I looked closer? The hairs on my arm? They prickled."

"I don't get it," he said.

"I slowed right down. Thought I might run off the road."

"You're making me—"

"Right in the yard? There was an excavator." Clamping her eyes shut, she saw the machine in her mind. "One of those big yellow CAT ones. Just sitting there. But ready for action."

Apparently Modele had hired someone to build an out-building, or pool, and they were planning to start soon. It was the worst damn luck. The heavy machinery sat way too close to where she didn't want it to be. Right next to the gnome lawn ornament, right where she had buried deep the Taurus Judge revolver.

She didn't tell Wesley she had pinched herself to make sure she wasn't imagining things. *Another* problem with the gun? A real mastermind, she was.

Now she blew out a breath.

God, come hell or high water, they had to retrieve it tonight. Or else.

But was the thing cursed?

48

The same day, Half-Assed Frank snatched up the restaurant kitchen phone. After willing his hand to stop shaking, he dialed Agent Ainsworth.

He couldn't stop thinking about payback against Weaseldick and his woman. He couldn't shake the fuckers from his mind. He hated them ten thousand percent.

He would cut their heads off with a hacksaw.

He would carve their hearts out.

"Think I'm going wacky," he said to Agent Ainsworth. "No, I goddamn *know* I'm going wacky. Starting to hear voices."

On the other end of the line, Ainsworth cleared his throat.

"Well, that'll go away."

Half-Assed Frank didn't think so. Every day now, the voices were telling him to split. To get the hell out.

"Yeah, right!"

Last night, limping to and fro through the dining room, he had toyed with the idea of rounding up customers on the street at gunpoint. A balloon payment to the bank was coming due. His suppliers were hounding his ass for payments too. He was about ready to cap them and then dump them into Norton Sound.

Could he get away with whacking his competitors? Blow their kitchens to bits?

Christ, he missed the life.

He fantasized about taking to the wilderness . . . mountains . . . rivers . . . someplace unmapped. But he knew he wasn't the type to build a goddamn cabin and hunt his own food, or to run off to some remote village.

When he pictured himself chasing a moose with a Glock and a baseball bat, he almost smiled.

"Nerves, you know?" Ainsworth said to him now on the other end of the phone line. "Right now you're safe. At least you're alive."

He sank back against a prep counter. Something stank. Bad fish?

"Am I, though? Know what I had for breakfast?"

"Frank, you got to—"

"Three goddamn glasses of Bardolino wine. Hell, maybe it was four. You know what? I'm *over* this shit."

49

Soon after scaring Wesley half to death by telling him about the .45's endangered location, Jules turned her Tacoma onto Smead Road. It wasn't much of a road, just rutted dirt. Here we go again, she thought.

Have to get that damn revolver.

Thick forest edged the road. The daylight was receding. When she glimpsed at Wesley, his face looked strained. Should she have even told him? Maybe she should've let him watch his stupid ball game. But wasn't retrieving a murder weapon the sort of thing a couple should do together? She hadn't pestered him the first time.

Oh, well. At times like this, it was fortunate she had Emma to babysit.

Who could have known it would be so hard to get away with one little murder and start a family?

"Christ," Wesley said.

"We'll get it."

He threw a hand up.

"What're we supposed to do if he comes out? Ask him a science question?"

"Don't sweat it."

"I think I'm getting, like, a rash on my arm. You know I don't like the—"

"Why don't you tell me ten more times? Isn't it nice to have a night out together?"

They hid the truck on a logging road. They then slinked across Modele's thick, closely cropped lawn.

Once she moved the lawn gnome, she watched Wesley dig a while in the weak light. When the hole was barely a foot deep, he stopped. What now? He stuck the shovel into his ragged pile of dirt and faced her, a hint of panic in his eyes. A bead of sweat trailed down his brow. Behind him, there were lights on in Modele's isolated Cape Cod house. Yet she didn't hear anything besides Wesley's loud breaths. She had a small flashlight tucked in her pocket, but didn't want to use it, unless necessary.

"Why the heck didn't you bury it in *our* yard?" Wesley said.

"Sssh! Keep your voice down."

"Why here?"

She smelled something yucky like diesel or oil from the nearby heavy machinery. For a second she felt like crying. Her hormones?

Chasing after a gun—what kind of mom was she?

But what if someone had previously seen her bury the .45, and finally tipped off the Staties? What if *they* had brought in the excavator? Or wouldn't they use a metal detector?

"You should keep digging," she said.

He wiped the sweat from his eyes.

"Can I just catch my breath?"

Yesterday Paige had called again. This time the bitch had demanded money, which Jules refused to pay. Who knew how that would play out? But the thought of turning over even one more nickel to her turned Jules's stomach. She would have to find a way to take care of Paige. Start fighting fire with fire.

Now that Half-Assed Frank might be back in the picture too, she and Wesley had to at least find the damn gun, and get rid of that problem.

But right now she felt a bad energy. It was dumb to linger out here. And weren't they making too much noise? The sky was a deep, navy blue. Slipping into black.

"Aw, crap. Gimme that shovel."

Wesley took hold of his lower lip with his teeth.

"Uh-uh. You got me out here. First, I want to hear this."

She grinned sheepishly.

Why bury the revolver here? It was a good question. And she still wasn't sure how to answer it.

"Because . . ." She stared toward the lit window of what looked like Modele's living room. Couldn't shake the feeling that something wasn't right. "I don't know, sweetie. I had to pick *somewhere*. Sticking it here gave me a sort of . . . kick. I even thought about maybe trying to frame him."

The light was fading fast. Night peepers sang out. She strained to see as her eyes adapted. Even up close, she could barely make out Wesley's worried face.

"What do you mean?" he said.

"He was always such a jerk."

"But—"

"Just be quiet a sec, listen. He was so mean. To everybody."

"It's so black out here! I can't see anything. We should go."

"Hold it down."

"Or let's at least put on the—"

"No."

She took a look into the darkness, to make sure they were alone. Gave her head a shake.

"Anyway, Mr. Science had horrible breath," she said. "And was a total lech. He even asked me to stay over after class one day, and pressed up against me. And tried to grab my boob."

For a split second as she had buried the handgun, she had considered calling a tip in to the cops, implicating Modele. Then she thought better of it, realizing she was being irrational.

Now, suddenly a large floodlight on a pole lit the yard.

What the—?

They both dropped flat on their bellies into the grass. All she heard was her pulse pounding in her ears.

"Ahh, that's better," Wesley said. "Phew! No, never mind."

She held her breath, listening for anything.

"Shoot. Hope that came on automatically."

The pole was a good thirty feet away. The light on top of it sat nearly ten feet above the ground.

Maybe in the past Modele had had teed-off students messing with his property?

"Now he's *definitely* going to see us," Wesley said.

"Think I just saw one of your balls roll by."

"Huh?"

"Let me think."

"I'll get this, 'cause I'm the man."

"Right."

"Maybe I can combat crawl, real, real, real slow, across the lawn. *Really* slow, I mean. You know? Like a prowling cat? Then you give me a signal. Two whistles? No, one. Or three?

No, one. I don't know. Anyway, then I'll, I'll . . . try and shimmy up the—"

"The shovel," she said. "Gimme it."

"How about on a count of three? One—"

"Am I speaking Japanese?"

"Okay, okay."

"If you've got a pen, you might want to take some notes."

"Notes?"

"Forget it."

She jumped up, raced across the lawn, swung the shovel hard, and smashed the light to bits.

Seconds later she was back with Wesley in the dark by their hole again. He made a little frustrated noise.

"How about if I—"

"Shhh."

There was an eerie and dark stillness. But she had an ugly feeling that someone else was near.

A voice rang in her head—*mistake, mistake, mistake.*

50

Half-Assed Frank clenched his hands and glared out the restaurant window at the low, gray sky. The street glistened with a sheet of ice.

Across the street stood a dumpy two-story bar and inn. A man with inky-black hair and small eyes crawled past it. He was either drunk, or he couldn't stand up in the damn wind. Half-Assed Frank shook his head wearily.

Screw the overdue bills, screw the headaches. This place was Loserville, U.S.A.

Who the hell wanted to live on tundra? He'd relocate his ass on his own this time. Disappear. Wasn't WITSEC voluntary, anyway? Hail smacked against the window. From below his right eye came a twitch.

He listened to the building strain, and the wind scream. Though he'd been trying to cut down, he jerked out a Camel and lit it. He then muttered.

"What else can I do? Herd lame-ass reindeer?"

In his mind he stuck his Glock into Weaseldick's mouth and pulled the trigger.

Bam.

J ules cocked an ear in Modele's dark yard.

"What's that?"

"Hah?" Wesley said.

She felt a little shiver of alarm.

"Quiet."

There was an uncomfortable moment of silence.

"Don't tease!" Wesley said. "You're freaking me—"

"I heard . . ."

Someone was there.

Moving closer.

She froze when a flashlight flickered toward them.

"Who's out there?" the old familiar voice said.

What now?

As she stepped back, toward the excavator, her stomach was turning somersaults.

"Show yourself now," Modele said.

Should they run?

Then again, Wesley was probably petrified with panic. And the open hole. Abandoning that might lead to someone digging further and finding the .45.

Should she have brought *another* gun?

The flashlight beam shot around. She heard Wesley breathing hard. Or was that Modele?

"What's going on out here?" Modele said.

Well, if nothing else, maybe she could bonk Modele with the shovel too. But in the bobbing beam of light, she made out Wesley drawing a fist back.

"Take this," he said.

With a grunt, he swung.

Apparently he missed. She didn't hear his fist make contact.

"Damn," he said.

The beam of Modele's flashlight shook as he hollered.

"You're in *big* trouble now, kids."

The shovel! She groped around herself in the darkness. She dug frantically into her pocket. Where the heck was *her* light? Had she dropped it?

Maybe she could kick him in the nuts?

In the bobbling flashlight beam, she caught a glimpse of Wesley's face. There was something in his eyes. Not panic.

Something else.

A second later there was a loud *smack*.

And a thud.

Modele's light lay in the grass. Shoot! Whose body had hit the lawn?

Modele's?

Or Wesley's?

Someone blew out a breath.

"Jeez," Wesley said at last. "That freaking *hurt*."

She burst out laughing in relief.

"Oh, my. Too much! That was . . ."

She looked at him and whistled. He then grabbed the flashlight. He aimed it downward and squatted down. Modele lay on his back in the grass. Still.

"Damn lech!" Wesley said. "He's out cold."

"Well, slugger, keep digging then."

He handed her Modele's light. Picked up the shovel.

"If he comes to," she said, "I'll whack him with the gnome."

Jules and Wesley took turns gouging away. Their pile of removed dirt grew and grew. When the shovel in Jules's hands clanged into metal, she cheered.

All right!

Maybe the gun wasn't cursed.

A while later she pitched it off the middle of the Champlain Bridge into Lake Champlain. The water was supposed to be over sixty feet deep here. If the revolver was ever discovered *here*, she'd throw up her hands, turn herself in, and confess.

She stared down over the walkway railing as the gun plummeted down into the darkness. It hit the water with a splash.

"Thank God," she said.

Now what? Her and Wesley's freedom was still on the line. There was Half-Assed Frank to deal with. And her sister too.

"Don't make me come to San Diego," she had warned Paige on the phone.

If she had to, she would. After hanging up on her sis, she had searched online and ordered something which might help her.

But for now, why not have a little fun? A misty fog was drifting in as she turned to Wesley on the bridge walkway.

Should she say it? That would be mean. Hadn't he just nailed Modele for her?

Oh, why not?

Why not keep him on his best behavior for a while?

"Come to think of it, sweetie, you're the only witness."

Under the dimly lit girders, all around them an inky void and fog, he nervously cleared his throat.

"Well, I suppose, *technically*—"

"To the water? It's a long, long way down, no?"

Fear seized his face.

"Oh my God."

"A hundred feet?"

He inched back, away from the railing.

"My heart. You're freaking me—"

"More?"

"Jules."

"Maybe you should be down there too."

With an uncertain look, he said, "Let's get the hell out of here."

5 2

———

"You sounded like crap on the phone, Jules," Bree said two days later. "Knew I should get my butt right over here."

Jules had inched Junior down for his afternoon nap minutes ago. At her front door now, she hugged her flame-haired friend tight. Bree was always up to something new with her hair. Today, her bangs were cut high and straight across her forehead.

Stepping around a scatter of blocks and toys, they sank down on the sofa. Though Jules made an effort to smile, it didn't hold. Bree patted her shoulder.

"Tell me. Get it off your chest."

Sunlight poured in the windows. But as Jules smoothed her stain-spotted dress, she felt worn around the edges. She inhaled deeply.

"I don't know. I . . ."

"Come on, girl, let it out."

Bree waited, and Jules shut her eyes. For a second her voice was trapped somewhere in her throat. She then cursed and told Bree how Wesley's shortcomings had filled her thoughts that morning. They had been sunning themselves in the yard, she'd confronted him—and one thing had led to another. So he'd torn off in his Mustang. Taking care of Junior was tough enough, she explained. And now her hormones were all over the map.

"Crap," she said. "Sometimes . . ."

"You're just going through a phase. Hell, at least all that Mob-trouble stuff is over with."

"Not even sure about that."

And Paige's threat? Jules almost mentioned that. The thought of it sent a wave of sickness through her. Yesterday, determined to strike back, Jules had hired a California investigator named Howard Crispin to track down the bitch in San Diego. When he found her, he was to search her trash for incriminating materials, and dig up any dirt possible.

"Wesley?" Jules said to Bree. "Sometimes I could kill him."

"All right, a really bad phase. You know he means well."

Bree dug into her purse. Plucked out a small amber-colored vial. Winked at Jules.

"Know you got another little one on the way. But a bit of this? Maybe it'll cheer you up."

Bree leaned forward. Shifting a vase full of wild flowers, she poured a tiny pile of coke onto the coffee table's glass top. Jules was tempted. Damn. How long had it been since she really cut loose? But she knew she shouldn't, as Bree started chopping up the crystals with a razor blade.

"Wish I could do more for you, Jules. Never easy, is it?"

"I'm not afraid of much. But losing him and Junior? That's my one big fear."

As always, Bree looked great. She sported a nose ring, pierced eyebrow, and the scooped neckline of her cropped yellow top dipped low. When she had two thin lines laid out, she rolled up a dollar. She smiled at Jules.

"You first."

Jules hesitated. Wasn't this something her baby sis would be more likely to do? Except Paige would be snorting crushed Oxys. And then stealing from whoever she had to, in order to keep going.

"You know, I don't think so. Really shouldn't."

"You're right."

"Well, maybe . . . a taste. Then that's it."

Jules bent down, rolled dollar in hand. She stared at the white powder. What the heck was she thinking? Her dream was to have babies. Healthy babies who would grow up to have great lives.

"Nah. You go, I'm cool."

A moment later Bree began to rub a circle on her back as she continued talking.

"Even though my hormones are revved, he acts like it's a favor touching me. He used to joke that insurance agents were premium lovers. What a load of crap."

"A shame, it's a—"

"God, men are such shits."

To hell with trying to save Wesley. Could anyone really save someone else? She made a grunty, frustrated noise. Still, even as she did it her mood felt lighter. Gazing into Bree's glittering hazel eyes, she let out a laugh.

Bree laughed too.

"God, it's true! Man. Oh, yeah, I didn't tell you. Remember Denzel? Detective Burpee?"

Jules stared hard at the little cop car she had given Wesley as a gag. It sat amid a spread of Junior's toys.

God, had Burpee had a change of heart?

Along with Paige and Half-Assed Frank, did she have to deal with him now too?

"What?" she said. "Of course I remember him."

"Whoa. You look like you—"

"Just tell me."

"He says 'hi' is all."

"Whew," Jules said.

"Saw him in town yesterday. He says he hopes you're doing well."

"That's cool. What a good, understanding man."

"Well, at least there's one out there."

Even without the coke, Jules felt a little high. Bree always managed to cheer her up. She admired the curves of Bree's figure, her sleek thighs. Her big eyes.

"Really glad you came by."

"Me too. We've always had fun, haven't we?"

They had spent countless hours grinding their booties onstage together. Naked or clothed, they had always managed to click. At the same time, they had supported each other's plans to move up from stripping. And later, partly thanks to Jules's cash help, Bree's new women's sportswear business had thrived.

When Jules brushed Bree's thigh with her hand now, her heart tripped inside her breast. How great it was to hang out with her beautiful bestie! Surging with a tingly charge, she tipped forward.

As she closed in, she smelled Bree's almond-scented lotion.

Surprising even herself, she gave Bree a tender kiss.

53

As Jules and Bree headed for the bedroom, Jules eyed the tiny cop car again. With all the threats piling up in her life lately, she hadn't thought of Burpee in forever. Even though she owed him her freedom, it had turned out.

Shortly after the assault on her home, Burpee had approached her on the back deck and smiled. She was still high from the battle's outcome. The air had never smelled fresher, sweeter. As Burpee reached into his pocket, she glanced out toward the birdhouses Wesley had installed. She laughed with joy.

She and Wesley had survived. What else could matter now?

Burpee handed her a flash drive.

"Here," he said.

She looked down at the tiny storage unit in her palm.

What the—? What could possibly be on that?

Porn?

His favorite comedies?

She gave him a puzzled look in return.

"I don't—I don't understand."

"That's my only copy," he said. "The last record of my own file on Eddie's homicide."

She tried to keep her face still but felt her eyes bug open.

A chill prickled her skin. He had been investigating them? Had he suspected them all along?

"Oh my—"

"You can check it out later. Or not."

She clutched the flash drive tight.

After her heart started up again, she looked him straight in the eye. She could read the decency in him. The kindness. She still had to worry about the bloody leaf. But at least this cop was off their trail. Thank God for that. But what should she say? How much did he really know?

How to sum up the hell she'd gone through? How her face once had been such a patchwork of swells and bruises, she barely recognized herself?

How Eddie had threatened to rape her with the Taurus .45?

Burpee gestured toward his gift.

"Just don't forget to get rid of that too. I'm hanging my ass out for you here, you know. This case is going into the Fuck-it file. But the thing about murder? It sort of *is* against the law. The law means something, it does. . . . Anyway, damn shame, all of this."

With a dazed feeling, she slowly shook her head.

"God."

He held his tongue.

"I'm—I'm stunned," she said.

He brought his brows together.

"Say, I never really figured . . . What about the size-15 footprints?"

"Ha!"

"Fair enough."

"At first? We thought we'd pulled it off near perfectly."

"Yeah. Well." He laughed gently. "Don't they all?"

54

Wesley slipped into the kitchen, clutching a paper cone holding a dozen red roses for the best woman in the world. Muffled sounds carried from the bedroom. So he crept down the hallway to surprise her. His sneakers made faint sucking noises on the floor.

What a royal pain in the ass he'd been. It was time to admit it.

As he stepped closer, a sound like a moan rose up.

He stopped. Held his breath, listened.

Strange.

Was that grunting? Was Jules doing some new pregnancy exercises?

Surprise her, he told himself. But something was making his body go on high alert.

His feet started moving, though. Whatever she was doing, she loved roses. It would be perfect! Unless Junior was off schedule today, he wouldn't be up for another hour. So they had plenty of time for—whatever. He felt a tickle of antici-pation. He loved her. He worshiped her. She was an angel!

She was great at everything—gardening, chess, homicide, cooking, and so on.

He peeked into the bedroom. Right as he was about to wave the bouquet, he halted.

His brain froze, his vision tunneling.

Had he walked into the wrong house? Was this really happening?

He blinked repeatedly.

Jules and Bree butt-naked on the bed! Caressing each other and moaning!

"Oh! Uhh!"

Lacy bras and panties lay mingled together on the rug. How sexed-up both women looked! Jules's face was flushed with pleasure.

He gulped as they kissed. Crushed the roses tight.

He couldn't stop looking. But even more urgently, he had to get out of there—freaking right away. Leave! He had to fling himself outside.

"Jesus, no," he heard himself say out loud.

Jules shot upright.

She turned toward him.

"Shit!"

She jerked a sheet up.

"Oh, Christ. Wesley!"

He spun around, his eyes blurry with tears. Bolting in wild panic, he thumped straight into the hallway wall.

———————

Later that night, Jules's phone rang. And rang.

After a while she yawned, massaged her eyes, and eyed the clock: 1:10 a.m. She groped toward the night stand. Was it her baby sister, calling to start more trouble? Half awake or not, she was not in the mood for another damn blackmail attempt.

No, it had to be Wesley. What should she—?

After she lifted the receiver, there was a long silence on the line.

Something caught in her throat.

"Honey?" she said.

No answer.

She wavered a moment, unsure as to whether to put the receiver down or not.

"That you?"

Still no answer. Just heavy breathing at the other end. Her thoughts churned around her head.

"Where are you? I'm so—"

Fear squeezed her chest as a deep voice boomed into her ear:

"I'm gonna get you. You're triple-fucked!"

Lying there in the dark, she felt her rage boiling up. She grumbled into the receiver. She then spit out three words:

"Kiss. My. Ass."

"No, quadruple, super—"

"If you even come *near* my family, you're dead."

55

At The Pines Motel in Burlington, Wesley collapsed onto a bed and frowned toward a crack in the window. Jules had betrayed him. It was all over! Their relationship. His life. The beautiful, sexy, crazy asshole he worshipped had crapped on his heart.

He felt ready for the psych ward again.

The slut! How many times had they done it? Ten? A thousand?

"How could she?" he cried out. "How the hell could she?"

What was next? Boning random dudes?

Hadn't he helped *kill* for her? Together, they had taken a man's life.

This is what he got for hooking up with a high-strung stripper. The kicker was, watching the whole damn scene had turned him on.

Silverware rang on a plate behind Jules as she spotted Wesley sitting at one of the red booths inside Mandel's Bar and Grill. He leaped up when she joined him, and flapped his hand at her in a vague wave. One look and she knew that, despite everything, he was still the only man in the world for her.

He had finally called her the day before. With a firmness that surprised her, he had insisted that they meet.

When he spoke now his voice quavered.

"Thanks for coming."

Meeting his eyes briefly, she sank down. God! How awkward was this?

"Well, think we both needed some time." She twisted her lips. "To put it mildly, it's been a . . . weird few days."

"Uh-huh."

"But I'm glad you called. Emma was thrilled to watch Junior."

She could tell Wesley had spruced himself up. He appeared freshly shaved and showered, and his light blue sport shirt was new. She wore a baggy gray hoodie and stretch shorts. But she had dabbed on lipstick.

"You look nice," he said.

"Thanks. I guess."

They ordered beer and a soda. They then sat in silence. Avoiding eye contact, they stared at the embossed placemats, the returning waitress.

For a while he picked at the label on his Heineken. At last he cleared his throat.

"I love you, don't want to lose you. But I guess I need to know how this . . . happened. Between you and her. The details."

She felt her throat tighten with unexpected anger.

Wasn't it bad enough worrying all alone about Half-Assed Frank showing up again at any moment? Ever since his recent call, she had a disturbing sense the psycho bastard was closing in. But Wesley was such a wuss, she couldn't bear to tell him.

Hell, then there was her meth-head sister. Well, screw her. Investigator Howard Crispin was still digging up dirt on the loony bitch. Maybe he even knew someone she could pay to go after her sis.

Now Wesley wanted a goddamn play-by-play of her hook-up with Bree? There was no knowing how all this was going to play out. Was she going to lose Bree's friendship? And Wesley too?

Then—after arranging babysitting, and taking her natal vitamin, of course—would she have to fight off Half-Assed Frank?

She could feel her pulse race.

"Told you on the phone, I'm *really* sorry," she said finally to Wesley. "But that's not good enough, is it?"

"Hey, I just—"

"Want details? I'll tell you exactly, then."

Wait.

Should she?

Did he even deserve an explanation? After all he had done?

He tapped his fingers on the table, impatiently.

In apparent agony.

"Come *on!*" he said at last. "Please, I mean. Please."

A laugh rang out near the service bar. Her voice rose.

"Not sure how it happened. Started kissing, we . . . got naked. Then went down on each other. Okay? Goddamn happy now?"

Nearby heads turned. Even a passing waitress stopped, loaded tray in hand. Wesley sucked down half of his beer as she continued.

"It was an innocent thing!" Squeezing both hands around her soda glass, she stared at it. "We did a teeny bit of coke—"

"What? But you're—"

"*She* did, I mean. I almost did, which was dumb. Way dumb. I know, I know. But I didn't. Anyway, being with her was . . . comforting somehow."

He gazed down at the table. His face colored.

"I got to admit. Watching you two?" He smiled. "It was kind of hot."

She locked eyes with him.

Did he really have a boner for her bestie?

"Yeah, well. Forget about it. . . . You let me down too, you know. A bunch of ways." He gave that a sad tilt of his head while she took a breath. "You haven't exactly been a ray of sunshine lately. And you're the one who dragged us into serious trouble."

Calling it trouble was putting it lightly. Was she going to have to dig defensive trenches around the house and pile up sandbags?

"I know, I know," he said. "I'm sorry."

For too long she'd had a sense that their prospects were hanging by a fraying thread.

"You really don't know."

"I'm crazy about you, Jules." His voice started to buckle. "You make it all mean something. I'd—I'd fight off a goddamn freaking dragon for you."

She looked down at the table and thought a moment. Opened her mouth again. Thought once more about saying it. Telling him about Half-Assed Frank's postcard. About the phone call.

"Jules?"

But what good would telling him do? He was loyal, he was gentle, he had a great butt. He had even risked his own life years ago, saving that drowning boy. But he was no dragon slayer. And this was stressful enough, as it was.

Why mention a wop psychopath?

Or the mysterious CD that had showed up in the mailbox today.

"Jules?"

56

Half-Assed Frank lumbered aboard a bus, his old fake passport tucked in his pocket and clutching his blue gym bag. Hours earlier, with a swell of longing for Vermont, he had taken an armrest-gripping puddle-jumper plane flight.

He'd had enough of Alaska to last a gazillion years.

The bus door shut with a sigh. He wedged himself into a seat then tried not to think or mind the stale air or sour odors. That lasted about ten minutes.

All at once he felt frightened and pissed as hell. The bus rumbled and shook. A mean wind scouring the snow drifts outside, he blew his breath out.

Screw Nome. Screw this stinking bus.

Some idiot behind him kept coughing. Across the aisle, a woman with scraggly hair mumbled to herself and nodded.

"The end is coming," she said to him after a while.

"You don't gotta tell me, lady."

"Cruel times. Suffering. Violence."

"You know," he said, "that's what I'm hoping."

A soda can rattled back and forth, back and forth, and Half-Assed Frank drowsed. When he opened his eyes again, he spotted a polar bear in the front seat.

What the—?

He blinked hard—and the vision disappeared. Christ!

"Revenge!" he yelled out a minute later.

"Hard times!" the scraggly-haired woman chimed in.

"Revenge!"

"Hey," said the driver. "Would you two hold it down back there?"

"Just drive, dickwad!" Half-Assed Frank said.

———

To be safe, Half-Assed Frank switched to a train at the next stop. As the train clacked across the plains of Alberta, a chipper-looking man in red suspenders tried starting up a chat with him in the dining car.

"You an American, eh?"

Half-Assed Frank tugged at a cuff of his velour pullover, the vibration of the rails running right through him. His immense chest swelled up as he threw the dumb Canuck a hard gaze.

"Get out of my face, you piece of shit. Should've been smothered in your crib. Screw you, screw everybody!"

The man in suspenders shrank back, and turned and stared out the window.

It was a beautiful trip—rushing scenery, lengthy stare-downs, no goddamn empty restaurant tables driving Half-Assed Frank up the wall. He had a butt-load of time to think, and he plotted away.

In a way, he could barely wait for the trip to end, though. Despite his own worries about getting whacked, the day the train clacked into Vermont he felt as if his soul had settled back into his body. Even the sheer ballsiness of his return had its own appeal. Right away the sky seemed brighter, the trees greener.

He eased back, admiring his new sideburns and mustache in his window reflection. Goddamn Weaseldick and his woman had a surprise coming. Now his thoughts circled around one question:

Would it be better to use a meat cleaver again?

Or a chainsaw?

57

———

When private investigator Howard Crispin called, Jules said, "Hang on, I just . . ."

She peeked out the window to make sure Wesley was still watching Junior. After their prickly discussion at Mandel's Bar and Grill, she and Wesley had reached a kind of truce. She still wasn't sure she could ever count on him to hold it together for her and Junior. And she suspected he wasn't sure he could trust her around Bree.

Yet given the sunny and warm weather, she and Wesley had recently farted around in the garden together, and splashed in Black Pond. Otherwise, she pummeled him twice—but only at the chessboard. And she hadn't told him about the mysterious CD that had recently showed up. Outside the window now, Junior sat in his sandbox wearing the cutest silly smile alongside his dad.

This call from Crispin was bound to be juicy. Her sis had to be involved in all sorts of dirty business.

"Okay," Jules said. "Go ahead."

Crispin's voice was gentle, deep.

"She's a busy one. Real busy." On the other end of the line, he gave a little grunt. Jules pictured him as bulky. Tough-looking. "Meth deals, rip-offs, hooking."

The last time she had seen Paige, Paige had spit on her. Not much could surprise her about Paige. But hooking?

Damn.

Jules puffed out her cheeks.

"That's my sweet sis."

"Name a scam, she's probably tried it. . . . Then there was the canvas bag."

"Bag?"

"In the back of her crapbox car. I had me a feeling, and when I broke in . . ."

"Yeah?"

"Inside were a Magnum revolver, a pocket-size semiautomatic, and another big-ass one."

When Jules peeked out the window again, Wesley was filling Junior's orange pail with sand.

"That doesn't sound good."

"None turned out to be registered."

A hot anger rose in her blood as she thought about Paige's threat. It was a damn good thing Paige lived so far away. But did she really know some of Eddie's old biker pals, like she'd claimed? What if Paige talked to them?

Shoot.

Murder, blackmail, revenge—life sure could get complicated.

"Just want to make sure," Jules said into the phone. "This is all . . . private. Right?"

"No problem there."

As Jules hung up, she knew there was no predicting Paige's next move. The last Jules knew, most days her baby sis could barely pull it together to brush her own hair. Still, if Jules had to, she would use Crispin's info somehow. Or maybe use something from her new *The Anarchists Cookbook*. Purchased on sale, which was cool, it had all sorts of wacko info on drug-making set-ups and so on. But most interesting was the explosives stuff: recipes to make bombs, and homemade hand grenades. What a way to settle a family dispute.

Gazing out the window at the dense woods, her face felt hot. Hormones? Maybe she could somehow pin the murder on Paige herself? Nope, the shocking evidence on the CD that had showed up in her mailbox recently screwed up her chances at that.

God. That chilling message.

Where the hell did it come from?

While in the yard the other day, Jules had spotted someone in an antique-y turquoise truck stuffing something into her mailbox, then roaring off. She had hesitated after retrieving the mysterious manila envelope. She felt something slim and hard inside it. She had a strong feeling that whatever was inside was sucky news.

What now? Could she hold off on opening it?

Her hands shook. With fear. She wasn't sure how much more pressure she could handle.

Still, she dug a fingernail under the tape on the envelope's flap. She started to tug at it, but stopped.

She felt a drop in her stomach. Took a deep breath. Breathed out.

Hell.

She had to know.

Fingers trembling a little, she ripped the tape off the flap. Inside the envelope was a regular-looking compact disc. It bore the Imation brand. The content and date lines were not labeled.

When she popped it into her laptop and clicked it on, she felt a stab of panic. Her lips parted in surprise.

Eddie had always used disposable phones—*burners*, he called them. But apparently someone had saved and copied one of the last voice mails that he sent.

It made her skin crawl to hear his voice again.

"*Be there soon,*" he said. "*I got a meet, then . . . Man, my Taurus .45? It's missing. Can't trust the bitch. The wifey, I mean. Never thought she'd—She's up to something. Later.*"

She slapped her laptop shut.

She could not seem to move enough air through her chest.

Crap!

She was dizzy with fear and adrenaline.

Another complication?

So much for keeping things tight. This was worse than the .45 nearly being discovered. Way worse. Because someone—probably Paige—was playing with her now.

She and Wesley had been extremely, awfully, horribly bad at this murder thing.

58

The next time Jules went to town, she wondered with a prickly feeling at the back of her neck if she was a moving target. She would deal with her baby sis. The voice mail recording Paige had sent wouldn't necessarily send her and Wesley to prison—but it sure could cause trouble if the Staties heard it. Still, just how close was Half-Assed Frank?

In town inside the Powderhorn Gun Shop, she eyed a stack of boxed double-aught buck shells. She then eyed the clerk.

Lately there had been no crazy threats from Half-Assed Frank. If *that* psycho made a move on her, she'd take him out. Somehow. But what if he was smarter than she thought? Just to be safe, she'd already had new deadbolts installed on her doors.

She had better be ready.

"Heck," she said to the clerk, "gimme all of those shells you got."

At home she also cleaned her Browning shotgun. Knowing the powerful way it would work was a comfort.

After sending Wesley out on an errand, she pulled on her ear protectors then Swiss-cheesed some targets hung between two saplings in the backyard. Staring down each silhouette, she visualized catching Half-Assed Frank square in the junk.

"Suck *this*," she said.

She wondered how many there would be. Probably only him. Her against him.

This time she would blast him within kill range.

"Come on and *come*."

With each pull of the trigger, the paper targets shuddered. Focusing on center mass next, she drew in the satisfying gunpowder smell. She shot away, hoping she wouldn't wake her little angel in his crib. She loved the feel of the gun in her hands, the kick and power of it.

Afterward, she cleaned her weapon again, and took a final look inside.

Okay.

Sipping at a glass of orange juice later, she debated meeting with Detective Burpee for advice. Hadn't he helped hold off the attack on her home? His bullets, it was later revealed, had dropped one of Cadillac Frank's goons that day. And from out of nowhere, he'd turned over to her the thumb drive holding Eddie's case file.

But what could she tell Burpee? That she'd received an unwelcome postcard? A disturbing phone call? She sure wasn't going to mention the incriminating CD to a cop. Even to a friendly one.

She supposed she could rat out Half-Assed Frank's recent Nome location to the Mob—but this was personal now. Way personal. And she would handle this without them.

Soon, she figured.

"War it is," she said to herself.

———————

The next day, Jules visited her neighbor Homer, who promised to keep an eye out for anyone who looked suspicious. And she kept on the alert. She slept with one eye open. Even when she got up to pee in the middle of the night, she checked for shadows.

She wasn't going to hide in the bushes all night, waiting for the bastard. Who knew when he'd show? But if he brought this fight to her doorstep again, she'd be prepared. A loaded Colt .45 waited under her truck seat while she was out in town. And she carried it on her while doing yard work, or airing Junior in his stroller.

Part of her was eager for Half-Assed Frank to make a move—so she could take him out. She did not want to look over her shoulder for the rest of her life. She would keep her baby safe, no matter what. And she would not let Half-Assed Frank victimize anyone ever again.

One afternoon she considered mounting the shotgun on the baby stroller handle. When she came to her senses, she laughed hard.

"Well," she said aloud. "Maybe not."

While fixing dinner, she thought about Paige again. She then came up with one more idea.

59

Where the hell was it?

Stuck behind a black Tahoe at a red light later that week, Jules thumped her pickup's steering wheel.

"Come on, come on."

She had the scent and this was a hunt now.

Where was he?

The light turned green. She gunned it. When a local bus pulled out in front of her, she whipped the steering wheel left. Veered around it. She squinted ahead through her windshield. Focused on the distance.

Car.

Car.

SUV.

Gotcha.

She felt a light charge, the thrill of closing in. There it was. The old turquoise Dodge truck again.

It sped up.

She accelerated hard.

She drove with internal momentum.

Wesley was home watching Junior. Home life, blackmail stuff—you had to prioritize. She had to keep things from twisting farther and ever farther off course. It was time to take control. Get this crap straight right here and now.

The same antique-y truck had slowed before her mailbox the day the mysterious CD had showed up. Out in the yard with Junior, she was just able to make out its first license plate letter: a *G*. Since then, Crispin had used his access to databases to search registration info for the few Vermont Sixties-era Dodge trucks still on the road. Not surprisingly, only one was listed as turquoise. And with a Vermont license plate beginning with a *G*.

Crispin had e-mailed Jules an address for the owner and a driver's license photo too.

Who the hell was Jann Tobey? In his photo, the guy had a broad face and an orange red beard. Something about his features was unsettling. They also seemed vaguely familiar.

Minutes ago on her way to his home address, she had spotted the old Dodge. She wanted answers. Who had burned that voice mail onto a CD? How did her baby sis get a hold of it? How did Tobey tie into Paige? Someone was controlling the flow of information for a purpose. A devious one.

Like a cop, she had to follow the evidence, see where it led.

Now, she kept a few vehicles behind the Dodge. For such an ancient truck, it looked in great condition. The old-style curves were striking.

Even though it was beautiful, she had a strong sense of it as menacing and evil.

She thumped through a pothole, passed a white minivan. Her breathing quickened as the other truck turned into Brennan Park. Stopping by the empty basketball courts.

She parked behind a tan cinder-block building, well out of sight. After climbing out, she curled her finger around the trigger of her Colt .45. She pulled back the hammer for practice. Then she tucked the .45 into her jeans.

She skulked along the tree line. When she had moved to within ten feet of the truck's rear, she pulled out her weapon.

Tobey hadn't moved. She still could see the back of his head. She swallowed dryly.

Was he waiting for someone?

A sense of dread coursed through her veins.

What was she doing here? These were bad people she was messing with. Was she stumbling right into the middle of something without realizing it?

Well.

There was no other . . .

Follow the CD, she reminded herself. Movement meant progress toward solving the mystery. She'd get to the truth.

Put on the ski mask.

Hold up.

Wait.

Darn. Where was it?

Should she go back to her Tacoma for it?

Yup.

As she returned, she skulked out of the trees toward the old truck from a different angle. Convinced she was about to make a breakthrough, she felt an electric buzz. She gripped her Colt .45 tight. Ready to mess some shit up.

Some hidden truth was waiting for her to reveal it. But when she moved closer, she did a double-take.

Wait a minute.

That was someone else behind the wheel of the truck. That wasn't Tobey.

It was someone who looked younger.

She pulled off the mask. Closed the hammer on her Colt and tucked her gun hand behind her back.

Well, whoever it was, the element of surprise couldn't hurt. She crept along the passenger side of the turquoise Dodge. Swung open the heavy door.

Behind the steering wheel, the driver started. A cloud of pot smoke wafted toward her.

The driver did not look like a vicious criminal. Hell, he looked about fourteen. Narrow-faced and gawky-looking. A smattering of facial hair. Blue eyes.

"Whoa, dude," the kid said. "You scared the—"

"Smells good."

"You, like, a ninja, or something? Sneaking up like that? You got some *moves*."

Now what?

Could her overall plan have been any dumber?

"I'm, I'm looking for the owner. Of this truck."

The kid gave her a goofy smile.

"Want some of this weed? Maybe you and me—"

"I'd, um, like to . . . buy it? The truck, I mean."

He shrugged.

"That's my dad you want, then. I doubt he'd . . . Anyway, he's, like, probably at work right now?"

"Where's that?"

"Tobey's Auto."

"Cool. That'll work. Thanks."

As she started to close the door on him, he gave her a wide grin.

"Hey, sure you don't wanna hang here? Shoot some hoops?"

"Uh, I'm good."

"Get naked?"

Her anger sparked.

Well, Jann Tobey, she was coming. The son of a bitch had some explaining to do.

60

Jules drew a deep breath as Tobey emerged from his flat-roofed little auto sales building. Cars that had seen better days hunkered down in the isolated, potholed-dirt lot; orange letters on their windshields announced discounts. He twisted his head around as he stepped outside. She had parked a long distance away, and then sneaked onto the lot and waited behind a rusty van. Now there was maybe ten yards between them. The air smelled of motor oil.

Her legs tingled. Fear?

For some reason, this guy had delivered the CD right to her mailbox. Had he been watching her home too? If so, why? Just how did he connect to her baby sis? Or to Eddie? The threat behind delivering the CD had to be tied to Paige and her constant need for cash. Even though her baby sis had moved away, she likely still knew half of the deadbeats in the state.

Jules tried to remember how to breathe regularly. What if Tobey spotted her before she was ready?

She felt the pull of a dangerous undertow.

According to Crispin, her investigator, Tobey had previously been convicted on all sorts of criminal charges—including various violent acts. Working at a strip club, she had learned to listen to her gut. Too many sketchy things went down there. There was a stillness about this whole car lot now that seemed ominous. Her strong instinct was to scoot. She still had time to get away.

She knew she was at a crossroads. This could backfire. Then again, it might gain her some kind of edge.

Before she lost her nerve, she pulled on her black mask. Feeling her energy building, she strode forward. She had to keep her family safe. She was here to strike back. How else could she connect the dots?

Tobey was heading for a pricey-looking chopper motorcycle.

"Stop," she said, her voice a little off.

He turned. Took a step toward her. His orange red hair fell to his shoulders. Yet his beard was neatly trimmed. His eyes, though—they looked dangerous. And crude, apparent prison tatts edged out from under his shirt cuffs.

She had a feeling of things coming together as she pointed her Colt at him.

"*Stop*, I said."

"Fuck you. Is it Halloween already?"

Jesus!

She finally recognized him.

That orange hair.

The realization made her heart momentarily stop.

Underneath the new beard, it was the same guy she'd seen with the rifle on Swamp Road, long ago. There really had been someone after her that day! Someone like Eddie's brother must have tried to use Tobey to take her down. After the one attempt, Tobey must have backed out.

Okay. Focus.

Now what was she supposed to say?

"You were seen on my friend's street. In Monkburg, days ago. Stuck something in her mail."

God. *My friend's street*? Would that lame lie pass his bullshit detector?

Oh, well.

He glared at her.

"Was taking a drive."

"Bullshit."

Now what?

At least she had the right guy this time. She still might break this mystery open.

"You need to put that damn gun *down*," he said.

"Nah, don't think so."

He was silent a moment, eyes on the gun. He spoke with a bit of amused menace.

"No?"

She managed to keep the .45 steady.

After she had told Crispin about Eddie's ties to bikers, what had Crispin told her? *If this guy Tobey's a biker too, stay far away from him.*

Tobey was way burly. Probably all muscle. This wouldn't have to get violent. Would it?

No stopping now.

He eased a hand toward a front pants pocket. For a knife? He looked tensed to charge. Her legs felt shaky, unsteady, but she stepped closer. She tightened her grip on her Colt.

"That's so not gonna happen," she said. "Hands behind your back."

As he took a deep breath, she saw his shoulders rise.

He made a grumbling sound.

"No way."

6 1

"*N*ow." In her free hand Jules held out plastic flexi-cuffs. "Just for you."

Even though Tobey wasn't dressed like a hardcore biker, she noticed that chromed metal spikes jutted from his black motorcycle boot tips. Likely for ripping flesh.

Some footwear for a supposed car dealer.

He glowered at her for at least five seconds.

"There's no—"

"You got no damn choice."

He inched closer.

And closer.

She didn't like the way this was heading. But she had made it this far. She wouldn't break now. She had to . . . If he tried to kick at her, he was going down.

"You won't shoot," he said.

She lurched forward. Jammed her gun's muzzle against his temple.

"Look around."

"Shit."

"See many witnesses?"

She cinched his wrists together. She then raised her .45 again. Braced in both hands, she pointed it. At his custom-looking bike.

His chopper had all sorts of chrome. The teardrop-shaped gas tank was painted in stars and stripes.

"I'll shoot it," she said.

His shoulders flexed as he apparently struggled with the cuffs behind him.

"Hell, no. God, don't."

She pictured the mysterious shiny Imation CD she'd received. Damn that disk. He had to know something.

She felt a growing sense of both dread and excitement as she said, "I only got one question."

"That's my—"

"You dropped something at my friend's house."

"I told you. I was—"

She bristled with anger.

"*Why?*"

He stared at her. She stared back. He shook his head.

Was that a refusal to answer?

She aimed right at the gleaming stars-and-stripes gas tank. Damn.

Not a good choice? Would that cause an explosion? If she had to, she would bang his face right onto those stars and stripes.

What did he know?

"Got no clue," he said at last. "I was *told* to deliver it, man."

Doubt tugged at her. Had she scrambled down the wrong trail? She willed herself to concentrate on what she was doing.

"Bull. How do you know Paige?"

He gave her a puzzled look.

"Who?" he said.

"Paige."

He answered firmly.

"I don't know any—"

"Don't freaking lie."

When she looked him straight in the eye, he broke eye contact first.

"Hey, I don't ride with the Pagans."

She raised her eyebrows. She didn't get it.

"I just take orders from them," he said. "That's it."

"Why shouldn't I shoot your—"

"I tell you, I'm not—Do the goddamn math."

She didn't say anything. Waited for him to fill the silence.

"I don't know squat."

A rush of disappointment hit her and she almost groaned. She believed him. When she first asked, he hadn't paused one bit in answering.

The Pagans had been one of Eddie's crack connections. And recently Paige had gotten to the biker gang somehow. But who knew where the original damn voice mail had come from?

She stood in stunned silence.

She thought she had known. Had been sure of it. She frowned, feeling even less in the know now. Somewhere she had made a wrong move, and she heard herself breathing harder with the realization.

She had a sense of a net that was tightening fast.

"So," Tobey said.

She cleared her throat.

"So."

Well, this sucked. Now she didn't know anything. She felt as if she was competing at chess again—but was about ten moves behind.

She ran her thumb along the grip of her .45. Hell, should she shoot out the chopper's tires? Ride off on it? Except for a kick-ass Ducati once, she'd only ridden dirt bikes before. She knew she could get the chopper started—but after that she would likely be too short to reach the ground with both feet. And what about her truck? Still, it would almost be worth taking it, just to watch Wesley's face when she roared up on it at home.

Nah, shoot it.

That day on Swamp Road, hadn't he planned to actually kill her? She felt the trigger strain against her finger. But why piss him off even further?

She let out a deep breath and said, "Sorry?"

62

———

The shooter let go with a half-dozen rounds.

Jules dropped her bag of groceries and dove to the pavement outside Shaws. She felt herself going cold with fear.

Damn! It was on.

Half-Assed Frank.

Finally.

But she was at least fifty feet from her truck. And handgun. She had tucked her credit card into her pocket for shopping, but had forgotten to grab her .45. Vision tunneling, she raised herself to a crouch. Then sprinted toward a tan Kia suv.

Her arms pumped.

Bullets sang in the air. They were quick hard shots. Maybe from a rifle. Maybe not.

Behind her a vehicle screeched out of the lot. She dropped and rolled. Crawled under the oily-smelling suv. Squeezed underneath the Kia on her belly, she lay breathless. Her right cheek pressed against the hard pavement. She wished she had the shotgun. Or at least the combat knife that Eddie used to carry.

Shit.

Now what?

She spaced out a second. Nerves? So, which way was her truck? She couldn't hide under here for long. She'd end up . . . She had to make another run for it. Look for her Tacoma. Arm herself. For a few seconds she concentrated on listening for footsteps. This wasn't the way it was supposed to go down! Her body began to shake with tension. She fought it, though.

Breathe. God, at least Junior and Wesley were at home.

When in the distance a pair of feet moved quickly to the right and disappeared, she felt her tension ratchet up. Half-Assed Frank must know her truck. The bastard had to be watching it. Maybe she was safer here?

She inched along the pavement. Poked her head out from under the s u v. Stared down a line of vehicles toward the storefront.

A light crashing sound came from near the shopping-cart collection area.

Uh-oh.

Casey Lambert, the developmentally challenged kid, was gathering shopping carts, muttering something that sounded like "Durka-durka." He was a sweet kid, who seemed to work hard. Was he okay over there?

Who knew?

Not far away from him, beneath a row of vehicles, the feet she'd seen a moment ago reappeared. A feeling of panic mounted in her chest. She had to warn Casey! The poor kid didn't know any better. Get back inside, Casey.

But if she yelled she wouldn't stay hidden. It was too risky to expose herself that way. No, she had to act—

Why wasn't he inside? Damn!

She scrambled out. Jumped up.

"Casey! Casey Lambert! Run! *Go!*"

Casey's round, friendly face wore a confused look.

"Julie?"

"Get back inside!"

Should she dive under another car? She swiveled her head to the left. A ridiculously low Mini Cooper.

She looked right.

A VW Bug. Nuh-uh.

When a flame spit from a gun in the distance, she ducked down.

Damn, she needed her Colt now.

"This a game?" Casey said.

There was her truck! A few cars away.

"No! Yes, yes, it *is*."

"Okay, Julie."

Well, screw it. She feinted left and then bolted right. As she closed in on her pickup, another shot rang out. The air moved by her head. From somewhere came a thump.

Her chest heaved as she halted next to her pickup. With trembling fingers, she inserted the key in the lock.

It wouldn't turn.

The wrong Tacoma?

No.

Not far away a chip flew up from the pavement. Jesus!

Wrong key.

Still panting, she fumbled in. Thank God. She shot her hand under the seat. Where was it? The other side?

She lunged across the seat.

No.

Every time she came to town she tucked it—

Well, almost every time, apparently.

Bummer. Wait, the glove box! She popped it open. Snatched her Colt .45. Outside, the rounds were coming from her left. So she pushed open the passenger-side door, dove out. Now she had some cover. And her gun. Its heavy bullets could blast a big man off his feet.

Crouching, she sucked air, trying to catch her breath.

Okay. Half-Assed Frank's postcard, the phone call—he'd been toying with her. Waiting to strike. But now he was going to be the one who needed protection.

She eased herself up slightly and eyed the rows of cars between her and the store. Windshields glinted in the sun. She listened, hardly daring to breathe. Another person was out there whose only purpose was to kill her.

Where was the bastard?

Somebody must have called the cops. Could she just haul ass out of here in her truck? Maybe. Maybe not. But it was time to settle this on her own. Take the fight to him. Get vengeance. Kill him now.

She eased closer to the windows of a tan Ford Explorer. Peered through. It had to be him out there. Didn't it? Or could Tobey have figured out who had threatened to shoot up his fancy chopper? Lately, it seemed she was up to her ass in bad guys.

Stepping away from the Explorer, she hollered.

"I'm coming after you!"

Wait.

What was that?

Well, it was time to—

Her breath rushed out of her lungs when a body hurtled into her. She tumbled to the pavement. Her Colt flew out of her hand and she saw white explode in her head.

Momentarily she was stunned.

What the—? Had she smacked her head?

Where the hell was her .45?

"You're a bitch, Jules!"

That voice!

She couldn't be hearing what she thought she was hearing. Maybe she *had* smacked her head?

Nonsense. Despite taking such a hard hit, she would never not recognize that irksome voice.

Her heart kicked her chest.

"Paige?"

63

What was Paige doing *here?*

Jules's drug-fried baby sis was supposed to be in San Diego! Goddamn it.

Jules shot an elbow Paige's way.

"You're the bitch, bitch!"

Her baby sister groaned. Then there was a lot of biting and yelling and rolling around.

Paige seemed weak but crazily determined. When she tried to rise, Jules reached out and grabbed her foot. Paige stumbled, fell. A packet of white powder dropped from her pocket. She snatched it up then slapped Jules in the face, and Jules shot her hand out and dug her fingernails into Paige's skin.

Jules finally landed a solid jab. She sat up. Lunged for her gun.

Grabbing a hank of Jules's hair, Paige held her back.

"Shit!" Jules said.

She aimed a fist at the center of Paige's chest. With even more fury, she walloped her again.

Paige yelped in pain.

Jules hammered her again. She then recovered her Colt. She sprang to her feet next to Paige's sprawled form. Jules shook a spinning sensation from her head and aimed her .45 downward.

Her head pounded. Her right hand smarted. She detected a smell like sour milk coming off Paige. Paige was doing some low-level moaning. After all her target practice, and waiting, Jules was tempted to shoot.

Someone yelled in the distance.

"Oh my God!"

Paige was family. But had always been trouble. Then, of course, there was the recent threat to rat Jules out to the cops. And the CD. Okay, okay, her only sis was a full-throttle bitch. She had even threatened Jules's life before, after Jules had tried to force Paige into rehab. But Jules had never taken the threat seriously.

They hadn't been close in years. Hell, had they ever been? Still, Jules wasn't sure she could shoot her now.

Hadn't Jules promised their aunt Ina that she would always look after Paige? Damn!

And where was Paige's gun?

Underneath her?

"Aw, crap."

Jules scooted around her Tacoma to the driver's side. Slapped shut the door that had been left open. Then she crouched down, while Paige apparently pulled herself together and stood. Now that Jules had some cover again and a better chance to look, she saw how crappy Paige appeared. Her ginger hair was ratty. Her face looked kind of sunken and wore a vexed expression. Although she was still young, there were lines along her meth-addled eyes. And scabs marred her face.

Despite herself, along with sadness, Jules felt an embarrassing little surge of satisfaction.

They'd always been competitive.

On the opposite side of her truck, Paige clutched a nice-looking handgun, though. A shiny big Desert Eagle, or a similar knockoff, pointed straight at Jules. So Jules kept her Colt up and ready. Jesus, this was like when they used to halt on opposite sides of a table, playing tag. But now they were armed. With both of their gazes focused on each other's gun hands.

"The hell are you shooting for?" Jules said.

Facing her squarely, Paige threw her a spiteful look.

"I've had it with you!"

"God! You scared the—I thought you . . . Never mind."

"All you do is rip people off," Paige said. "And, and, smoke it all away."

"Paige."

Paige shook her head. Twisted up her face. Her lip had started to swell from their tussle.

"You're sick, Jules."

"That's *you*. You got it all—"

Paige struck the truck roof with a palm.

"Your brain is scrambled!"

Jules groaned to herself. Maybe somehow she could use the info investigator Crispin had turned up to scare off Paige? Nope. Mention that, and it'd probably make her sis even more freaking pissed.

"The cops must be on the way," Jules said. "You better split."

"You're working for them, aren't you? The goddamn DEA!"

"What?"

"Spying! Seen you in those black helicopters. I know."

Jules blew out a hard breath, touched her jaw. It felt tender.

"Listen, I'm going to . . . grab my checkbook from the truck, write you one."

Paige condensed her eyebrows as if she didn't understand.

"No more shooting," Jules said, "and I'll toss the check out the window when I leave."

Paige lowered her Desert Eagle.

Raised it.

Lowered it. Then raised it again with a tense, readied look. She sucked air with a whimper which sounded close to crying.

"You squealed to my probation—"

"To try and get—" Jules felt her face heat up. Did she really have to explain herself to her sister? "Only to get you some help."

That had been a big mistake. But a long time ago. Back then Paige had been sent back to jail.

"So, what about you?" Jules continued. "Lately, lately, you— Those crazy calls. And *you* fucking tried to blackmail me."

The siren was getting closer.

Her .45 still up and ready, Jules stared down her agonized-looking sis for an instant longer. God, she was thin. She was probably aching inside, desperate to get high again. Sometimes she wouldn't even shower because she thought clogged pores helped hold in a drug longer. Would she even make it into her thirties?

How close had her own life come to winding up so bleak?

"Get some help with the money," Jules said. "You wanted money when you called. Take it."

Paige laughed darkly.

"Screw that."

Hell, that was just like her fuckup sis, never agreeing to anything. If she didn't give a shit about help, couldn't she see that she could at least take the money and then smoke or snort it all away?

Paige started making a grumbling noise. What was going on in her head? Neither of them was about to give in, it seemed. Was Jules really going to have to off her own sis?

A sudden fear that she'd never see Junior again overcame her. She tried to force the thought down.

Sweat ran down her neck as Paige said, "You and your filthy secrets."

Jules didn't want to shoot.

She had to shoot. She would not let Paige win.

Wasn't Paige already living in her own circle of hell?

"Damn it," Jules said to herself.

Keep aiming for the bitch's body. The muscles of Jules's trigger hand were flexed tight. Who knew what Paige might say to the cops? She had to have another copy of Eddie's voice mail.

"Paige, it's—it's your way out."

"No!"

In a flash, Jules remembered holding Paige's little hand years ago, when a brutal case of the flu had landed Paige in the emergency room. Jules could still feel the warmth of their entwined fingers. *Family is what counts*, their aunt Ina used to tell them. When their aunt's health had failed, Jules had tried to provide order, tried to put food on the table.

Now Jules softened her voice, made it even more sympathetic. "You can do it."

Paige worried her lip. Otherwise, she didn't respond, which Jules took as a good sign. She took a breath.

"I'm out of here. The cops got to be close. In a sec you better run your ass off too."

"You never did—"

"Good luck, Sis. I mean that."

For a long, long time, Jules had tried to be her sister's keeper. She fed her, cleaned her up. She researched rehab places for her. It was a horrible thing to see when Paige was jonesing— Paige would shake, beg, cry. Maybe this time Paige really would get help? Probably not. But at least now she would have one more chance.

With a swell of both sadness and relief, Jules grabbed her door handle.

"Funny thing is," she added, "there's someone *else* out to kill me."

Paige scratched hard at an arm through her orange shirt.

"Boo-hoo. I'm crying for ya."

God, she was a bitch.

"Anyway, next time you want to visit? *Call.*" Jules thought about that. "No, just don't. Wait! What about the CD?"

"Huh?"

"The voice mail!"

"Don't know what you're talking about."

64

The next day, Jules strutted before Wesley in the living room in a new sheer peach-colored negligee. Her right shoulder was still sore from tumbling to the pavement outside Shaws. Her right hand ached as well. Thank God she had screeched away before any cops showed up yesterday. She hadn't heard from them either, so apparently Paige had escaped too.

This morning, Jules had propped the Browning shotgun by the front door. Just in case of any other trouble.

"Went shopping today," she said to Wesley now. "Like this new nightie?"

Without looking up from his sports magazine, he said, "You never explained about the new locks."

"Did you even hear me?"

"Or that new bullet hole in your windshield."

"Hey."

"Or that scratch on your—"

"Check *this* out."

Gazing up from the sofa, he threw his magazine aside.

"Holy wow, Jules."

God, she was horny. After all that ruckus with her baby sis, she ached for some good naked fun.

All she wanted now was to feel her man between her legs. Something to clear her mind, renew her.

Earlier as she finished up changing Junior's diaper, the sucky reality of her and Wesley's situation had sunk in. If Paige had been honest about the CD, somebody *else* was messing with them. She bit her lower lip as she pondered. Could it be one of Eddie's buddies? Maybe the Pagans were planning to blackmail her? It could also be Eddie's prick brother, Travis. Probably none of them would even hesitate to slip a wire around her throat.

Whatever was going on could lead to some dark places. Clearly, someone wanted *something*. But why had they waited so long to send the CD?

Screw you, whoever you are, she thought.

Now, aching to fool around with Wesley in her new negligee, she ran a hand across her boobs.

"Not much to it, but it does make me feel pretty naughty."

Wesley grinned widely as she pulled at his belt buckle.

"Let's get you out of these," she said.

"Uh-huh."

She eased his jeans and pale blue boxers down. Pushed him back onto the throw pillows.

"Let me . . ."

"Oh, yeah," he said.

"Like that?"

"Ohhh, honey. Yeah. Ohhhh. Give, give it to me, Bree."

Her face heated up.

She drew back, threw him a stern stare.

"*Bree?*"

When she jumped to her feet, the dumbass gave her a pleading look.

"Hey! Don't stop."

"Did you say 'Bree'?"

"Course not. I—"

"You did!"

He jerked up his boxers and jeans and sat up. She stomped down hard on his foot.

"Ow! Shit, that hurt . . . . Wait, don't take that off."

"Shove it up your ass."

———————

Wesley fled for Skunk's Lounge with a whopping sense of despair. The sky flashed with veins of lightning. Inside the nearly empty bar, he sank onto a stool. The place smelled as if someone had mopped it with stale beer. The letters "NAT" slashed across the bar top before him.

"Jameson's, Jimmy. A double. On the rocks . . . . Just like my crazy relationship."

He gave out a weak laugh. Jimmy, thickset, with beady eyes and a red nose, shook his head in sympathy.

"Can't be any nuttier than mine. Some days? I want to kick the woman right in the butt."

Off to Wesley's right sat a large woman in a pink sweater. Pool balls clacked behind him. Slouching forward, he drank, and drank.

After a while his head swarmed with worry and booze. He squinted through the dim light at the tattered stuffed skunk behind the bar.

"You got it good, pal. Good! Ah, Christ . . . . Hey, Jimmy, it moved!"

Jimmy grabbed two freshly washed glasses and slotted them up to dry.

"Yeah, sure."

"It did."

"Problems—everybody got 'em except me."

Wesley studied the brown slop at the bottom of an abandoned mug. Well, at least he wasn't out digging for a damn gun. But what about Jules? Now she probably really did want to pitch him off the Champlain Bridge.

Jeez!

For a second he had a sense of consequences hanging in the air—like an anvil ready to drop on his head.

He threw some cash on the bar. It had been a long time since he had felt so alone. But, but . . . when life handed you shit, you had to make lemonade. Or something like that. Hell, he'd figure things out. He was tired of thinking. Maybe before he talked to Jules, though, he could slip on the bulletproof vest.

Outside, he let out a long burp and then zigzagged across the lot to his car. He fumbled in. But he felt water sprinkling on his head. Quickly the rain poured down. So he cranked up his window. Somehow he still seemed to be getting wet. Did he have the top thing down? Or up? Oh, well.

In a high-pitched voice, he mimicked Jules.

"Shove it up your ass!"

It took him two tries to get the key in the ignition. The car then lurched forward, and he screeched out of the lot, laughing.

"Whoo!"

The Mustang weaved all over Pratt Road. Tires hissing on the wet pavement, he swerved across the dim lines in the center of the road. A moment later he drifted away from them. Then back again.

What was with this freaking road?

Rain rushed against the glass, splattering everywhere. Even though his lights were on, he couldn't see shit. When he finally remembered to flick on his windshield wipers, the road shone with water.

Tunes! Shooting over a low rise, he pawed at the floor for his CDs. Lowered his bleary eyes.

A car horn blared.

"What's—"

Looking up, he swallowed hard.

Straight ahead between his clacking wipers shone the lights and hood of another car. With a wild bolt of fear, he jammed his right foot down and yanked at the steering thing and the wheels bit down but then locked, the road slipping away. All he could do was hold on. Shooting off the road, the car slammed into a ditch with a gouging racket.

He hurtled through the air, headfirst.

———————

"Mother of God!"

Half-Assed Frank shook his head in disbelief, clenching his Caddy's steering wheel. God, it was hard to see. Whoever the hell had been heading the other way, they couldn't drive worth a shit.

That was damn close.

Easing off the gas pedal, he crept on. Burger wrappers covered the floor. The rain slammed at the windshield, and the pulse behind his eyes drummed.

65

Wesley survived his car crash without one broken bone. Like a bumpkin circus daredevil, he rocketed headfirst out of his Mustang right into a nearby hay bale. Once he smacked into it, his brow and shoulder blade hurt like hell, tiny stars drifted before his eyes, and he passed out.

When he came to on his back, it was light out. His brain and body ached. Damp hay clung to his face as he eased his head to the right.

"Oww."

What the—? A sopped field? A hay bale? His brain did not want to work. Nothing came at first, then a bit of a blur and the image of a rushing car . . . . Then jerking at his steering wheel in panic. Shooting into a ditch.

Hell, he'd been thrown clear. He was alive. Sort of.

Had he run someone off the road? God, he had enough on his conscience already.

He planted his hands flat on the ground. His wet clothes stuck to him as he rose to his knees. Shakily, he then dragged himself up.

"Ohhh . . ."

Grimacing, he prodded a goose-egg rising from his brow. It was painful to touch. He ran his tongue over a cut on the inside of his lip.

Well, he had to . . . Jeez. What? Get home to Jules. Apologize? But where was his . . . ?

Slowly, he turned toward the road, slack-jawed. His Mustang sat half in the ditch. He slogged closer, stumbling in a dip as he neared the hood.

When he squinted this way and that, the front-end damage looked slight. The right bumper caved in a bit. One headlight was busted and flared off like a lazy eye. There were no obvious leaks, though. Still, no matter how many times he blinked, the car was freaking tipped. The back wheels sat a foot off the ground.

He let out a weak groan.

Brakes squeaked behind him, so he eased around and then plodded up onto the road shoulder. Burnt-rubber tracks swerved along the pavement.

A ruddy-cheeked guy in an Agway cap climbed down from a huge teal pickup. Silvery silhouettes of naked women glinted on the truck's mud flaps. Spitting out a wad of tobacco, the guy considered the tilted car. After a while he made a whistling sound.

"Shoot. Lookit that."

"I know."

"You okay?"

———————

A little later, Jules glimpsed a figure outside behind her home's side-door curtain, and her vision tunneled.

The figure lingered there.

He was back, he was here.

She grabbed her shotgun. Took cover alongside the fridge. Aimed. She pulled in a deep breath to gather herself, then another. Her ears strained as they both waited.

Other than the hum of the fridge, it was dead quiet.

Finally it was time.

It had to be Half-Assed Frank.

She'd taken out the trash only minutes ago. Hadn't she relocked that door?

No.

Shit!

She eyed the knife rack. Grabbed the largest one. Slapped it on top of the fridge.

Out of nowhere, she remembered they needed milk. Was there time to jot it on the grocery list on the fridge door? Well. Probably that could wait.

She had to focus on this killing.

But what about baby food? Okay, baby food and milk.

Kill.

Then add to the list later.

Junior.

Nobody was going to touch him.

She held her finger steady on the trigger as the doorknob turned. Come to me, she thought.

A weird, scary silence followed. Her tongue felt parched. It seemed to take forever for the door to open.

Just what was—?

"Damn!" Wesley said.

The blood drained from his face.

He gaped at her, stood very still. Apparently terrified that if he moved, she'd pull the trigger.

A moment later the dumbass shambled in, looking horribly hungover and battered. He held himself stiffly as if he was sore. Something that seemed to be dried blood stained his gray sport shirt and an ugly lump on his forehead. His eyes looked poached.

As she stepped forward, she sure wasn't feeling any warm fuzzies for him.

Was there even a *chance* he'd ever straighten out?

Ha!

Screw. Him.

"Well, well, well. Look who decided to show."

He noisily cleared his throat.

"You—You really *are* pissed."

"Give the man a prize." She looked down a moment. The shotgun. "Oh!" She gave him a sheepish grin. "Hands where I can see 'em!"

"You kidding?"

"Maybe."

She laid down her gun. The sorry-looking fool muttered something she couldn't make out.

"What the hell happened to you?" she said.

"I . . . slipped."

She eyed the welt on his brow and crinkled her face in disgust. It looked like he had a jellyfish stapled to his head.

"Ew! Yeesh. What happened?"

"Fell?"

She made a little noise.

"Don't."

"Hmmm." He was having trouble keeping eye contact. "I was trying to . . . avoid a baby deer?"

"Don't start," she said. "I thought that maybe . . . I thought something else."

Briefly the other day, she had also been in a panic that Half-Assed Frank had appeared. Looking out the window, she caught a glimpse of a new-ish sedan, which was creeping by. The driver was a male, with his hat pulled low. His dark silhouette seemed to be staring toward her house. When she pressed her face to the glass, the driver floored it.

The brief glimpse gave her a chill.

Paige might be history now. Likely, she was hitting the pipe hard. But Jules knew the big showdown with Half-Assed Frank was coming. After spotting the suspicious car, she had asked investigator Crispin to check with the feds on Half-Assed Frank's whereabouts. And last night she had kept her shotgun close.

"I barely slept," she said now.

"Okay, a little, um, accident." Wesley winced. "Got the worst headache."

She popped a few almonds into her mouth and studied his forehead as he wobbled before her. Over two inches across, the bruise appeared crusted, slightly purple. A ridge of dried blood shot down the center.

When she sniffed the air before him, he smelled of wet grass. Or hay. And booze.

She shook her head.

"Mm-hm."

She was exhausted, physically and emotionally. She didn't know whether to slap him, for worrying her so. Or to smother him in kisses in relief that he was basically okay.

Somehow, she let out a loud laugh. After all her worries, it was a great release.

"You know," she said, "we should clean that thing on your head up."

"Were you really going to shoot—"

"Hydrogen peroxide, or something. And maybe slap on a bunch of Band-Aids."

"Man, could I use a hot shower. And Tylenol."

She gave him a peck on the cheek. Before he headed off to clean up, shouldn't she explain the shotgun, and so on?

Was it finally time to bring him into the loop?

Or would he totally freak out?

Very possibly.

Still, if they were being stalked . . .

She swallowed.

A sense of anticipation flooded her body. It just might be a relief to share her burden. She readied herself to catch him, though, in case he passed out from the news. As it was, he looked as if he might fall on his face at any moment.

"You know, you probably don't want to hear this," she said. "Been meaning to . . . Anyway, take a breath, it's . . . scary stuff."

"I really just—"

"But—But somebody is out to hurt us. And *somebody else* . . . Well, they're trying to blackmail us." She had to fight down the fear rising in her. "We're in real trouble."

Swaying slightly, he stared at her.

There was no surprise on his face, no fright. No large, surprised eyes. For a moment her hopes lifted. God, was he going to step up and help her handle this mess?

Or had his accident scrambled his brain?

"There's something else running through all of it," she added, "and I don't know what yet."

Finally, he gave out a weak sort of laugh.

"Hilarious, honey."

What?

"Wesley—"

"You're too much."

"Hey, you're not—"

He cut her off with a tremendous yawn.

"But, but . . . cut the jokes, okay? Please."

Taking in his bruised brow, bloodshot eyes, and rumpled clothes, she gave a big exhale. Oh, well. He was a total mess right now. Obviously he wasn't ready to . . . She reached out and massaged the back of his warm, tight neck.

It really *was* hard to believe how much trouble they were in.

That night in the bedroom, Wesley watched Jules shimmy out of her tube dress. She faced him and grinned widely, then lit candles. He knew the crazy tension was about to erupt into some smoldering sex.

Before long, despite his soreness, there was no stopping them. Candles flickering low, they both finally collapsed into a deep blissful sleep.

The next morning, Wesley guided Junior into red overalls and fed him. He then prepared for a day out with him.

"Come here, you little monkey," Wesley said at last. "Ready? One, two, three!"

When he scooped Junior up, Junior murmured into the curve of his neck. Jules had seemed a bit tense, in general, lately. Her pulling the shotgun on him? That had been a bit unnerving. Maybe she needed a day to herself.

"Time to give Mommy a break, kiddo."

By the front door, she slipped her arm around his waist. Her face glowed. She pecked Junior on the forehead, and squeezed Wesley's butt.

"Have fun, guys! I love you so much."

"Love you too. You're the best, Jules. The best."

He caught her glancing toward the window. At times he had a sense she was watching for strangers lurking outside.

Even on a good day, she could be so irrational.

"Be careful," she said. "Keep your eyes open."

"Huh?"

"Just be careful, Wesley."

"Yup."

"Listen. There've been some things on my mind, some things . . ." Her eyes moved toward the window again. "Tried telling you yesterday, but, well, you were in *no* shape to get it."

"Honestly? I barely remember the day."

"We need to talk. When you get back, I'll explain everything. Now don't forget to pick up the things. You know, at the—"

He mock-saluted her.

"We'll get it." He met her sweet eyes and did not look away. "Enjoy the peace and quiet. You know, I know we've had our stresses lately. But, well, I'm sure the worst is behind us."

"Right. Um, sure."

He floated out of the house, diaper bag, a bag of toys, and son in arm. He wore a baggy pair of shorts and an I'M NOT NORMAL t-shirt, a purplish welt on his brow, a hickie on his neck, and an ear-to-ear grin.

The door closed behind them and then a metallic *thunk*.

One of the new locks she'd never fully explained.

66

Eleven miles south in Philo, Half-Assed Frank crept through Pine Hill Cemetery's gateway in his freshly stolen Caddy ATS sedan. He had been so wired he had barely slept for days, and oversized sunglasses covered his burning eyes. A Glock 19 sat behind his belt.

Beneath his powder-blue porkpie hat and shades, he still felt a bit shaken by his near-death brush with some nutcase driver in the crazy-ass rain the other night. Headstones all around him, he couldn't help muttering about it now.

"Could've ended up laid out here. Like all these stiffs."

He yawned. For a brief moment he considered curling up and taking a good, long nap.

Well, soon enough he'd have *Weaseldick's* ass, right? Revenge, at last! He would wipe him the fuck off the map.

Hell yeah.

He killed the motor. With a grunt, he squeezed his way out and scanned the evergreen-lined road. To his left, flowers wilted in a pot before a pink gravestone. Was he really going to kick someday? Could there really be a heaven? Pearly gates and shit? Who the hell knew?

He limped on through a row of headstones. Yet somehow his mind and body wouldn't quite snap to.

Close to a clump of elms rose up Sal and Pino's marble markers. As he neared them, he pulled up short, a roaring in his head. He swiped six pink roses from a nearby plot. Clutching them tight, he hulked there before their graves, frowning.

"Hey, boys, been a while." He swallowed. "Miss you, you dumb shits."

He stared at their headstones, memories whirling up in his mind. The furry line of Pino's eyebrows. Repeatedly threatening to whack Sal. The three of them sharing smokes and cookies on Mount Mansfield, then hauling ass after Weaseldick as he streaked around in drag.

Forlornly, he stared at each stone.

"You guys never let me down, did you? Hell no. So you roughed up, shot the wrong guy sometimes, Sal. Big deal. Had some times together, didn't we? Great damn times."

They had been twisted, stone-cold killers. They had been good people.

Something swelled up in his chest.

His eyes teared up.

"Well. Christ. Ah, Jesus . . . . Rest in peace, *goombahs*."

He hoped the two of them were having a blast in heaven. Maybe they were banging big-boobed airhead angels right now. Or maybe they were sitting on a cloud edge, puffing on Camels, some dumbass strumming on a harp in the background.

Squatting, he plucked some stray weeds. He then tenderly dropped three flowers at each headstone.

"I'm—I'm sorry."

He turned and lumbered away. When an uneasy feeling seized him, he sank onto a big-ass rock to collect himself. Ever since their first days sticking up poker games, the three of them had come a hell of a long way together. Stealing cars had been a hoot. Jabbing pistol barrels up the noses of business stiffs had been even more fun.

And now? Now, those days were history. Like an idiot, he'd turned snitch. And how was he rewarded? With a big screw-you—dumped in ball-freezing Nome.

A wave of sorrow swept over him. Warm tears slid down his face, and he turned his head. A truck with a camper shell rattled down the road to the west. No one else was around, though. Tugging off his shades, he dabbed his eyes.

Shit. Shit. Shit.

He felt such a heavy sadness that he just wanted to lie down and let it crush him. Maybe he should just stick his piece right into his own mouth—end it all, right then and there. He pulled out his Glock. Stared at it. He could let his pains and worries bleed quickly away. Here he sat, in the middle of a cemetery, after all.

One simple squeeze would—

But what kind of chickenshit end was that? Tucking his Glock away, he stared off toward a double headstone. Rubbed his face. The hits themselves were going to be a piece of damn cake. But his ass was wanted now too. He might as well be lugging around a sign that said RAT. Starting up the Caddy lately, it was hard not to worry about some wiseguy screwing with it as well. Probably it would be a bullet, though.

Maybe they'd even rip out his tongue for singing to the feds. Or stuff a bird in his mouth.

Sweating a little under the glare of the sun, he whipped his head around. And what about the goddamn feds? He had bailed on the WITSEC program. That whole lame-ass program was voluntary. Still, would those asswipes be looking for him too?

Who the hell knew?

All that mattered now was payback—whatever the cost. He heaved himself up and limped on past grave after grave.

From his powder-blue hat to his lavender sneakers, he burned.

Who did he have to thank for all that shit? Who had goddamn wrecked everything?

Weaseldick!

67

Wesley had a zillion errands planned. But after unstrapping Junior from his car seat and picking up baby food, then lugging him to Dr. Peters's office in Burlington for a check-up, he decided to enjoy the sunny weather. Letting out a yawn, he turned onto Main Street.

"Let's get out of this car."

He checked the rearview mirror. Making loud spluttering sounds, Junior gaped out the window at—something. Up ahead, Lake Champlain stretched out tranquil and blue. Once they reached Waterfront Park, Wesley waited for a roly-poly man to hitch up his pants and move, then eased his slightly dented Mustang into a parking spot.

"Okey-dokey, here we are."

He lugged Junior's purple stroller out of the trunk. Handing Junior his sippy cup, he plopped him into the stroller. When Junior made some fussing noises, he patted his back.

"Let's go, kiddo. Come on."

They strolled past a line of evergreens toward the glassy aquarium and science center. A red kite danced high above— and something flitted about at the edge of Wesley's mind too. Sensing someone behind him, he flicked his eyes about and listened.

Fear tiptoed up his spine.

"Got a bad feeling, Junior."

Why had Jules told him to be careful?

Lately, she had spent a lot of time double-checking doors and windows. Even weirder, not long ago he had scooped up a pile of books, intending to read to Junior. Below *Green Eggs and Ham*, he was stunned to find another book, which had instructions on sabotage and bomb-making. Later, when he caught her sprinkling baby powder outside the front door, as if hoping to capture footprints, he figured her pregnancy was driving her totally bananas.

But maybe the weirdest thing lately was the Taser gun she'd given him. "For your birthday," she said. Which was two months away. She insisted he bring it with him whenever he was out of the house. To humor her, it sat on the Mustang's front seat now.

Now, he began to have a funny sensation in the pit of his stomach. Why all the secrecy? Why the Taser? It seemed obvious he might have missed a hint or two that trouble was coming.

He sped the stroller along the walkway. Yet nothing he saw raised an alarm.

A weary-eyed woman smiled at them.

"Isn't he a cutie!"

Once he wheeled Junior inside the aquarium, the displays— zippy frogs, whiskered lake sturgeon—and Junior's kicks of delight distracted him. The building teemed with kids. They swarmed around Wesley and Junior and the glowing tanks.

As he and Junior turned away from a flounder half-submerged in sand, two girls with straight blonde hair wriggled close. Junior looked mildly pleased. A smile spread across his mouth. When the girls gawked up at the crusted-over welt on Wesley's head, he felt like another exhibit. He scooted the stroller forward, backward.

"Hi, girls."

The shorter girl pointed up toward his brow.

"Mr. Bumpy Purple Head!"

They both giggled, and scampered away.

Minutes later he eased Junior into the freshly cut grass outside. With a pealing shriek of pleasure, Junior zipped across the grass on hands and knees. Wesley stared out at the lake and felt the past rise up. He took a breath, squelched the memory. That didn't matter anymore. The present was about strength. A little boy chased a girl in circles around a cooler nearby.

"Gonna git you!"

"No-o-o!"

A stubby ferry glided into its slip to the south. Wesley shut his eyes, facing the sun, until Jules's comment flashed back into his mind.

Why *had* she told him to be careful, earlier? For a moment she had looked so—

"Gonna git you!" the boy cried again, somewhere behind him.

Wesley popped his eyes open. Looked around.

When he looked down, Junior was gone.

Christ!

Wesley's heart crashed back and forth against his ribs.

Where was Junior?

Where?

"Gonna git you!"

Someone had—

No. There he was.

Thank God.

A few feet away, Junior had a beetle smushed up by his mouth.

"Uh-uh. Don't eat that."

Wesley brushed away the bug. He told himself he was being ridiculous. On a beautiful day like today, why worry about anything? He ruffled Junior's whorls of hair.

"Come on. Back in your stroller, hotshot. Let's roll."

"Ba!"

"This is cool, just us dudes, right? Finally we can talk about guy stuff. I ever tell you about the time I tried to rob a . . . ?"

Wheeling along the path, Wesley ogled a pair of perky-paired young joggers. The women jiggled by, pumping legs and arms, heads held high.

"Now there's something, Junior. That's worth growing up for. Not too shabby, huh?" Wesley laughed. "Just don't ever even try to figure them out."

Then it hit him—a terrible, sinking feeling that things were about to fall apart.

68

Approaching True Value Hardware on Stevens Road, Half-Assed Frank tugged his Caddy's steering wheel to the right. Now, almost ready, he had a feeling of pulsing urgency. A nerve in his left eyelid hopped.

Weaseldick had to go. Fuckin' A.

After he screeched to a halt, he whipped his shades onto the dashboard, and his Glock under his seat. He then climbed out. Eyes narrowed, he limped briskly to the door. Inside, he was approached by a scrawny clerk.

The clerk stopped in front of a pyramid of paint cans and gave him a wholesome smile. Overhead the fluorescent lights buzzed faintly.

"Can I help you, sir?"

Half-Assed Frank did not smile back.

"Your damn chainsaws?"

"Right over here." They passed a display of orange wheelbarrows, turned. "Nice day, no?"

"Great, just great."

"Well, let's see. Got this Jonsered 2054 on sale. It's got a 3.5 horse engine, and—"

"Just need something light, but strong enough to . . ."

"Yeah?"

"Well, never mind that."

"Also have this 2050 Turbo. Maybe—"

"All right, enough crap already." Half-Assed Frank shot a finger forward. "Gimme me that goddamn one."

———————

Half-Assed Frank mashed his Caddy's gas pedal, zooming back onto Williston Road under the blazing sun. On the front seat sat a can of gas and oil. And his new chainsaw.

It was almost time to boot up his receiver and find Weaseldick with the unit he had planted in the Mustang's bumper the day before.

He had done some snooping in Monkburg too. But things hadn't gone well there, previously. So, he had decided on using his tucked-away Bear Mountain cabin. He could barely wait to get started. He had momentum and it felt good. Hate was no damn fun if you kept it to yourself.

Now, this was the day.

His anger swelled, the fuse burning low.

"You're screwed, Weaseldick! Gonna mess your life up."

Outside the window, tract houses crowded alongside a churned-up field. When traffic bunched up behind a shit-box compact car, he pounded on his horn.

They were idiots. They were asswipes, all of them.

On the next straight stretch of road, he gunned his Caddy around all five cars.

"Screwed! Gonna kill the fuck out of you."

69

Wesley wheeled Junior behind a gold Jeep in Waterfront Park's parking lot. Stopping within sight of their car, he raised his hands to play peekaboo with Junior. As he peeked between his fingers, sweat ran down inside his T-shirt. Nearby, a shoe scuffed along the pavement.

"I see you, kiddo! I see—"

He froze. And that was when he felt it. Felt *him*.

Through his fingers, looming before him, he spied Half-Assed Frank and felt a twist of alarm in his gut.

"No."

Where the hell did *he* come from?

Half-Assed Frank wore new sideburns and a mustache, a goofball hat, and dark shades. But even through spread fingers, his agitated fleshy face was unmistakable.

"You cocksucking son of a bitch."

Wesley felt fear shaking him.

"Oh, God."

"You never write, you never call."

"Oh my . . ."

Half-Assed Frank rammed a pistol muzzle into Wesley's gut and laughed derisively.

"Peekaboo."

Peekaboo?

Wesley felt his fists clench. Felt the anger in his face. No freaking way would he let—

Pulse pounding, he knocked Half-Assed Frank's arm away and slammed a fist into his face. So hard that the bastard was driven backwards. Wesley then shot forward, drove a savage kick into Half-Assed Frank's shin.

Grabbing the stroller's handle, he barreled with it to his Mustang's front door. Scrambled to unlock it. Snatched the yellow plastic Taser gun off the seat.

If Half-Assed Frank wanted a freaking fight, he'd give him one.

His chest heaving, he raised the Taser. Darted his eyes back to where the big bastard had been.

No one was there.

His eyes jumped from car to car, watching for activity.

Where had he—?

Damn, damn.

Wesley couldn't hear him. But he still felt him.

Holding his thumb on the Taser's on-switch, he told himself to stay cool. He had to be strong for this. But he could feel the burn of eyes from somewhere. Imagining a swarm of bullets punching through the air and into his chest, he took in several deep breaths.

He then sensed a sudden movement to his left. All right. He felt his heart kick into a higher gear as he thrust out the Taser and activated the probes.

Take that!

A zillion volts, you bastard!

The probes made contact.

In the shoulder of a lanky teen in a muscle shirt, who jerked violently. The wrong person.

"Shit," Wesley said.

His throat clotted with fear, Wesley bashed his fists against the dark inside of a moving car's trunk.

"Let me out of here! Let me out."

Outside, a car swished by. His old bookie yelled back from up front.

"Shut up!"

"Don't you touch my kid."

"He's right here. He's—"

"Hey, anybody! I'm in here, help!"

Shortly after Tasering the wrong dude, Wesley had ended up with the muzzle of Half-Assed Frank's pistol jammed into his right ear. Then he had been forced into the trunk.

Now beneath him a little blast sounded in the exhaust pipe. Flinching, he thunked his noggin by the wheel well. He grimaced, bit his lip.

This couldn't be happening! Hold on, his cell phone! What an idiot he was. Of course. He could . . .

He patted his pockets, groaned.

He then groped wildly around him for a tire iron. Nope. Pitching to one side, he yanked back the carpet trunk mat. He slapped his hands around. Shit, nothing there, either.

What about . . . ? Had the bastard tampered with the emergency release? Squirming around, he kicked hard where the trunk latch should be, trying to force it open.

"Shoot."

He hated the feeling growing inside—that he had brought all this upon himself. Regardless, he had to use his fear. Get pissed. He banged his fists again.

"Come on, let me the hell out of here."

Half-Assed Frank's voice boomed back.

"I'm gonna drink your blood from my shoe. You're mine, you fuckstain. Mine now."

When the car jerked to one side, the sudden motion threw Wesley around. Then the car jostled over a bump. He pitched up. Flopped down.

"Christ, what're you *doing*?"

A few seconds later they rolled to a stop. Maybe for a traffic light? Were those shoes scraping on pavement outside?

"Hey, you out there! *Someone!*"

"Can it, already. Or I'll drag you out, cut your damn balls off now. I'll leave parts of you everywhere."

70

Half-Assed Frank tore southeast along Interstate 89, stomach churning. He blinked at the dark line of hills ahead, frowned. It was nice to be driving around with some dumb shit in his trunk again. And his shot at payback was finally at hand. But why'd he feel so damn uneasy?

Go figure.

A slat-sided pickup dawdled ahead in the passing lane, so he thumped on his horn. Whipping by on the right, he flipped the driver the bird.

"Stupid hick! Go screw your mother."

A small herd of cows eyed him from a pasture.

He craned his head forward, squinching his achy eyes up. Was some moron really sitting at the edge of that huge stretch of bare rock above the road? SAVE THE LEDGES! said the idiot's large hand-painted sign. The clown had to be protesting the road-widening, or some-fucking-thing.

Half-Assed Frank raised his eyebrows. Stolen baby in the car seat, Glock under his own seat, and the baby's father in his trunk, he muttered, "What a freak. Freaks everywhere."

He kneaded his eyelids. Checked his mirrors. Why'd he feel like he was the one who needed saving? Did somebody see something in Waterfront Park? Or was a wiseguy onto him?

Hell, maybe the feds, cops, and Family were all tailing him. Whatever.

When he turned toward Weaseldick's kid, his heart melted a little. He reached out to muss the little tyke's curls. He enjoyed smacking people with crowbars, and had never been accused of being touchy-feely, but he did have a soft spot for bambinos.

The baby gave a tiny yawn. There were cookie crumbs in the corners of his mouth. This one was so little. Those teeny fingers and jutting ears killed him.

"Nothing to worry about, right? Maybe we both just could use a nap."

Blinking repeatedly, he shot off the interstate and onto the exit for Bailey.

What the hell. Well done.

Heading into a stretch of low hills, he slowed down. Dully, he admired the sweeping view of the Onion River and valley. Before long the road started to climb, and he began to work his way up boulder-strewn Bear Mountain. Despite his fatigue, he brightened.

Ahhh.

With a slight grin, he passed a cluster of beat-up houses. Nearby sat a house trailer, a rusted-out car on blocks out back. Then came pine trees, pine trees, and more pine trees. When the pavement ended, gravel clanked up against the car. He sank a fingertip on the window switch and it hummed down. He breathed in the piney air and then gave out a big-ass yawn.

"Almost home, Weaseldick. Close, real close."

Feeling a growing pleasure at what was to come, he half-sang.

"O—ver the river and through the damn woods, to my lit—tle cabin we go ...."

He felt his pulse picking up a notch.

It was motherfucking time.

71

Half-Assed Frank trudged Weaseldick into his rustic log cabin at gunpoint, spots swimming before his eyes.

"Park your ass."

"What are—"

"I said, sit the hell down."

With neon-blue bungee cords, he lashed his guest to a ladderback chair for a welcome. As he cinched the cords tight, the goddamn pussy wiggled, eyes huge.

"Let us go."

"Boo-fucking-hoo-hoo. I'll tell you what, you son of a bitch. Why don't I—"

"Don't do this, *don't*."

He made a dismissing sound. Shook his head.

"I am doing this."

"Untie me. Just—"

"Hold still, moron."

"Oh, God."

He smiled, in a cold way.

"Cozy? How's that, now?"

"What the fuck!"

"Screw you, you piece of dogshit. I've been waiting and waiting for this. It's time to pay." He waved his sleek, black Glock in the dumbass's face. He pointed it directly at his forehead. "*Capisce?*"

Point made, he limped back outside to gather up the bambino, shotgun, chainsaw, and an armful of kiddie books and toys.

"Now where'd you drop that pacifier? Know I saw it just ..."

———————

Inside the cabin, Wesley wobbled his head in disbelief.

He could barely focus. Or breathe.

When he babbled out loud, his voice sounded like it was coming from someplace else.

"What the hell do I ... ?"

He was surrounded by solid log walls. Dry-mouthed, he stared down at the braided rug. Would he leave wrapped up in it? This was so ...

He had to shake his fear off and do something.

Any-freaking-thing.

Crazily, he struggled to work free. He squirmed, he rocked. Sweat beading on his brow, he grunted.

Twisting this way and that, he nearly toppled face-forward onto the floor.

When Half-Assed Frank lumbered back inside and glared, Wesley gulped hard. He checked himself and tried to stay cool, then did his best to make his voice work.

"C'mon, let's fight. Man to ..."

His eyes jumped from Junior to mountainous Half-Assed Frank. To the chainsaw. And shotgun. The skin on his neck crawled, and he wished he were back in the trunk.

A mosquito whined by, and returned. Bouncing around his eyes, it settled below the lump on his brow. He thrashed his head about. Winced as it drilled into him. Right away his forehead felt extra itchy. Itchy, twitchy, all too aware a horrible ordeal was coming, he watched his psycho captor ease Junior onto a stuffed chair by the fireplace, and choked up. His innocent baby boy plopped back in his overalls, grinning toward the moose antlers above the mantel.

The words *I did this, I did this* ran through Wesley's head.

Was this his punishment for helping with Eddie? Maybe he *deserved* this.

Then again, so what if everyone he knew ended up wanting to kill him. You don't just give up!

He thought of his late brother. A proud soldier. Tough as nails. All rippling muscles. Drew had given his life trying to save a buddy. Well, he was tough too. Pretty tough, anyway. Now, he felt the start of his strength coming back, and he straightened up.

"Well, okay," he whispered to himself.

He had to save Junior. And keep Jules out of this, wherever she was.

Turning to Half-Assed Frank, he clenched his hands.

"You don't spare me."

Half-Assed Frank loomed closer.

"Huh?"

Humiliation burning in his chest, Wesley said, "I mean, *scare* me."

"Ooh, tough guy. Look at me, I'm shaking."

Wesley bucked against his tight bonds.

"Let us go!"

A vein on Half-Assed Frank's temple started to tick. His eyes narrowed. Watching the fury flash into them, Wesley froze.

A hard wallop landed on his head. It exploded in bright pain. He felt as if he had been hit by a club.

He gasped. Gripped the chair seat.

He shook it off, tried to come back.

"C'mon, show me, you miserable shit," Half-Assed Frank said. "Show me what you're made of."

All at once, Wesley felt his face turning dark with anger. He couldn't allow himself to roll over. He worked his wrists, felt the cords bite.

"I'm so not kidding! I'm not laying down. Could use a good fight right now. Come on, damn it."

———

When Half-Assed Frank clamped his fingers around Weaseldick's neck, the dumbass's eyes popped with alarm. Half-Assed Frank felt him wriggle, squirm. He then eased his grip so Weaseldick could breathe.

Grinning, he tightened his fingers again.

After letting go, he smacked a piece of duct tape across Weaseldick's mouth. He sucked at his teeth, barked at him.

"You dumb shit. You turd. You just wait. You're gonna get yours. You *and* your woman, together . . . You're already dead, you know that?"

Done, he dropped into his ash rocker. He blinked a few times. Yawned then thought of something else and turned his head.

"One question, Weaseldick."

Weaseldick stared at him.

Waiting.

Unable to respond.

"If I shoot you in the mouth, think your teeth'll come out the back of your head?"

Weaseldick moaned.

Except for the freaked-out man tied up near the cobbler's bench, it was a tastefully decorated camp. The cedar logs were neatly chinked with plaster. Braided rugs adorned the floor, and a photo of Half-Assed Frank's lightly mustachioed mother graced the fireplace mantel. Just like his Mama had taught him, plastic slipcovers shielded the easy chairs.

While the baby cooed, plucking at his stuffed dinosaur, and Weaseldick cast a wild look at the floor, Half-Assed Frank brewed some espresso.

"You don't spare me? That's rich. What a jamook."

Once the espresso was ready, he plopped his butt onto a stool at the pine-slab kitchen counter. For a while he slurped at his tiny cup and munched away at a plate of sugar cookies. Every so often he closed his aching eyes and saw flashes of color.

Should he just give Weaseldick a serious headache now—with a bullet in the head? There was also the chainsaw. Then there was the bambino. The little guy complicated things. He couldn't even think about that. Not now, anyway. He'd been amped up since the snatch, but God could he also use some . . .

He felt his head tip forward. Shook himself out of a half-snooze. He still had to . . . call Weaseldick's woman too. Tell her that, unless she showed up nearby—pronto—Weaseldick was a dead man.

A few feet away, the baby bunched up his face. His chin quivered. He then bawled.

"Oh, come on. Hey, hey."

Half-Assed Frank forced his eyes open wide. Damn, maybe now was the time to go make a call. Who could nap or think with all that racket?

When he checked the bambino's diaper, the cute little shit was dry.

"Tired? Maybe you can take a nap."

He threw some chairs and blankets together for a crib. He patted the baby, lowered him down. The little guy settled down right away. So Half-Assed Frank grabbed his shotgun, and slapped the side of Weaseldick's head just for the hell of it. He then lumbered onto the front porch.

The pond shone a pale green. Blankly, he gazed toward a spiky clump of cattails near shore.

Now he had to draw in Weaseldick's woman. She would come armed. He had no doubts about that. But he had that shit figured out. He had planned on whacking Weaseldick first. But no. Even better, he wouldn't kill the shithead until he whacked her.

Weaseldick would see her dead first—dead because of him.

———

Soon afterward in Bailey, Half-Assed Frank leaned against his Caddy's hood outside Dairy Queen to steady himself. Only a few of his ex-goombahs knew where his cabin was. Still, if someone was trying to track his cell phone, he wasn't going to take any damn chances now. A DQ chocolate milk shake just might hit the spot too.

Cars swished past on Towson Road, and a bitter smell wafted from the Dumpster to his right.

A cottony-haired woman shuffled by, lugging a huge purse. She stared at his face, then tisked her tongue against her teeth. He shooed her away.

"Take off, you old bag."

"Well!"

"Go screw yourself."

As he first spoke into the phone to Jules, it seemed like he was dreaming.

"I'm giving you one chance," he said into his phone. "One goddamn chance."

"Bullshit," said the voice on the other end of the line.

"Or your little family? They're done. Dead."

There was a long pause.

"If you even—"

"So, listen good . . ."

Right before hanging up, though, he remembered one more thing.

"Oh, yeah. And bring some more damn Pampers."

72

Jules flung herself into her pickup and raced to Bear Mountain. Utility poles flew by. A box of powdered doughnuts, box of Pampers, her Nikon 10 x 50 security binoculars, and the sawed-off Browning sat at her side. The shotgun would provide wide coverage at short range. Little outside registering in her roiling mind, she downed one doughnut after another. Slate-gray clouds huddled to the east.

This was unbelievable. Goddamn unbelievable.

Clenching the powder-dusted steering wheel, she sped on, deeper into the hills. She needed an outing—but this was not her top choice. Done scarfing doughnuts, she screamed.

"I'll kill him! I'll goddamn kill him."

When she finally thought about it, she wasn't sure if she meant Half-Assed Frank or Wesley.

She swerved around one corner, then rechecked the directions she'd written down and made a hard right on the next. Her jaw was clenched tight.

She wished she had seen what was coming. Wished she had come up with a plan. Wished she had held Junior for hours that morning. Wished she had at least spoken up as Wesley and Junior left the house.

Before racing out, she had dialed Burpee, her proven ally, repeatedly. But hadn't reached him. So, she would do this on her own. It felt like fate now.

What she would do to that sick bastard Half-Assed Frank would be brutal. What she would do to him would be righteous.

Oh, the shit was on now.

"Hold on, Junior," she said. "I'm coming."

Halfway up the mountain near a screened-in shack, the pavement turned to gravel. Trees crowded in upon Jules.

A little further, a ROAD CLOSED sign blocked her way. Hurtling along in her angry daze, she almost ran it over.

Shit!

Her hands choked the wheel. She stomped her brakes. The Tacoma lurched and swayed to a stop. For a moment she just sat there behind the steering wheel. She forgot what she was doing. She nearly burst into tears.

Pregnancy brain!

At times lately her mind seemed to have been reworked into baby fertilizer.

God, she needed a sharp mind right now. Well, what *was* she supposed to do now? Drive around the road sign?

Or . . . what?

Junior.

Her baby.

Something smelled of a setup, a trap.

But she had to get to her baby.

The air sat heavy on her face. She sensed something in the bushes to her left.

With deep foreboding, she turned.

When Half-Assed Frank shot out of the brush, pointing a black pistol, her heart clogged her mouth. It was a trap. Weaving slightly, he gestured her out of her pickup. He was taller than she remembered. And even beefier.

"Out of the truck now. Out!"

The shotgun.

She had to . . .

The giant bastard stepped closer. The muzzle of his pistol closed in toward her head.

Damn.

He threw her a pouchy-eyed look of contempt.

"And—easy now—the Pampers, put 'em on the hood."

Mind racing, she did as he said.

She felt hot and a bit faint.

"There. Okay?"

He spotted the sawed-off, grabbed it. He snatched up her cell phone from the dashboard and hurled it into the brush.

"You don't move an *inch*. Unless I say so."

She looked down. Her baby bump stuck out a bit, but she was just beginning to show. Powdered sugar dusted her cotton print dress. All worked up with fear and surging hormones, she didn't know what to say.

"Can't help eating so much, I'm—I'm expecting."

His face twitched.

"Oh, Christ."

"This is—"

"You got a damn bun in the oven?"

She began to tremble, then braced herself against the truck and willed herself to stop. She sucked in a breath.

"I feel kinda . . ."

She swayed on her feet. Clenching her eyes shut, she pictured Junior's sweet round face and pulled herself together. There was only one thing to do. This was her chance, and she didn't dare wait any longer. Maybe she would never save her wacky sister. But right now she would save Wesley. And Junior.

She swallowed very slowly. Felt herself growing darker and tighter. Felt a growl in her throat.

She wanted to remember this moment. She wanted to look straight into Half-Assed Frank's eyes when she killed him.

Slowly, she lowered a hand.

Aunt Ina used to say *Evil don't die*—but today it would.

Blood roared in her ears. The distance between her right hand and her ankle seemed like a mile.

Half-Assed Frank was moving closer.

"What the—" he said, looking down toward her ankle. "What's *that*?"

Inwardly she swore. When he stepped next to her, she had the impulse to bolt. Thick forest cover was only a few yards away. Without thinking about it, she separated her feet.

He was going to kill her.

Maybe torture her first.

But she wasn't sure her legs would move fast enough. And if she took off, how would she find Junior and Wesley?

There had been no time for anything. Except to grab the shotgun. And Pampers. And doughnuts. And to try to reach Burpee. And make one other quick stop on her way.

Now, her mouth opened and closed.

She decided to play dumb.

"Huh?"

Her insides tightened as he pointed toward her lower leg. They both stared down.

"There," he said.

"I don't—"

He jerked her tiny Raven .25 from its hiding place in the rim of her high-top Converse sneaker. Making a whistling sound, he pocketed it.

"Crap," she said.

When he frisked her, he found the mean-looking Ka-Bar combat knife strapped to her right thigh.

"Double-crap," she said.

————————

As Jules inched up to the camp's porch with Half-Assed Frank's pistol muzzle stuck in her back, her heart twisted. Near the door sat Junior's yellow rubber-duck squeeze toy.

"Oh, God."

"Easy now. . . . Nice and slow."

She turned her head, her chin tilted up defiantly.

"You better not have touched him, believe me."

When she jerked the door open, she almost yanked it off its hinges. She buzzed with adrenaline.

Junior looked okay, thank God.

She would keep him safe, no matter what it cost her. She tried to put on a happy face.

"Hey, sweetie!"

"No fast moves, I said."

"Don't you worry, Mommy's here. You'll be fine."

Wesley was pale as a ghost, though. She pressed a fist to her mouth. What an ugly lump on his brow! He'd been roughed-up, tortured.

"Wesley!"

With a swell of disgust, she remembered the welt was from his car-crash. Just one in an endless string of screw-ups.

"You . . ."

He raised his fingertips in a lame wave. She saw his mouth moving behind the duct tape. The bridge of his nose was swollen, as if he had been punched recently. When she stared back with obvious irritation, he flushed.

She felt herself vibrate with emotion.

"You ass."

She nearly ran over and smacked him too.

———————

Jules changed Junior's diaper at gunpoint. As she finished, he gave a shrill cry.

"Of course, sweetie. One sec."

It was time to prioritize. She had to feed the baby, kill Half-Assed Frank, and then . . .

Smiling hard, she fed Junior two wedges of apple. She then eased his pacifier into his mouth and kissed his tiny brow.

"Good little boy! I love you, love you so much. Now, you hold on, Mommy will take care of everything."

As she put him down by a stand made of bent twigs, his pacifier bobbed in his mouth. The energy rising inside of her, she drew in a long, slow breath. Her body went rigid with determination. Her brain began working at high speed.

She was an innocent mother!

Except for the murder.

And the insurance fraud.

This was the man who stood before her and all her plans. One more bad guy to take down. Hell, it had been a while since she killed one.

Briefly, she studied a solid-looking lantern on the counter. A half-full bottle of booze. The cookware atop the old stove. Half-Assed Frank.

In her head she measured the distance between him and her. She exhaled.

Speed was critical. She would have a second. Or less.

How long had she had to look over her shoulder, waiting? It was time to end this thing—and now.

He was the Devil.

Feeling the insistent throb of her pulse, she lunged for an iron pan to pulverize his skull.

"You goddamn—"

But she was too far away.

Heaving forward as her hand settled on the skillet handle, the bastard jammed his pistol's muzzle against her temple. His cold black eyes grew fierce.

"Hold it!"

"Shit. Shit."

She was so scared and pissed off she trembled. Still, she had to be relentless. When he pulled the gun back, she balled her hand into a tight fist. With a white-hot fury, in one explosive move she leaped up and swung. She hammered him in the throat, waited for him to falter.

His knees buckled in response.

He gasped.

Grimaced.

His pistol, though, held on her.

For a moment he simply stared at her.

Pain pulsed through her knuckles. She had landed a solid jab. But she had missed his windpipe. She heard her own breath short and raspy in her chest. At first she couldn't read his face. She then caught a disturbing flicker of excitement.

"Oh, my," he finally said, "this is gonna be fun."

He snatched up some nylon clothesline from a crate on the floor.

"Have a damn seat."

"No! No! Shit."

A smirk itched the corner of his lips.

"Please, you're company."

As he lashed her to a nearby ladder-back chair, her throat choked with rage.

"Not so tight!"

"Abra-fucking-cadabra. Here we are. Welcome to Bear Mountain."

73

After seven quick loops around Weaseldick's woman's chest and thighs with the rope, Half-Assed Frank felt like sitting down too. Jerking the end to tighten a final double knot, he leaned over her. He saw the lace trim of her bra down the front of her dress. She had the looks and body to give a guy some serious wood.

"Stick a cork in it, all right? Hear me?"

The ballsy hottie stared back, eyes hard. Her face was dark with anger. Despite her tiny size, she had a certain goddamn force to her.

"You hurt one hair of my—"

"I got to say it again? I said shut up. Shut the—"

"I'll hurt you, I really will."

They glared at one another.

As he stared down, he also considered duct-taping her little mouth. His eyes burned, though. He felt too beat to bother. So he clamped a hand around her tiny wrist, squeezing his fingertips into the bone.

"You ain't gonna hurt nobody."

"What do you want? Tell me. You have a chance still to—"

"Try anything else, you're dead."

"Screw you," she said. "I will kick your teeth out."

Studying her defiant face, he thought about the baby growing inside her—the itty-bitty body, the teeny hands and piggies. Making an exasperated noise, he let her wrist go.

———

Wesley gaped on. His sopping wet shirt clung to his skin. Jeez, how had things gotten so wildly out of hand? What an idiot he was for getting Jules and Junior involved in this mess. She looked fit to explode. She wouldn't even glance at him.

He seemed to have a stone in his throat as he stared down at his pinky stub. What else was he about to lose? They could still just be hostages, couldn't they? But now she was here too, who was supposed to pay the ransom?

The cat?

There wasn't going to be any ransom. They were screwed!

Half-Assed Frank would mount his head and stick it over the fireplace.

———

Less than ten feet away near the loft ladder, Jules held her mouth tight. Her wrist ached. Quickly she glanced at Junior, sucking away on his pacifier. She glared at Wesley. She eyed Half-Assed Frank's pistol, to remind herself exactly what was at stake.

After the nightmarish time Eddie had bound and beat her, she had vowed she would never again end up trapped like that. That was her past, and she would leave it behind for good. No more toxic guys, no more violence. Yet here she was.

She'd heard her heart hammering then too. Bound on the bed, she'd cowered, eyes wide with terror. Unable to save herself.

Now, her breathing became louder.

Inhale? Exhale?

She goddamn couldn't goddamn breathe.

She was not that cowering woman anymore. She was not, she was not . . . It was time to show some ovaries.

Slowly, she caught herself.

She would fight with her last strength. If she had to, she'd chew her own arm off to get free. Then she would grab the wop bastard's gun and shoot him in the prick.

She tried a secret shimmy. With all the force she could muster, she flexed her ass, chest, and limbs, stretching the rope to the limit. Her chair creaked—but the rope cut into her skin and barely moved. Despite all her practice wiggling for cash, she couldn't create any slack.

Shit!

Breathe.

Turning back to Half-Assed Frank, she felt her face harden. *I'm so going to kill you*, she told herself. Promptly she blew up in a blazing fury.

"Blow it out your ass, you son of a bitch!"

Damn! Her hormones!

The big goon tried to pour on the evil eye in return. Head held high, she glared straight into his bleary eyes.

For a few tense seconds, they stared in silence.

Did he really think she would back down first? Well, screw him.

She didn't blink. Did not allow an eyelash to flutter.

Soon he did blink, and yawned loudly. She gave a *whew* of relief as he let out another, long yawn.

"Oh, yeah?" he said. "Well, screw you too."

"I want my baby."

"Think I don't remember you from the titty bar? You ain't nothing but a stripper."

She winced, picturing herself dry-humping a vertical brass pole.

"Not any—"

"Flashing your boobs."

She spoke through clenched teeth.

"I didn't stay what I was. I did not stay one!" She composed herself and calmed her voice. "That all you got?"

"Something else? How about . . . ? I, I knew about Eddie."

No way.

"What?"

"Never liked him. But he could be useful."

She thought about it.

"That's total—"

"The Pagans? I had ties with them too. And that night one of them spotted an old white Mustang, racing away from the Gorge. He said it crossed right into his lane. Almost fucking dumped his bike."

Her world started spinning in the wrong direction.

Bullshit. She didn't remember that.

Maybe in the heat of the moment, though . . .

"The couple he saw inside?" he said. "They sure sounded like you two to me."

Well, crap. Who *hadn't* known about Eddie?

Just how many things hadn't she paid attention to back then?

"Did Eddie call *you* that night? Did you send me—"

"You liked that?"

"But how ... ?"

"Eddie? He called one of my *goombatta*. I paid for that message. Then had it dropped off. I've had it a long-ass time."

She nodded, the pieces falling into place.

"Christ."

He gave her a creepy grin.

"That was just for ... fun. It's gone now. I got a hell of a kick putting you through that." He scoffed. "But let's get something straight: I own you now."

Half-Assed Frank sat dead still, his mind blank. After a while he dragged off his hat and sneakers. Thunder rumbled in the west. With a distant kaboom, raindrops pattered against the tin roof. He slumped back in his rocker. Did he have some kind of fever?

"Get up, moron," he said to himself. "Move around."

Heaving himself up, he poured a glass of grappa, and sipped at it. The rain drumming down above, he stared off into the distance. Somehow he ended up in his seat again.

Christ, with barely any shut-eye in days, he was acting like a major retard. A minute floated by. When a bat fluttered down from the rafters and across the room, he startled. He nearly blasted it with his Glock.

As the rain stopped, he still felt that crazy hottie's eyes boring into his skull. *Don't mess with me!* they said. The same eyes that had blazed back at him over two shotgun barrels long ago. Right before unloading on his ass.

Still, his mind drifted. He blinked his eyes, until the baby dropped his pacifier.

"Whaaaaa!"

Half-Assed Frank waggled his head to wake himself the hell up. Ignoring Weaseldick and Jules, he grunted to his feet, eased the little cutie up, and jiggled him to calm him. Despite the racket and his own fatigue, he gave a snort of pleasure.

"Coochie-coochie-coo. What's the matter, bambino?"

With a tug of concern, he felt the little guy's fresh diaper. A wet tushie, again! Mentally cursing, he laid him on the counter. The baby chewed on a drool-covered fist as Half-Assed Frank dragged out a diaper. This was some plan he had. How did he end up babysitting?

Working the little tyke around, he fumbled his way through a change.

Smiling dully, he took the baby in his arms. When the little guy fussed, giving a low cry of tiredness, Half-Assed Frank felt a pang of affection. He sank down again with him, dragged his piece from his waistband, and thunked it onto an end table. Lowering his voice, he made an attempt to sing.

"Rock-a-bye ba-by, in the tree top . . . when the wind blows, the damn cra-dle will rock . . . ."

74

Jules stared at Junior and Half-Assed Frank, blood whacking at her temples. For a brief moment Junior squawked and thrashed his arms and legs. Half-Assed Frank's big goddamn head nodded, and his eyelids fluttered. His gravelly voice slowed, and grew fainter, and fainter.

"When ... the ... bough ..."

His mouth fell open. His chin sank onto his chest. Her sleepy-eyed, beautiful, precious baby batted his eyelashes and settled down too. He yawned. His teensy lips pooched out. He and Half-Assed Frank both held still. They then drifted into sleep.

If she could get out of these damn ropes, this was the perfect time to snatch his gun.

Her wrists burned and ached from the steady pressure she was applying.

Come on!

Nuh-uh.

She bowed her head. Cursed to herself. She took another long moment, but then was ready to try again.

Some of the feeling was gone from her fingers. But she felt a pang of hope when she realized she had forced a slight bit of play to the rope around her hips. So she worked harder, furiously, pulling the closest knot tighter but hoping to produce more slack.

Frantically, ignoring the rope's bite, she kept at it.

Screw these . . .

She started to feel a twinge of encouragement as she managed another zillionth of an inch. But that was it.

All she'd ever wanted was to settle down. Raise her own family. But now—

She thought she heard something.

Listened closer.

The clock above the stove was an older model. She heard it mark off precious seconds. But there was another sound as well.

Outside.

From the porch came a loud squeak and the scuff of uneven footsteps.

She stiffened.

A floorboard creaked.

One step.

Another.

The noise stopped. Then came another sound. Something like a . . . hiccup?

She watched Half-Assed Frank's eyes flip open. The fat bastard blinked hard. She saw the fear steal into him.

"Who the hell?" he said.

The hairs on the back of her neck prickled as the footsteps outside scuffed closer. Then stopped.

Could this be good news? Was it Bree's old buddy, Detective Burpee? Had he tracked Wesley's cell phone or something? Would he help save them again? The way things were going, she doubted it. But could things get any worse?

Maybe it was her drug-addled baby sis, clenching an AK-47.

No, it had to be Burpee.

Her last hope.

Every cell in her body rang on high alert, and she took a deep, quivering breath.

Slowly, the white doorknob turned.

The door hinges creaked.

And the door swung open.

75

———

Half-Assed Frank's chest lurched. His senses revved in alarm.
Shit.

They'd found him!

Toad-eyed Nicky the Mole Testa, the jewel thief, teetered in
the doorway. Was he imagining things? No, goddamn Nicky
clutched what looked like a Sig Sauer piece. A lit cigarette
dangled from his lip. He reeked of whiskey.

Nicky hiccupped. Squinting, he aimed his eyes toward the
baby Half-Assed Frank was lowering to the rug, then toward
his tied-up guests. The cigarette fell from his mouth.

His voice came out ragged.

"*Gesù Cristo*! What the hell's—*hic*—going on here?"

Half-Assed Frank snatched up his piece. He steadied it,
face clenched.

He felt a sharp excitement, knowing that soon someone
would be hurt.

"Screw you. Your mother takes it up the ass!"

Wobbling to his left, about fifteen feet away, Nicky raised his piece too.

Both guns roared.

One muzzle flashed after the other. The reports were loud as fuck.

When Nicky sank to a half-crouch, Half-Assed Frank dove from his seat. A hail of bullets missed their mark. Nearly all at once, slugs tore into the doorjamb, the moose antlers, the box of Pampers, the photo of his mother on the mantel.

Glass shattered.

A candlestick toppled to the floor.

As the reports boomed across the cabin, a round passed next to his head, and the baby's mother bucked in her seat, screaming amid the racket.

"Stop! Stop it! Stop!"

The bambino squawked.

"Whaaa!"

"Stop—No, wait, shoot each other!"

Slugs thunked into the log walls. Blue gunpowder smoke and muzzle flashes filled the air.

Nicky's pistol locked dry.

He stared at it.

Half-Assed Frank took to one knee. Squeezed the trigger again. Nicky jerked backwards. His mole-covered face bunched up in pain, he clutched the crimson spot blooming on his chest.

His eyes were wild and afraid. Blood leaked between his fingers.

"Rat . . . bastard."

He stumbled. Thudded down on his side, his semiautomatic clattering across the floor. His face was losing color quickly.

He made some chesty, gurgling noises. Threw in a final hiccup.

Then he lay there dead, alongside a disk of blood. His eyes open, staring at nothing. Junior's rubber-duck squeeze toy at his feet.

Half-Assed Frank staggered to his feet, feeling dazed. Yet his gun was still up and ready. The room stank of gunpowder. Shell casings lay everywhere.

"Jesus H. . . ."

He slammed the door shut. After bolting it, he plunked down his Glock 19 and butt again. His eyes jumped around.

What a shitty way to wake up that was.

He torched up a Te-Amo stogie and puffed away, trembling. What were his chances now of hiding out from his old *goombata*? The heat was on. It was just a matter of time. He had a bad feeling about everything.

He rose, twisted his pinky ring round and round. If he wanted to save his ass, he'd better get moving.

"Where the—"

Hearing another squeak like the one that had given away Nicky on the porch, he snapped around.

Another wiseguy?

His body tensed.

Feeling his desperation mount, he snatched up his piece again. Just how many goodfellas were out there?

Out of the corner of his eye, he then glimpsed the baby. The little shit was pulling away on his pacifier. His happy-eyed ladybug squeeze toy was at his side, which he must have just squeaked.

Half-Assed Frank set down his piece, then wiped his sweaty palms on his shorts.

———————

Wesley took in Jules's oh-so-disappointed look, and dared a glimpse of the dead body and pooled blood on the floor, and winced.

He would not give up hope. He refused to give up. But all of a sudden he couldn't stop moaning.

Half-Assed Frank finally shot him a furious look.

"Stop that. Shut the hell up. Now, or I'll ram my Glock right down your throat."

He fell silent.

The bullet-riddled cabin walls closed in.

He felt himself fading out and he dropped into darkness.

76

Jules shook her head—Wesley's moaning had also been getting to her. Now, though, the hush was unbearable. She felt dazed with fear herself. But when Junior gazed up at her with his angelic eyes, she fought back the panic welling inside of her. Feeling a lump of love in her throat, she beamed him a smile.

"Hang on, little one, Mommy's here."

She couldn't wait to hold him again. She would hug him for a hundred years. Thinking about her baby-to-be as well, she knew she could face anything but losing them.

Bunching up her mouth, she glared at Half-Assed Frank again. He sat there without moving. His dark eyes stared toward the end table. At his pistol. She struggled to force up her arms, couldn't. The rope dug into her limbs, and she shifted the weight from her sore buns. Cramped and stiff, she clamped her eyes shut. A chair creaked. Junior cooed in the background.

If Half-Assed Frank was going to whack them, it would be soon.

She huddled in her hard chair, aware of the cold hollow in her chest. When she opened her eyes and faced the bastard, he looked spent. Troubled too.

Christ.

Well, she'd had to fight to be free before. The bad things that had happened then had not killed her. Now she would fight again.

There was something she couldn't put her finger on. Yet it was coming to her. An idea nudged at her mind. She then felt a little charge in her blood.

Biting at her lip, she tried to compose herself. Her bladder was ready to burst. God, the pain was sharp. And along with everything else, thanks to her heightened sense of smell lately, the bloody body by the door was already starting to get to her. Whoever the guy was, he wasn't looking too good either. She wasn't going to be able to sit much longer without peeing herself, or tossing her cookies. Or both.

It was time for a . . . What did the wiseguys call it? A sit-down. Well, that was fitting.

A lump clogged her throat as she gathered herself. She eyed Junior and then turned back. Clamping her legs together, she spoke up in a soft voice.

"Look, I'm expecting. You—You know that. I got to pee bad." Her stomach growled. "And I'm starved, and really, really want some potato chips."

She smiled, slightly, and let her words float in front of Half-Assed Frank.

Not a muscle stirred in his face.

The clock over the stove ticked away.

This was a deadly chess match. One she had to control. Mentally, she crossed her fingers. She then nodded toward the doorway.

"Look—the Mob's onto you. You know you can't stay here."

She watched the psycho bastard's Adam's apple bob up and down. Saw the confusion and hint of fear in his face. She caught his gaze and tried to keep it.

"But for starters, I think I know a place for you." As she paused, her heart swelled with gratitude for her flighty hippie aunt Meadow. "An abandoned commune, where you can hide."

Were her words falling on deaf ears?

Yup.

Nope.

She saw his dark eyes going to work. They had brightened with interest. Her excitement grew. So far so good.

He nodded slowly, as if to himself. Hell, she owned *him* now. He had fallen for her gambit. Didn't he know it was the queen who always had the most power in a chess match?

Soon, though, he raised his pistol and aimed it.

Directly at her head.

Damn!

She nearly peed herself.

77

—————

Half-Assed Frank blinked hard. He breathed in, tightened his grip on his piece. Crooked his finger around the trigger.

Weaseldick's woman's sexy little face showed a flash of concern.

Shooting first and thinking later was almost always the answer. Hadn't she already shot him? The buckshot had torn into him. Blowing off pieces of his flesh. What pain! For a long time he had relived that moment, obsessed about it. He should cap her ass right now.

Do it, he told himself.

But he felt a tingle of curiosity. What the hell was she yakking about? Was it some trap?

"Now listen—"

"You listen: I'm talking about a local spot. But where they'll never, ever find you."

"I—"

"You understand? You don't want to die, we don't want to—we're so on the same page. *Nobody* else gets killed. How about that?"

"Why the hell should—"

"You know," she plowed on, "a girl's got to be prepared. There's also twenty-four grand I brought. In the bottom of the Pampers box. I'm sure you could use that." She waited a beat. "Cash. And you can save yourself. You let us live, I show you the perfect hideout. That's it, end of story."

He made a low whistling sound.

It was a good ten seconds before he responded.

"You shitting me?"

She wrinkled her nose.

"Oh, it stinks in here."

Fatigue had filled his head with goddamn cotton. He blinked at her small rounded belly. Blinked down at the floor, and back at her. On one of her cheeks there was a faint white crescent scar. Who knew how she had gotten that? The truth was, she scared the crap out of him.

She seemed a bit oobatz. Crazy.

"Well—?" she said.

"So bushed now, I can't . . ."

With his free hand, he pinched the bridge of his nose. Weaseldick had it coming. The cocksucker. The asswipe. He wanted blood. But the bambino . . .

When he gazed into the baby's shiny eyes again, he felt his face twitch. The little tyke sat there, making raspberry sounds. The kid was so full of life. Unlike Nicky The Mole. He swallowed. And him, if he didn't figure this thing—

A cell phone blared, and he gave a start. Turned.

The damn thing was Nicky's.

His Glock trembled.

Who could be calling?

He felt a thud of dread.

Was it Crazy Joey? Crazy Vinny?

Louie the Lumper?

Lefty Guns?

Nicky sure wasn't going to answer it.

As the ringing stopped, he had a prickly feeling he was being watched at close range. He glanced toward the windows. Darkness was closing in. How long could he make it without a good place to lie low? Maybe he should have left the ghosts of his past alone.

"Fuck me," he whispered.

He turned back and met her gaze. Still unsure of how to answer her. Her eyes were pleading.

"Can you put the gun down?"

"And if I just whack you? Blow your shit away?"

She drew her full little lips in, as if pulling her shit together. Her voice rose a hair.

"Then you're stupid. And you deserve whatever happens to you. Because without a better hideout, the Mob whacks your ass too."

He didn't say shit.

"If you want me to beg, I will." A wet shine appeared in her eyes. "Cry? No sweat. Right now my hormones . . . Just don't hurt my baby. Babies. Anything but—"

The plan, was all he could think. This wasn't the plan.

"You had the cd," she said. "Even back then, you could've turned us in. But you didn't."

"Too easy."

He had put the X on them. He had *dreamed* about this day.

But what damn choice was there? In his mind he still heard Nicky's death throes. That lame-ass, final hiccup. He pictured Nicky's eyes as the light died in them.

Did he have it in him to whack a baby? And what if he just iced Weaseldick? Wouldn't she then end up after him too? He sure as hell didn't want the Mob, the feds, and a hothead hormonal widow on his trail.

Bump off both parents—and then what? Bring the bambino on his next shakedown?

"Put it down," she said. "You still got a second chance. You know it."

He felt trapped in her gaze, unable to break the contact. When Nicky's cell phone rang shrilly again, he felt the stress settling on him like a cement overcoat. His gut told him she was being straight. But was there a stripper anywhere who didn't know how to con? Right now she was handling herself pretty good, even with her clothes on.

He palmed sweat from the back of his neck. Well, if she *was* trying to play him? Then . . . to hell with it, he could cap her. Them. Whatever. And pistol-whip Weaseldick's corpse. Then he could grab the damn cash and scoot.

Better check to make sure the money is actually there, though. He pushed himself to his feet.

"You'll do the right thing," she said.

As he moved toward the counter, he kept his trap shut, wondering just what the right goddamn thing was. His tied-up hottie wore a hopeful, expectant look on her face. His piece was still pointed her way.

This whole thing was beginning to burn his ass. What was left of it.

He reached inside the Pampers box.

Diapers.

Nothing else.

He faced her, his finger ready on the trigger.

"You, you . . . What the hell! There ain't—"

"Deeper! God, reach down in there."

He tried again.

There it was. Bundled cash.

He opened his mouth, about to say something. He just didn't know what. When he spoke, he was surprised by how fast his voice was.

"Okay, okay."

He lowered his piece and gave a sharp exhale.

"Screw it. Maybe we can work something out."

He saw the tremendous relief begin to flood her face. Heaving a breath, she beamed him the world's biggest smile. Her voice jumped up a couple of notches.

"Whoo, yeah!"

He felt a kind of grudging respect for her, and gave a weak laugh.

"It's funny . . ."

"What is?"

"*My* hands are tied. I mean, what the hell."

"Thank God."

He puffed himself up a bit. Pointed a finger of warning at her.

"But don't you dare screw with me. Or I'll chew you up in a damn second. Am I clear?"

She nodded.

"Crystal clear."

"I want you to say you understand."

"Yup, I get it. Of course, of course."

"All right."

She looked at him for a long moment, then put on a pleasant expression.

"Well! It's been . . . We really don't want to overstay our welcome." She stared toward Weaseldick. Her voice dropped to a conspiratorial tone. "But there's just one thing, though."

As the bambino gummed a crayon and squealed, the two of them made a deal. This time around, she told him she would save his butt—as long as he helped her punish Weaseldick.

———

As the duct tape ripped from his mouth, Wesley came to with a jolt.

He screwed up his face in pain, let out a gigantic gasp. He then gulped down extra air. His limbs had gone numb. He didn't know how long he had zonked out—it might have been seconds, it might have been hours. He didn't remember being slugged, but it must have been a brutal blow to have knocked him out. Now, he felt queasy as his body geared up and flooded with more adrenaline.

Something huge was about to happen! Jeez!

His shoulders rose and fell with his quickening breaths. He was going to freak out. He was going to crack—just like the freaking ice had the day he rescued Tommy Jenkins.

He felt the intense, naked fear. Felt the cracks, felt them spreading . . .

Cracking, cracking, cracking, everything coming apart.

No, he had to pull himself—

What about the thought diversions Dr. Chi had tried to teach him? The presidents. List them in order.

Who the hell was that first guy? He was on the damn dollar! Oh, Christ.

What was he doing?

He could do this.

Hadn't he once been a competitor, a fighter? Game after game, he had blown a baseball by hitters. He had been ferocious.

He straightened his back now. *Jules, I'm sorry. I will keep you safe. I will, I will.* It was time to make a stand. But he needed a moment. One more moment.

His mouth seemed to be full of sand.

Finally, he cleared his throat, and felt the fire come up in his eyes. He was determined not to flinch under Half-Assed Frank's gaze.

"Let them go. I will fuck you up, dude."

Limping back to his seat, Half-Assed Frank stifled a yawn. "Don't think so."

"Well then, I'm the one who screwed up, kill me."

Half-Assed Frank faced him, wearing a smirk.

"Okay."

"J-Just leave them the hell alone."

Half-Assed Frank scrunched his eyes.

"Want me to whack you in here? Or outside?"

"Do it outside," Jules said. "It's already pretty messy in here. *And* smelly."

Wesley felt his mouth fall open.

"Honey, what're you—"

"But if you kill him quick and untie me, I can finally pee," she said. "Then again, well, maybe you want to torture him first?"

A chill of fear made Wesley shiver. He glanced desperately back and forth between Jules and Half-Assed Frank.

Half-Assed Frank burst out with a short, harsh laugh. He then butted back in.

"Before I whack you, you help me get rid of Nicky with the chainsaw. Legs, arms, head."

Wesley gaped at the bloody, rank dead guy. The body reminded him of Eddie. The rushing rapids at the Gorge. All those gunshots . . . He could feel Eddie's phantom looming over everything. A wave of guilt rolled through his chest. And he gave out another long moan.

When he turned his head back, Half-Assed Frank threw him a mean-ass stare.

"You're gonna suffer . . . to your last damn breath. What do you think about gutting him, and eating his liver?"

Wesley squeezed his eyes shut. Twisted his head back and forth.

He hated getting shot.

An eternity later, Jules nodded to Half-Assed Frank. She then turned back to Wesley.

"All right, enough. Relax, Wesley."

"Relax? *Relax?*"

"It's over."

He blinked. Drops of sweat were running into his eyes.

"How the—"

"I'm pissed at you. But everything else? It's okay."

It took a moment before he managed to speak.

"Huh?"

"We worked things out, and were breaking your balls. Jesus, after all this, don't die of fright on me now."

Half-Assed Frank untied Jules. He watched the little hottie stretch awkwardly and rise on legs that looked stiff and sluggish. Making a face as her nerves fired back to life, she wobbled.

"Whoa."

She started to sink, then managed to stand. She opened and closed her hands, then shook life back into them. Massaged her little wrists to restore the circulation. Rolled her sweet body from side to side, as if trying to work out a kink.

Yet when he finished untying Weaseldick, her face changed. She seemed to be reading the situation. Preparing for something. Then her eyes narrowed. A hard glint came into them, and her cheeks flared red.

This suddenly felt wrong.

She exploded across the room.

Pure rage.

Coming right at Half-Assed Frank.

He recoiled, another surge of blood beginning to shoot through his body.

"Hey!"

This wasn't the goddamn plan either!

He had come to admire her. She was tough. And smart. But the bitch had lied.

It had all been a trick.

He felt something black descend. Now he had to whack them both anyway. What a mess the cabin was going to be.

79

Jules charged forward.

The bastard!

He had brought this nightmare on them. She was done sitting, thinking. It was time to act. To get her own revenge.

Finally.

Her temples thundered.

A surprised-looking Half-Assed Frank had raised his pistol. She bolted past him. Throwing Wesley a severe look, she drew her fist back.

"Damn you."

"Now, honey—"

She'd had it. For too long she had been carrying everything. And she'd goddamn had it.

Before Wesley even had a chance to fully stand, she walloped him on the nose. The force knocking him off his feet, he stumbled backwards and tumbled over the cobbler's bench to the floor. The air huffed out of him. Now one more body sprawled on the floor.

He looked wildly up at her.

"My back!"

"Oopsa-daisy, Daddy fell."

"Shit. Nearly, nearly . . . broke my spine."

She eyed him with weary disgust. She shook her head hard.

"You damn jerk."

As she loomed over him, he pulled himself to a sitting position. He shook and still looked wigged out.

His eyes darted right and left, like he was looking for a way to escape. They were big with shock. He jerked up a hand in a calming gesture.

"Don't! Stop it."

She grumbled to herself. After realizing she was still making a fist with her sore right hand, she tried to relax it.

"All right, your hand. Give it to me."

Reaching down, she then helped him up. His legs were still half asleep apparently, and as he stumbled around again, she couldn't help but laugh. She gave him a restrained smooch.

"Take a breath, okay? That's it, though. I'm done talking to you for the rest of this kidnapping."

Half-Assed Frank laid his pistol on the fireplace mantel. He then stepped close, gripping the fireplace shovel.

"My turn."

With a look of disgust, he clocked Wesley flush on the top of the head. It connected with a metallic *thonk*.

Wesley's face contorted with pain.

"Jeez."

Half-Assed Frank leaned back and swung a big leg up. Her man let out a bark of a cry in anticipation. His eyes crossed when Half-Assed Frank's foot drove hard into his crotch.

Clutching the rocking chair to hold himself up, he let out a long, agonized groan. He crumpled to the floor.

Well, maybe that had scared some sense into Wesley. Maybe it had punished him a bit.

"*Stop*," she said. "That's enough."

There was a hardness to Half-Assed Frank's eyes now.

"Nope, don't think so."

Although half of her wanted her man to suffer even more, Jules drew herself up. No way could she bear to see Wesley really get hurt.

"I'm telling you—"

"I'm liking this too much," Half-Assed Frank said. "Why stop?" His cold dark eyes glared straight at her. He laughed a crazy laugh. "Then how about I nail you to the floor, and bang you good?"

Well, okay.

Don't you dare mess with me, Half-Assed Frank had said earlier.

But it was time now.

The bastard had victimized others for years. He had dared to threaten her family.

Her muscles tensed.

Although her right hand had stiffened and was difficult to close now, she grabbed the back of Half-Assed Frank's shirt and yanked it up over his head. The fireplace shovel clanked to the floor. He struggled to free his arms.

The gun? Where was—?

The blood barreled through her heart.

"Cunt!" he said.

She stumbled when one of his big fists smashed into the side of her head. The force of it was unexpected and immense.

The floor began to rush toward her. Then she found her balance.

Shit.

Her head felt off-kilter too.

What had—?

She had only a blurred vision of him. She tried to shake off the blow. She blinked. Blinked again.

As her vision cleared, she drew herself up and scanned the nearby counter.

That screwdriver?

Why not?

She dove forward. Glowering, he turned toward her. She barely had time to pivot and snatch up her weapon and he swung at her again and she ducked his fist. The fingers of her banged-up hand, though, would barely close down on the screwdriver's handle. For an instant she thought she might drop it.

Clenching it as best she could, she drew a careful bead on Half-Assed Frank's throat.

He glanced toward the fireplace mantel.

Damn.

His pistol.

She stepped closer.

"Don't you dare mess with *me*," she said.

She had one chance to get it right. Had to strike fast. To hell with this predator.

She plunged forward.

She connected with every bit of strength she had, felt the bastard's throat flesh give. Rammed the screwdriver through.

She felt the blade go deep. Heard him gasp.

His look was a mixture of shock and pain. Blood shot from his throat around the screwdriver's yellow handle.

She stepped back as he staggered and then dropped to all fours.

"You lost," she said.

Finally.

It was over.

Checkmate.

No?

Arm over arm, he belly-crawled toward her.

She stared in disbelief. She then felt something dislodge in her chest, felt the fear.

What the—?

Crap!

Panting, he pulled himself onto his knees. He raised his head. His dark eyes bored into her. He raggedly sucked in air. Christ, he was about to climb to his feet. He should be bleeding out. He should be dead. Was he really going to keep coming at her?

Her own breaths came hard. She was not sure how much fight she had left.

As his hand reached toward her ankle, clutched it, and tightened, she felt a paralyzing terror.

80

Holy goddamn shit!

Jules's heart beat up her neck and into her skull. This wasn't over.

A thought fluttered through her mind: *Evil don't die.*

Half-Assed Frank's mouth was a straight line now. Blood gurgled in his throat.

A cold panic starting up her spine, she kicked free. What the hell was she supposed to do now? She had used up everything. She had the feeling of just not being strong enough. The thought that she might lose.

Her brain engaged and disengaged.

But she—

The bloody giant kept coming at her. With crazed determination, he advanced.

Grab the damn gun.

Apparently recovered, Wesley stepped up. He made a face. Pissed? He stood tall and strong. His fists were clenched. She saw his jawbone work. She had a sense he knew this was his moment to prove who he really was.

His tone was surprisingly firm when he said, "Got it, I'm all over it."

He grabbed the iron skillet. Raised it high and clocked Half-Assed Frank in the head.

"How's that feel?"

Half-Assed Frank groaned and put out an arm. Looking for some way to brace himself.

"Come on!" Wesley said. He was trembling with rage. "Crazy is here, baby! You son of a bitch. Told you I was taking you ..."

He screamed again. But this time it was a warrior noise. He walloped Half-Assed Frank once more.

"That's gotta hurt."

Half-Assed Frank pitched forward, hitting the floor with sickening force.

Well, it was about time for Wesley to help out! He did have some guts.

At last!

He had grown a pair.

Why did she always have to kill all of the bad guys? Still, she wanted to finish this herself.

"Gimme that."

She flexed her aching fingers to help restore them, then snatched the skillet from him, and pounded Half-Assed Frank's head for a long while. Until she thought her arm would drop off.

Was he still moving?

She whacked away again.

"Okay, sweetie," Wesley said. "Okay. Okay."

She threw in a final, solid smack.

A small moan escaped from Half-Assed Frank's lips.

Was his body just releasing air?

Or—?

Her arm shook as she raised the skillet.

Three more whacks.

"Oh, yeah."

"Brains on the floor," Wesley said. "That should do it."

She was panting.

She spit onto Half-Assed Frank's body. She took a deep breath, released it slowly. She then dusted off her hands.

"There. You made the mistake of messing with my little family."

She had killed him. One more bad guy.

Her plan all along.

———————

Junior looked up at Jules. Eyes widening, he broke into a grin and waggled his arms. Her heart broke, in a happy way.

How close she had come to failing. She had barely been able to con Half-Assed Frank into a fake deal. And then she had hoped to take out Half-Assed Frank when he first untied her. But he had raised his gun.

Now, she had done it.

Screwing with her family? She had known all along that he would have to pay.

"Junior!" She scooped him up, twirled him around. She felt hot tears rolling down her cheeks. "Here you are! Oh, that face."

"Ga-ga-ga."

"You sweet, precious thing. Thank God, you're okay."

She hugged him tight. She buried her nose in his neck to smell him, and nuzzled his soft plump face. His little breath smelled sweet, and she kissed his cheek. Stroked his curls. His teeny fingers clutched at her shirt.

When she tickled him under his neck, his eyebrows lifted in delight.

"You're the best little boy. Now I'll be back in one sec. Maybe Daddy will find you a snack."

Handing him off to Wesley, she stepped around the bodies, the blood, and raced to the bathroom. For a moment she gazed at the knotty-pine paneling and thought she was going to be sick. She heaved twice over the toilet, bringing nothing up, and then exhaled in relief.

After jerking down her panties to pee, she let go in a steady cataract for close to a minute. It felt glorious.

She scooted back, smiling.

"Wow, that's better."

Soon she attacked a bag of potato chips.

81

Minutes after leaving Half-Assed Frank behind, Wesley buried the Tacoma's gas pedal. To keep from shaking, he held onto the steering wheel as hard as he could. He still felt the cold muzzle of Half-Assed Frank's pistol pressing into his gut. Half-Assed Frank's voice kept right on rattling in his ears. In his mind, he still saw the flames from the fire he and Jules had set before they raced away from the cabin.

His words came out loud, panicky.

"Well, I showed him! Sure did. I crushed that."

Jules blew her breath out.

"Never got to use my kick move on him, though," he added.

When he glanced her way, she didn't look happy. He could read the accusation in her eyes. She gave a short incredulous laugh.

His only thought was to get away. Despite the dark, he drove like a maniac. In a kind of trance, he sped up for corners and ignored the brakes as if the pickup was a Maserati, and they hurtled down the gorge. The beam of their headlights bobbed with every bump. Pine trees whizzed past outside. She kept shaking her head.

"You can be so thoughtless sometimes," she said.

As the land began to flatten out, they rocketed around a sharp curve and the tires thumped along the shoulder. The steering wheel wobbled in his grip. The truck bounced and jounced. He jerked the wheel to the left, and she clamped her hand on Junior's car seat.

Annoyance flared in her eyes.

"Slow down! You're going to kill us yet." She made a grumbling sound. "God, sometimes I think you got a death wish."

Tugged at by an unreal feeling, he didn't respond.

"Just slow down, okay?"

Jules patted Junior's downy curls with her sore hand. There were red, tender ridges on her wrist from struggling with the ropes not long ago. Gently, she jiggled his car seat. Junior scrunched up his face, cooed, and her heart pinched with love. She kissed both of his hands.

"You sweet little baby, good little baby. Who's precious? You!"

She dug into the last of Half-Assed Frank's potato chips. Finished with them, she sang.

"Oh, the wheels on the truck go round and round. Round and round, round and round. Wheels on the truck . . ."

Afterward, drawing her shoulders back, she studied Wesley in the dim light coming off the dashboard. He still looked pale and a bit in shock. He was still breathing hard. She could smell his nervous sweat. He cleared his throat.

"What's—What's wrong?"

"You got to be kidding."

He gave her a clueless look.

"Still mad?"

"Don't get me started," she said. "You know, *I* should kill you."

"Still mad."

"Jesus, what a weird day. God! This was a new low. A new damn sucky low. Not exactly a Family Fun day."

He made an airy gesture with his hand.

"Well," he said, "it was—"

"You know, I would love it right now if you stopped talking."

"*You* try being me. It can wear a guy—"

"Enough."

He stared straight ahead.

After feeling along the side of her head where Half-Assed Frank had clocked her, she eyed the star-studded sky. She then rocked Junior's seat again, smiling at him as he sucked at his juice cup. Her back ached. Her wrists burned. She felt exhausted. When she kissed the top of Junior's head, his curls smelled of cigar smoke. Outside, the headlights swept across a set of bleachers at the edge of a dark field. Junior gave a sudden hiccup, and she let out a loud breath.

"Junior, you poor little boy. Not even one year old, you already been kidnapped."

She gave Wesley a little look. Maybe she should have tried to tell him about the threats earlier? But he was the one had started all this crap with his idiotic gambling.

Way back, she had promised herself she would save him. No matter what. But he sure as hell didn't make it easy for her.

Still, it was all about trying.

Who knew? Maybe someday she would even give Paige another try—gun-free.

"Your Da-da sure is a screw-up, no?" she said now to Junior. "Some role model."

———————

Wesley scrambled to think of something to say to Jules, biting at a nail on one hand and clenching the wheel with the other. He racked his frazzled brain. But he couldn't find any words. What could he say? Sorry he got the family kidnapped? It won't happen again? Nobody's perfect?

A diesel truck roared past. She cradled her belly. Stroking it, she half smiled. After a moment he shrugged.

"Love you too, honey."

"Mmf."

"You know, this could've happened to anybody."

"Oh, shut up. Would you? I can barely wait to see what you got planned for tomorrow."

"You blame me for everything, don't you?"

She massaged a wrist.

"Watch the road."

As he drove on, though, she gripped his right hand and held it tight. Her hand felt soft and warm. Headlights flashed by and her eyes shone. They glanced into each other's eyes, then away. She gave out a weary breath.

"You all right?"

He shivered, as if he could shake off a thought.

"I did not like being in that trunk. Hell no. Or—"

"God, I ache. And I could wolf down a huge salad with avocados."

Thinking about all he'd been through in the day, he shook his head and whistled.

"I'll never sleep again."

The day had been a bitch. All day, it seemed, he had a gun practically stuck up his butt. It had been enough to put him over the edge. His nerves still clanged. And his nose and noggin and nuts still felt sore.

The hardest fact to face, though, was that she was right—it was nobody's fault but his own. He was a screw-up. He knew that. She'd blown a gasket, but he'd deserved it. In a big way. Letting go of the wheel briefly, he scratched at the scab on his brow. A twinge of pain shot down his left leg. Regret washed through him, and he felt the corners of his mouth tremble.

He swallowed. And swallowed again.

He had been so stupid. If only he could turn back the clock. This whole thing sure was a black mark against him.

"I'm sorry," he said finally. His voice was tight with emotion. "Truly. For everything. I feel like such a . . . you know. My bad."

She waited a moment before saying, "Big whoop."

A couple of miles further down the road, Wesley reached the top of a slight rise. He had begun to gather himself, thinking that someday, somehow, he was going to change things. Maybe he would even find a way to be brave. Or a little brave. He was no blunderer. Hell, who was he kidding? Together, though, they would make it. They could start from square one and were going to get things right.

What was the last thing Drew had told him?

You stay strong, bro.

"Say, Jules, I never got to . . . Did I tell you about the letter?"

"Huh? What letter?"

"Didn't I? The one that came the other day? The one with the leaf?"

She stared hard at him.

"What?"

"Well, parts of a leaf. Little bits. Kinda crumbly really, in a baggie."

She thumped his arm.

"The point! Get to the point."

"It came that day we fought, and I—"

"*Now.*"

"The envelope was addressed to both of us. From that cop, Burpee."

She kept staring.

"Oh my—"

"The note said that was a final gift. Something he'd snuck off with."

The corners of her mouth rose.

"cs-29."

"Said he'd held onto it for quite a while. Which supposedly had something to do with, like, wanting to keep us honest."

She sure looked pleased. It took her a moment to speak.

"That's so . . ."

"Some gift! What's up with *that?*"

"Phew."

"Jules?"

"Never mind."

Wesley slowed the truck to a crawl.

"Look, honey!" he said. "Look."

Rita's blinked an orange neon sign. The outside of the restaurant looked homely as they come—a pocked stucco block with saggy window awnings. Deep ruts scored the dirt parking lot. But in red lettering across the front window it advertised an all-you-can-eat buffet, and Jules grinned wide.

Seeing the further softening in her, he gave out a loud "Whew!" of relief.

She licked her lips and gave him a long, hard look before responding.

"I love you, Wesley. I do."

He slipped his hand under his shirt and made his heart appear to flutter.

"Ditto."

He knew with a sudden certainty that she believed in him, that she always had. They shared a smile and it made him feel good. Better than good. Like a truly lucky man. She laughed.

"But if you don't pull over, I will kill you."

"I'm on it."

"You know, back there? At least you *did* try and sacrifice yourself."

He drew himself up with dignity. Felt a sudden surge of pride.

"True that."

"We're all just trying, right?"

"Maybe I am pretty great."

"Good work with the skillet too. In a way, I guess you proved yourself a hero, again."

He pulled in and parked, amused at the strange turns life could take. Through the restaurant's big glass windows he saw a friendly-looking waitress filling a coffee mug.

"Well. I'm definitely not ordering Italian."

Jules let out another bright laugh and then gave him a soft-lipped kiss. When she spoke again, there was something playful in her voice.

"Maybe now I can show you. My secret, I mean. You know, I guess sometimes you *do* get what you wish for."

He looked at her, puzzled. He saw what looked like triumph shining in her face.

"What do you mean?"

She clicked open the glove compartment and took out a small black cloth bag.

"I found this on the seat of that mole-faced, dead guy's car."

She pulled the drawstring open. Inside nestled what looked like emeralds, sapphires, and rubies. Dozens and dozens of them.

"Dinner's on me," she said.

ACKNOWLEDGMENTS

The author would like to gratefully acknowledge those who helped with the writing of this novel. They include Jen Howard, Lindsay Guzzardo, Jeff Driscoll, and the ever-awesome Jane Ryder.

Also, Hez, Jane . . . this book would never have happened without you. Thanks for the way out, Rob K.

Many thanks to all who helped.

AFTERWORD

———

My sincere thanks to you for reading and taking this journey with Jules (and Wesley) and me. If you're moved to leave a review on your online retailer or on Goodreads or pretty much anywhere else, your efforts would be greatly appreciated. But no problem if it's not your thing. I hope you enjoyed the book, because that's what matters most.

ABOUT THE AUTHOR

———

Mark Petersen loves to travel due to his (literal) Gypsy blood, but he spends most of his time in Vermont. He presently works as an addiction counselor, and has previously been employed as an archaeologist, construction worker, and truck driver. He attended law school for one day. That was enough.